ESCAPE: BOOK TWELVE OF BEYOND THESE WALLS

A POST-APOCALYPTIC SURVIVAL THRILLER

MICHAEL ROBERTSON

EDITED AND COVER BY ...

To contact Michael, please email:
subscribers@michaelrobertson.co.uk

Edited by:

Pauline Nolet - http://www.paulinenolet.com

Cover design by Dusty Crosley - https://www.deviantart.com/dustycrosley

COPYRIGHT

Escape: Book twelve of Beyond These Walls

Michael Robertson
© Michael Robertson 2021

Escape: Book twelve of Beyond These Walls is a work of fiction. The characters, incidents, situations, and all dialogue are entirely a product of the author's imagination, or are used fictitiously and are not in any way representative of real people, places, or things.

Any resemblance to persons living or dead is entirely coincidental.

All rights reserved.

No part of this publication may be reproduced, stored in a retrieval system, or transmitted in any form or by any means electronic, mechanical, photocopying, recording, or otherwise, without the prior written permission of the author except in the case of brief quotations embodied in critical articles and reviews.

READER GROUP

Join my reader group for all my latest releases and special offers. You'll also receive these four FREE books. You can unsubscribe at any time.

Go to www.michaelrobertson.co.uk

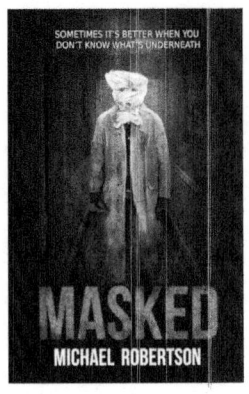

ESCAPE: BOOK TWELVE OF BEYOND THESE WALLS

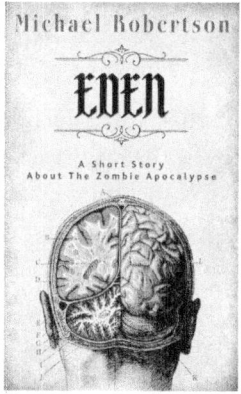

CHAPTER 1

Joni led the line, her calves aching from where she walked on her tiptoes. Down the sloping entrance ramp into the garage, the night at their back. One of many entrance ramps. The guards were so brazen. They were in control here. Always had been and always will be. They could leave the garage open. The implants prevented the prisoners from getting close, and who else would be brave or stupid enough to waltz in and out of here whenever they damn well pleased? If they admitted Joni did this, they'd have to admit they weren't as in control as they made out. Although, he wouldn't be able to avoid it when she cut his throat. But not now. No, not now. That time would come. Soon enough.

Little Chick, the one she'd fed and nourished, whom she'd rescued and looked after, scowled at her every time they spoke. "And you still reckon they don't know we're here?"

Her pulse throbbed in her temples. Dizzy with her fury. Intoxicated by what she'd do to him when she got the chance. Joni paused. "They will do if you don't keep your voice down." She dropped behind a tank, and the others copied her. Seven of them in total. Thankfully, the injured one had stayed back at her place. Chopped Liver. Not chopped liver anymore, but his wounds were still too fresh for him to be gallivanting around the prison. Stay at home. Rest. Heal. He could also tell them what happened and where. Twenty screens. A good view of the place. Or at least better than theirs in the underground garage. Besides, she already had a herd of elephants behind her, taking one who struggled to walk might have been the final nail. "Fail, pail, snail."

The scowling little chick scowled harder. "What are you talking about?"

"Fail. If you don't shut up." The end of Joni's reply took flight around the cavernous garage. The echo grew wings and soared through the place, searching for any listening ears. She should have worn her helmet. At least it would have hidden her face. From them. From him. She rarely wore it down here, but she usually worked alone. She could trust herself to be quiet. She could be as quiet as a mouse on her own. She'd been in and out of this place for years with no trouble. Had she pushed her luck today? Only one way to find out.

Little Chick Artan duckwalked along the side of the immaculate vehicle until he was a few feet from her. He pointed at her face, his teeth bared. "Don't you dare tell me to shut up."

The small and fierce one. The pocket rocket, Olga, grabbed Artan by his shoulder and spun him around so he faced her. She pressed a finger to her lips and leaned close to him. "Shh! She'll stop telling you to shut up when you shut up."

Little Chick bit his bottom lip. He chewed back his response, his flushed face lit up by the garage's fluorescent glare. Only a baby, a little chick, but well on his way to owning the physique of a man. His broad chest swelled when he breathed in through his nose and sank as he released his rage. He kept his words to himself.

Joni reached the end of the tank and braced against its cold steel body with her right hand. She peered around the front along the garage. Their surroundings like everywhere else in this damn place. Brushed steel. Rough concrete. Damp in the air. Being here leached the light from the sky and the spark from Joni's soul. No matter how bright the fluorescent glare, this place turned her dark. Although, he'd taken most of her glow when he'd brought her here. And maybe she'd never get it back, but she'd take his. An eye for an eye. A spark for a spark.

Six in the line behind her. They all leaned against the immaculate tank. They watched her, all bathed in the clinical glare from above. Enormous eyes in tired faces. Bags beneath their glassy stares. Shadows pooled in their sallow cheeks. Little Chick at the front. More shadows than the rest put together. His angular face still locked in a heavy scowl. Joni reached out to him, but he turned away. "You're worried about being down here?"

"Of course."

"They don't have cameras." Joni shook her head so hard it made her dizzy. "As long as we keep quiet, and you do as Joni says, we'll get the hoverboards and get out of here. Okay?"

"You're sure they don't know we're here?"

"Dog with a bone. Won't let it go. Won't trust Joni."

"What?"

"No." Joni shook her head again. Her palm cold against the tank. Her thighs ached from her crouch. "Won't trust her. All Joni's done is look after him. What can she do to prove to him she knows what she's saying and he can rely on her?"

"Rewind time." He raised his voice, the harder letters of his words snapping around the garage. "You locked me up. You *tied* me down. You kept me away from Nick."

"Nick was sick. Slit. Ripped. Needed to be on his own to heal. Not be near someone shouting. The angry little chick was no good for Nick."

Before the little chick replied, Olga Pocket Rocket grabbed him again. She leaned close. Just inches between her and Little Chick's faces. "And from the way you're behaving, you needed it. I agree with Joni. You were best kept away. And don't forget Joni rescued us. She nursed Nick back to health."

Joni's hand trembled when she rested it on Olga's arm. She'd had so little human contact in such a long time. The warmth of another person. Even through the fabric of her clothes. She'd spent years watching the prisoners on her screens. She'd fantasied about being one of them. No matter how wretched their lives, they had one another. "Thank you for backing Joni. For seeing she means well. The angry little chick has a valid question, and Joni doesn't mind him asking." She pinched the air and twisted an invisible dial. "But he needs to turn down the volume."

Joni shook her head at Little Chick. She whispered, modelling the behaviour she needed from him. "No, they won't know we're down here." A glance back at the rough concrete ramp leading back out into the dark night. She raised a finger. "First, very few guards do the night shift. Most nights, none go out. Lazy pigs." She raised a second finger. "There's no surveillance in here. They say they respect the guards' privacy, so there's none anywhere in the block. Laughable really."

Artan shrugged. "What is?"

"They respect their privacy, but they don't respect them as people. They treat them like shit. Like they own them. They crush them." She ground her jaw and balled her right fist. "Destroy them!"

The others paused. Even Little Chick's brow softened.

"Anyway …" Joni rapped her knuckles against the side of her head and laughed. "To the point. Joint. Anoint."

The friends glanced at one another. Joni's mad. No secret there. But she also cares. And she knows things. Not everything she speaks is nonsense. They'll see that. They'll learn Joni has a lot to offer. Give them something more solid. Concrete. Steel. Heal. Feel. "They think we're far away. They'll be watching and waiting for us to come close. Cameras everywhere, they'll see us approach." She tapped her nose with her right index finger. "They don't know we're already here. Joni's lived in their shadow for a long time, and they've not found her. They never will. He never will. They'll be looking elsewhere. And there's a lot of elsewheres to look. This is a big place."

William, the reluctant leader of the group. The one they all turned to when decisions needed to be made. Tall, dark, in love with his beautiful girlfriend. And who could blame him? Beautiful, beautiful girlfriend. William said, "Surely they'll be looking for us after we've robbed them?"

Aches streaked Joni's thighs. She'd crouched down for too long. Her palm still cold against the tank. She peered around the front of the immaculate vehicle again. "All of them immaculate."

The beauty. His beauty. Matilda. She frowned. She looked from Joni to the tank. Closed her mouth. Her brow softened. "The tanks?"

Joni nodded.

"The tanks are clean?"

Joni nodded again.

"Why *are* they so clean?"

"No battles here. Not in this place. They act like an army, but they're not. They fight no wars, despite having the supplies and equipment to take on half the north. Massacres? Yes! Oh yes, massacres in abundance. But they don't even break a nail doing massacres. A state-funded terrorist organisation. Massively overpowered compared to their enemy. They press their boots to the necks of the prisoners. No wars here. Nothing to see. The most they have to do is wash away the blood and move on. Murder washed away. Lives, families, and histories not even allowed to dry on the bodywork. Instead, diluted by a guard's hose and flushed down the drain."

Matilda moved next to Joni and peered around the tank. The garage was still empty. "Do they ever lock this place?"

"They could. But they don't. They think they're untouchable. Why would anyone come in here? The prisoners can't cross the lines to get close enough. Might as well leave it open. Let the guards come and go whenever they please."

The scarred barbarian, although built like a warrior, hung his head. Deep shame. Fear. A lack of confidence. Hawk, his voice too loud. "But we can cross the lines."

"Shh." Joni flapped her arms. Without the tank for support, she fell to her knees. The tiny concrete pinpricks speared her kneecaps. "Keep it down, frown, they'll go to town. We'll drown in blood. Mud. Diluted flood."

Olga elbowed Hawk in the ribs. "Lower your voice!"

The scowling Little Chick's frown returned. "Are we going to move on or not?"

"Joni's polite. Joni answers questions when you ask them. If you want to go, stop asking me things. Do you want to go?"

Six heads nodded at her. All she needed. Joni stepped from the tank's cover and froze.

Matilda bumped into her. The rest of them stepped forwards, pushing Joni farther out into the garage. Joni barged back. Six people behind her. She should have come alone. She could move freely on her own.

Two guards had entered the garage.

Joni shoved again. Her versus six of them. They needed to retreat. Now!

A man and a woman. Dressed from head to toe in grey. They blended in with their dreary surroundings. Guns hung from straps across their fronts. Semi-automatics. Pistols on their hips. Tasers on the other side. Grenades hooked on their belts. The man's voice bounced off the walls like a wayward bullet. "Double fucking shifts! Doesn't he know we need our beauty sleep?"

"You might, Carragher."

The man's laugh boomed through the garage. "Rate yourself, don't ya?"

Their steps continued towards Joni and her new friends.

The man snorted a laugh. "I suppose someone's got to, right?"

"Screw you."

The guards walked in time. Their steps beat a death march. The click of their heels. They progressed with an inevitability and a guarantee. They were closing in. They would always guard this place. And if they found you, they'd fuck you up. Maybe Joni should just get out of there now. She'd been on her own before she'd met this lot. She could do it again. She'd said she'd help them, but how could she if they didn't help themselves?

She backed into them again. Met resistance. Six bodies slowed her retreat. Her pulse matched the rhythm of the guards' steps. Pounded in her ears. She can't do this. She's not ready to be seen. For him to find her. She's going to find him. She's the one in control. Taking it back. What he stole from her. He won't own her again. She clenched her jaw. Never again. She needs to get out of there. She didn't promise to keep them all alive. Didn't promise she wouldn't abandon them if they left her vulnerable. And what did they expect? As a collective, they were a liability. Like they were actively working against their own well-being. She had to leave now. Run. Leave them to fight the guards. All bets are off. She can jus—

The six moved more than before, and she fell onto her arse. Finally, they got the message. Gracie, the quiet ginger one at the back of the line, vanished around the rear of the tank. The others followed.

The guards' steps like a tiny axe to Joni's temple.

Clack!

Clack!

Clack!

Joni shoved again. Speeding up the retreat. On her own, she would have been long gone. But just as the guards' feet appeared at the front of the tank, Joni vanished around the back. The last one to hide from their sight. Resting a sweating palm against her thumping chest, she rode her heavy breaths. "Too close. Closer than close. Roast. They'd be toast. Make the most. Nee—"

A sharp sting from where Joni slammed down against the concrete, knees first. Shoved forwards by Matilda, who pressed her finger to her lips. Like Joni needed to be told. Joni knows this place better than anyone. Better than anyone ever could. She knows when to be quiet. But maybe she was being too loud. She nodded. Joni's a coward. Can't stick up for herself. She's afraid of everything and everyone. Why else would she be living in the shadows? Why else would she have let him do what he did?

Matilda didn't scowl like her angry little brother. Little Chick. Kindness lit her features. Filled her heart. Drove her pulse. She raised a thumb at Joni and mouthed *you okay?* So beautiful.

Joni halted mid-nod and snapped a hand towards Gracie. Reached in her direction and mouthed a silent scream. No!

Olga grabbed Gracie to prevent her from going the other way around the tanks.

Wagging a finger, Joni shook her head. Don't go that way. They never go that way. Sure, they were docking and in sleep mode, but the drones and dogs were that way. She'd never passed them. Never been in their line of sight. Never risked it and she never would. Maybe they couldn't wake up, but would she want to test it? No. Absolutely, positively not. No thank you. Drones and dogs. Spit-roasted hogs. Dried-out frogs. Commune with the gods. No thank you, sir. No thank you.

Gracie shrugged. What had she done wrong?

No time to explain.

The steps moved farther away. Past the line of tanks and out of sight. Several clicks and thunks, followed by the whir of two electric engines. The guards drove two circular motorcycles, the chains humming against the rough road. Eight-foot-tall rings. Twin chain tracks. They hit the exit ramp with a *thunk* and accelerated out of there.

The hum quietened to nothing. Matilda raised her thumb again. "Are you okay?"

"Joni's always okay. She's been this way since back in the day. How else can she survive?"

Olga Pocket Rocket leaned closer. She raised her eyebrows. "The boards?"

Joni's vision blurred with her vigorous nod. "Of course. Of course. Follow Joni."

Every one of them nodded in return. At least they were quieter now. Knew the dangers. Had now seen the dangers. One of many. Guards. Guns. Dogs. Drones. Prisoners. Everything and everyone in this place wanted a piece of them.

Joni crouched while she ran. Keep low. Behind the tanks. Away from sight should any more come down. Double shifts. Night duty. Maybe they're not as safe as she's telling them.

Maybe he's taking this threat seriously. Maybe things were changing around here.

Breaking from the last tank, Joni ran to the wall of wheeled boards. Stacked from floor to ceiling in their charging rack. She pulled them free one at a time.

The scarred barbarian, Hawk, took the first one and laid it on the ground, but Olga grabbed his arm and shook her head. She leaned close. Kept her voice low. "Carry it. Run with it. We'll learn to ride them outside. Away from here."

Her throat dry, her pulse pounding, the hairs on her body standing on end, Joni nodded. "She's right. Carry them out at first. Get away from here. We can ride them then. Need to learn. Not hard, but not easy either. Need time. No time here."

Hawk's thick arm bulged when he lifted the board and wrapped it in a headlock. Joni continued to free the boards. Seven in total. Nick didn't need one. Wouldn't be coming out for a while. Needed to rest. Chopped liver. Can't deliver.

The last board free, Joni gripped it beneath her arm like the others. She could ride it out of there, but instead, she ran from the garage, leading the way back through the tanks, back up the ramp out of there, back into the glow of the moon. Its silver light accentuated their brushed-silver surroundings. She kept to the shadows. Always to the shadows. A life in the shadows. But for how much longer? The tables will turn. She'll step into the light, and he'll be the one cowering in the darkness.

CHAPTER 2

William covered his mouth with his hand. It hid his smile, but not his snorting laugh.

"What?" Hawk's lips tightened, and he threw his arms up. When William didn't reply, he tutted, stepped back on his wheeled board, leaned forward, and jumped off again with a yelp when the board moved. "What's so funny?"

The muscles in William's face twitched, and he nearly covered his mouth again. Instead, he pressed his lips tight and shook his head. "Nothing." He zipped over to his friend. He stood about a foot taller than him because of the hoverboard. "It's hard, I get it. I had to learn how to drive one of these things when I was being shot at. Olga was like those two." He flicked his head at Artan and Matilda, who were already zipping up and down the road. "She was a natural. And like I've already told you, I had a nightmare. The only thing that helped me was the fact that my complete lack of control made me entirely unpredictable. How could they shoot me if even I didn't know which way I'd turn next? Come on, give it another go."

His arms out to the sides like a tightrope walker, Hawk stepped onto the board again.

"It'll only move when you have two feet on it. And it responds to subtle movements. You don't need to do much."

Hawk's tongue poked from his mouth, and he flapped his arms when the board slowly edged forwards. But he stayed on. "Look, I'm doing it."

William beamed at him. "See, when you get used to it, it's super instinctive. You'll be fine once you get the hang of it."

They were on a long, straight, and wide road. The moon shone down on them like a lantern. Olga stopped close to Gracie, aiding her like William aided Hawk.

Joni had paused about twenty feet away. The silver moonlight on her back, the blue light from her device shone on her face. She divided her attention between her device and looking up and down the road. When she did cast an eye back at William and his friends, she looked through them rather than at them, her brow creased, her teeth bared. "We ready to move on?"

Olga gave a thumbs up on Gracie's behalf.

William waited for Hawk to zip forwards, turn one hundred and eighty degrees, and zip back. A grin lifted his usually stoic demeanour. The poor bastard had had little in his life to smile about. He nodded, so William copied Olga's gesture and showed Joni his thumb. "Can we take it slow?"

"Yep."

Joni said it more to her screen than William and had already set off. Had the yep been for him? Had she even listened? Should they trust her? She clearly had a loose grip on reality. But what choice did they have? If the key to their safety lived in the mind of a lunatic, what could they do but scatter their hopes and dreams in the winds of madness and pray they landed close to their destination?

"You ready?" William patted Hawk's back.

Thrusting his arms out for balance again, the rigid Hawk leaned so his board rolled forwards.

They picked up speed, their tyres humming against the rough concrete. William travelled with his friends, the road wide enough for them to move as a pack. Joni, the lone wolf, a little farther ahead. The tall walls loomed over them on either side. They cast deep shadows, but the road's width allowed space for the moon to light their path.

"Keep an eye on these." William pointed down at the small pip of light by his hoverboard's left wheel. About a quarter of an inch in diameter. The boards didn't have a front or back, so the lights were on the right for some. A small green glow. "That's the board's charge."

Olga said, "When that flashes red, you're screwed."

William smirked. "So eloquent as always, Olga."

"Why say twenty words when a couple will do?"

"When it flashes red," William said, "the charge is about to run out and the board will soon stop working."

Hawk, standing on his board like the next messiah, circled his arms backwards as if he might fall off at any second. "How long do we have left when they flash?"

"Not long," Olga said.

The moonlight caught the slight sweat sheen on Hawk's face. He lowered his arms a little. "That happened to you?"

"Yep." William nodded. "It's when we decided we had to do the rat run. We were on foot and surrounded by guards."

"Speaking of guards …" Artan looked behind. "Should we be worried?"

Joni shouted back at them, "Not on the night shift. Oh, no, not on the night shift. No, no, no." Locked into her slight lean forwards, she shook her head repeatedly and remained focused on where they were heading. "Not about the guards. Oh no."

ESCAPE: BOOK TWELVE OF BEYOND THESE WALLS

Artan raised his eyebrows at William and coughed to clear his throat. "Are you talking to us, Joni?"

"No guards." She shook her head again, her raggedy blonde hair trailing out behind her. "You asked about guards." The hum of their wheels against the concrete grew louder. She set the pace. They needed to keep up. "There are no guards in this place at night-time. Or very few at least, even with the double shifts. Even with the guards moaning in the garage. Chances are, they've found somewhere to rest for the night and are pretending to be out doing their job. Don't need to worry about the guards at night-time."

Gracie said, "What about the dogs and drones?"

Joni's entire frame tightened, her slim shoulders snapping up to her thin neck. "They don't rest." She shook her head again. "Not like the guards. Not lazy. Never lazy. But ..." She thrust her hand into the air to show them her glowing device. "Joni knows where they are at all times. Knows how to avoid them. Stay with Joni and you'll be fine. The dogs and drones are the eyes of the guards. Avoid them and we—"

"Avoid the guards?" Hawk thrust his arms out again. The quickened pace clearly tested his confidence.

"Exactly," Joni said.

"Hi all!"

William jumped, his heart kicking.

Artan gasped and pressed his finger to his right ear. "Nick?"

"You can hear me?"

"Yeah."

"At last. I've been trying to speak to you since you left. I wonder why it didn't work until now."

Artan smiled. "It's working now. That's all that matters."

They all wore an earpiece. The tiny little things were so small William had forgotten about his. Nick had remained at Joni's and sat in front of her bank of screens. From there he could provide them a different perspective on the prison. He saw the world through the eyes of the dogs and drones.

"How are we looking from your perspective?" Were Matilda not next to him, William wouldn't have heard her through his earpiece. He only got Nick's reply.

"It all seems clear. Joni's right. If there are guards, they're probably resting somewhere. I've not seen a single one out tonight. Are you all okay?"

"Fine!" Hawk still had his arms out.

The hum of their collective progress, of rubber against rough concrete, had grown louder. William squinted against the cool headwind.

"They've not seen me yet, you know?"

William saw his own confusion on the faces of his friends. Joni had gone to the effort of shouting to be heard, so she must have meant it for them. He leaned forwards to quicken his pace and pulled level with her. The hum of their tyres changed momentarily when they crossed a white line. "Who hasn't seen you?"

"The guards. No, the guards haven't seen me. Nor the dogs and the drones. In all the time I've been here, I've been as quiet as a mouse. Lived in my underground house."

"How long have you been here?" The others matched William and Joni's pace, but kept about ten feet back.

"Dunno." Joni threw her scrawny shoulders up in a shrug. Her blonde hair streamed out behind her. "Twenty to twenty-five years."

"Years?"

"At a guess, yeah."

"Jeez."

Slim. Lithe. Joni leaned forwards a little more. The motors in her hoverboard whined with her acceleration.

William could match Joni's pace all day, but the ten-foot

gap between them and the others increased. Hawk and Gracie rode at the back.

Joni turned right.

William wobbled at her sudden change in direction, overshot the turn, spun around and followed her, entering the narrower road with the others. Maybe they had the right idea of holding back a little. Hard to predict someone like Joni. They could only ride on her coattails and hope they ended up where they needed to be.

"How are you feeling, Nick?" If Artan struggled with keeping pace, he hid it well.

"Fine. You?"

"Better for hearing you. Are you all healed?"

"The worst of it, yeah. I don't know what Joni gave me, but it helped. A lot. It was some kind of special ointment."

Hawk rubbed the scars on his neck. William bit back the need to ask if he was okay.

Joni snapped into another left turn. Now fifteen to twenty feet ahead. William led the following pack. Matilda and Artan shot around the bend after him. Hawk took the turn wide and slapped his hand against the steel wall. But he remained on his board. Gracie slowed to take the turn, Olga beside her.

William leaned forwards again and caught up with Joni. "You need to slow down."

Joni eased off. "What do you think will happen when you're in the last section of the prison?"

The others caught up. When none of them replied, William said, "What are you talking about?"

"The final ten percent of the prison."

"You're speaking like we know about it," William said. "What about the final ten percent of the prison?"

"It's hard to get through. So very hard. Joni wouldn't try

it. Oh no, Joni knows what she can and can't do. She can't do the final ten percent. Very few can."

"Prisoners?" Artan said.

"No. Not prisoners. No prisoners in the final ten percent. They wouldn't last two minutes. Which is precisely the point." She pinched the air as if the point she just made had become tangible and it needed collecting.

William frowned as hard as his friends. "What are you talking about, Joni?"

"The last ten percent of the prison. Close to the south exit."

"Go on."

"It's too close to the south exit."

"Too close for what?"

"For prisoners. They don't want them there. Want it to be hard for anyone to get through. That small amount of insurance. Peace of mind."

"Who doesn't want them to get through?" William said.

Artan jabbed a finger at his temple. "You're mad in the head, Joni. You talk in riddles."

"Artan!" William waved him back.

Artan eased off and fell in with the others.

William tried a softer approach. "Who wants peace of mind, Joni?"

"The people in the south. They want to know if there's any trouble in the prison, the prisoners won't be able to get to them. The last thing they need is an army of angry prisoners on their doorstep."

"And that's where the final ten percent of the prison comes in?"

"Gold star for you. Joni knew you'd catch up eventually."

"What's it like?"

"What's what like?"

"The final ten percent of the prison?"

"Oh, that. You don't want to go there."

"But that's where we're going."

"You are?"

"You know we are."

Joni slammed several hard knocks against the side of her head. "Stupid, Joni. Stupid. Stupid."

"All right." William reached a hand in her direction, but stopped short of touching her. Joni hung in the balance. Even slight physical contact could tip her over the edge. "Calm down, yeah?" He raised his eyebrows at the others, his cheeks bulging from where he blew out. "Now tell us about the final ten percent of the prison."

"You don't want to go there."

Artan flapped his arms. "We know we don't want to go there!"

William glanced at Matilda, who reached out to her brother and frowned at him.

"The final ten percent of the prison is a fail-safe. If the prisoners ever overrun the prison, they'll find it hard to go south because it's a maze of walkways and roads."

"Like here?" William said.

"Yes, but tighter roads with so many twists and turns. And—"

"And?"

"Booby traps. A shitload of booby traps."

"And there's a route through?"

Joni nodded. "Of course."

"Good. What is it?"

"Dunno."

"Dunno?"

"Only the guards know. Joni doesn't go that far south. Nothing there for her. And even if she wanted to go there, she couldn't. The route changes all the time. Learn it one week and it's different the next. Only the guards know what it is."

"So we're screwed?"

"Maybe. Maybe not."

"What?"

Joni leaned forwards and sped up. "Joni's teaching you to move fast. If you're quick, you might outrun the booby traps. You might get through."

"Run?" William said. "That's the best you've got?"

"That's all there is. Unless you can work out the way through. So we need to move faster. You all need to be faster. That's what this is about. This is why Joni is taking you through this part of the prison. Practice. You need to be fast on the boards. It might keep you alive."

"Well, that's made me feel better." Artan shook his head. "Are you hearing this, Nick?"

"Loud and clear."

"Joni's here to help where she can. She's not here to make you feel better."

"No," William said, "I don't suppose you are."

"But what she can do is give you practice around here. Get you better on the hoverboards, so when you need to, you can move fast. If you can't be safe, at least you can be fast."

"You must know something about the last section of the prison?" William and Joni had once again opened a larger gap between them and the others. Hawk and Gracie were struggling to match their pace. But they needed to be faster. Maybe they needed pushing.

"There's more everything in that section. More dogs. More drones. More booby traps. Drones, dogs, and booby traps, oh my." Joni frowned into the wind and remained fixed straight ahead. Her board's motor sang. They were close to top speed.

William sensed it this time and pulled back. He rode halfway between Joni and his friends.

Joni snapped right into a plaza like many they'd already visited. The space occupied by two massive buildings. There were trolleys scattered throughout, much like they'd seen in the plaza with the catapult. They were half-filled with seemingly useless tat.

Gracie yelled. The turn had been too sharp and too fast. William winced as she flew from her board and rolled over the rough concrete before she came to a sprawled halt.

William cupped his mouth with his hands. "Joni! Slow down!"

Wild eyes. Wild blonde hair. Joni came back. She divided her attention between her device, the fallen Gracie, and the entrance to the plaza. She tutted and shook her head. "Too slow. Won't last five minutes. A waste of Joni's time and patience. Too slow. They have a death wish, and they're trying to take Joni along for the ride."

William said, "What is this place?"

Joni scowled at her device. "Industrial section." She looked back at the plaza's entrance. "Manufacture."

"What do they make here?"

"Whatever they're told to make. The biggest workforce in the UK. What else are prisons for? They work for nothing. Well, they get fed."

"That doesn't sound like much compensation."

"Oh, you have no idea. They live like royalty comp—" Joni's jaw fell. Her face illuminated by the backlit glow from her screen. "Dogs and drones! We need to move. Now!"

Olga and Matilda helped Gracie back onto her board.

Joni's long hair whipped out behind her as she spun around and shot away from William.

Gracie back on her board, William gave her a thumbs up, which she returned. He led them out of there after Joni.

William left the industrial section first. Joni pulled away from him, and he pulled away from his friends.

Across the wide road, Joni shot into a residential plaza.

William waited at the entrance. One eye on where Joni had gone. One eye on his friends.

Artan exited the industrial plaza first.

William followed Joni. The residential square like many he'd already seen, this one crammed with small houses.

A mazy route through the place, Joni got farther and farther away. William cupped his mouth and filled his lungs, but he let his call die with his exhale. The place still. Everyone must be asleep. Shout now and he'd wake them up. And no matter how much noise he made, she wouldn't wait. His shouting would only add prisoners to the dogs and drones already closing in on them.

Back the way he came, William met Artan at the residential section's entrance. Artan slowed to a halt, and William shook his head.

"She's left us?" Artan said.

Nick in their ear. "What's going on?"

Artan tutted. "She's left us, Nick. I knew we couldn't trust her. She's mad in the head. She's a snake. And she's left us for dead."

"For dead?"

Matilda, Olga, Gracie, and Hawk burst from the industrial plaza.

Although replying to Nick, William raised his voice so the others heard. "She sensed drones and dogs on our tail. We weren't fast enough to keep up."

"So she left you?"

"I'm going to kill her," Artan said.

Clack-clack!

Clack-clack!

The dogs' mechanical steps called through the quiet night. Hawk looked back at the plaza. "If we live that long."

Artan stamped his foot. "Shit!" His board spun to the right and nearly bucked him off.

His face as pale as the moon, Hawk checked back again. "We need to hide somewhere. Get away from here."

"They'll still find us," Artan said. "Joni left us because we're screwed."

William waited for Olga to look at him. When she did, he nodded back towards the industrial plaza.

Olga chewed on her bottom lip.

William shrugged.

Olga nodded.

"Tilly." William grabbed her warm hands and stared into her wide brown eyes.

Clack-clack!

Clack-clack!

"Why don't I like this?"

"You, Artan, Hawk, and Gracie need to find somewhere safe."

"Where?"

Nick came through to them. "Come back here. I can guide you. Head for the guards' tower, and I'll get you the rest of the way."

"Good." Artan nodded. "When we get back, I'll cut Joni's throat for abandoning us."

A mess of worry lines on her face, Matilda squeezed William's hands. "But what about the dogs and the drones?"

Clack-clack!

Clack-clack!

"We'll deal with them. Olga and me."

"What?"

"Meet us back at Joni's, yeah?"

"What are you doing, William?"

"We don't have time for this." William kissed Matilda. "We'll see you soon." He pulled his hands from her ever-tightening grip and followed Olga back into the industrial plaza.

They shot across the abandoned square, back towards the sounds of the dogs.

Clack-clack!

Clack-clack!

Olga led the way at full speed. She exited the plaza.

The sound of the dogs on their left, she turned right.

Gatling guns whirred, and bullets tinged off the nearby walls.

William followed Olga down a narrow street on the other side of the road. The bullets sparked against the steel wall. A ball of flames heated William's back.

The tight road contained his board's hum. The tall walls blocked out the moon's glow. The deep shadows made William's already tired eyes sting. He searched the darkness for their route through. Where would Olga take them?

The path snapped left and right. William gritted his teeth, chewed back his adrenaline rush, leaned into his acceleration, and followed Olga's mazy path away from the drones and dogs. Hopefully they had the pace and trickery to lose them.

The dogs' mechanical gait overrode the drone's hum. But where there was one, the other would be close, hovering over them, ready to fill their target with lead. The machines entered the smaller road.

Clack-clack!

Clack-clack!

Already too close and they were gaining on them. These destructive creatures didn't need the light. They'd hunt you down and kill you whether they could see or not.

CHAPTER 3

Gracie stood in a daze and stared across the plaza. Artan snapped her out of it by knocking into her, sending her stumbling from her hoverboard.

"What was that for?"

He snorted an ironic laugh. "What? You expecting Joni to come back and help us? That ship's sailed, sweetheart. That snake left the second she got a chance. Don't believe her kooky act and faux sincerity. She's as ruthless as everyone else in this place. Her cogs are all turning, and her plan is her own. But at least she's shown us the truth."

"Which is?"

"Whatever we need to do, we do it alone."

"Hey!" Nick came through to them. "I'm with you too!"

Gracie stepped back onto her board and checked behind.

"And we haven't got time to worry about them. William and Olga can handle their business. We need to handle ours."

The residential plaza, a maze within a maze. Alleys ran in every direction, some of them too narrow to pass through. The moon shone on the sprawl of one-storey houses, their flat roofs a brushed steel mirror for the silvery light. The tight paths were bathed in darkness.

"But don't worry." Artan had remained nearby. "I'll make sure we get through this alive and back to Joni's place. Someone has to cut her throat when we see her."

Hawk also stood in a daze. He stroked his throat.

"Sorry." Artan raised a hand in his direction. "I didn't mean to …"

Matilda pressed a finger to her ear. "Nick, are you in contact with William and Olga?"

"No. From what I can see, the last thing they need is me jabbering in their ear. I've muted myself on their channels."

"But you can see them?"

"Well, it's dark, so not really. And the view keeps changing between the dogs and drones, but I'm getting the idea. They're being chased."

"Are they getting away?" Matilda turned her hands over one another as if the action could somehow spend her anxiety.

"I think you should focus on what's ahead of you. You need to get back here. Can you see the guards' block?"

The houses were low enough to give Gracie a clear view across the plaza. The gap in the tall wall, their exit out of there, framed a section of the vast and ugly building in the distance. "For now, yeah."

"Good." A slight metallic hiss to Nick's response. "Then head for that, and worry about everything else later. You're no good to anyone dead."

They were standing still, but Hawk thrust his arms away from his body again to help him keep his balance. "Won't it be easier for us to go around?"

Artan pointed at the guards' block. "But we can see where we need to go." Even though he spoke with a whisper, his voice carried across the plaza as a gentle call to the hundreds of sleeping residents. "If we try to go around, the walls will block our sight."

Hawk's brow locked in a hard scowl, and his face twisted. He had plenty of things to say, but, clearly, none of them were a valid argument against Artan's logic. He leaned into his board and moved slowly forwards, deeper into the residential section.

"Also"—Gracie raised her eyebrows at her scarred friend—"we can't be sure we've lost the dogs and drones. I don't want to risk going out there and bumping into them. And if they end up chasing us, we stand a better chance of losing them in here."

A distant *clack-clack* called through the prison. Faint and growing fainter, but anxiety still gnawed at Gracie's gut.

"Do you think they'll be quick enough?" Matilda faced back in the direction William and Olga had gone. Her mouth hung ajar.

Forcing her tight lips into the approximation of a smile, Gracie's voice wavered, betraying her attempted confidence. "Yeah, I'm sure they'll be fine."

"Nick's right." Artan zipped over to Matilda and Gracie. "We need to focus on what's in front of us. I don't think getting back to the guards' block is going to be easy. We need to get moving now."

Artan led the way, Matilda behind him. They zipped along one of the wider alleys running through the plaza and vanished around a corner, their speed low to keep the whine of their boards' motors to a minimum.

Gracie rolled next to the trundling Hawk. "You ready?"

"No. I th—"

"Shit!" Artan's voice echoed in the alley.

Hawk glanced back at the plaza's entrance.

Gracie tugged on his still protruding arm. "Come on." She led the way after Artan and Matilda.

Artan had jumped from his wheeled board and stood in the middle of the path.

"What's happened?" Gracie's whisper carried through the square.

Artan threw a hand toward his board. "It's out of charge."

The small red light beside the left wheel blinked. Gracie chewed the inside of her mouth.

"Better one of ours than William's and Olga's. We can deal with this." Matilda pressed her finger to her ear again. "How are they getting on, Nick?"

"Same."

"Same?"

"Yeah."

"The drones and dogs aren't gaining on them?"

"You need to focus on you, Matilda. You need to head to the guards' block."

"Can you—"

Gracie rested a hand on Matilda's forearm, and her friend flinched.

Matilda pressed her earpiece again. "Can you put me through to William?"

"That won't help. They're moving fast, and it's really dark. They're safer if we leave them to concentrate."

Tears glistened in Matilda's eyes.

"So what do we do?" Gracie said.

Hawk pressed down on the air with his hands. "How about we keep the fucking noise down?"

"What about Artan's board?"

"What can we do?" Artan threw his arms up in a shrug. "It won't magically recharge."

Hawk stepped from his board. "We might be better on foot, anyway."

"*You* might be."

"Do you have a better option, Artan? You can have my

board if you like, but that means you have to let me ride piggyback."

The next one to step off, Gracie pointed towards the guards' block. "Come on, let's keep moving."

Since William and Olga had left them, Matilda had divided her attention between where they were heading and where she wanted to go. Gracie took her hand and helped her step down. "Come on, Tilly. We've made the choice to head for the block. We need to focus on that."

"Easy for you to say."

"You think I don't care about William and Olga? We can't help them right now. We need to make sure we're waiting for them when they get through this."

Matilda sighed and stepped from her board. "At least we're quieter on foot."

Like when he'd been on the boards, Artan led the way. A fierce boy at the best of times, he seemed spurred on by his fury at Joni. His broad shoulders hunched, he jogged and leaned into his progress.

Now they were off their boards, they had the freedom to move along all but the narrowest of alleys. Gracie followed Artan's lead, the path so tight she only had an inch clearance on either side of her. Any tighter and she'd have to turn sideways to progress.

The group halted when someone shouted in a familiar but entirely unrecognisable language. Gracie's heart pounded, her pulse a bass drum throb in her ears.

Click!

A nearby door opened.

Click!

And another one.

A flash of white passed the end of the alley. Someone ran whilst carrying something. They moved too fast to see exactly what. A bat or club. A weapon of some sort.

Another person tore past. The moonlight licked his long knife's blade.

"They know we're here." Hawk's breathing quickened. He turned one way and then the other. Someone else flashed past the alley behind them. Both ends covered. "We're screwed."

More shouting. More people woke up.

"I knew we should have gone around."

Artan bared his teeth. "Have you got anything useful to say?"

People flashed past every few seconds. They clearly had somewhere to be. That somewhere wasn't the tight alley. But they'd find them soon enough. Surely just a matter of time? There were too many of them to fight. Far too many. Even if they only met a small group, the residents were armed. Gracie dropped to one knee, linked her fingers, and held her hands out as a step for Hawk. "Get on the roof. Now."

It took for Matilda to do the same for Artan before Hawk moved. He stepped into Gracie's hands, the grit on the soles of his boots sharp against her palms. Gracie grunted as she boosted him higher.

With both Hawk and Artan on the roof, Gracie held her makeshift step towards Matilda.

"No." Matilda remained down on one knee. "You go first. I can get up on my own."

"You're sure?"

"Just hurry, Gracie."

Gracie stepped on Matilda's hands and pushed off, boosting herself so she caught the lip of the roof. Her boots scraped against the brushed steel wall as Artan and Hawk grabbed the back of her shirt and dragged her up.

Lying on her front, Gracie rolled over just as Matilda sprang up onto the roof next to her. "What the …?"

Matilda hunched down and pressed a finger to her lips.

A stampede tore through the alley they'd just left. Men and women shouted. Footsteps pounded the ground.

His eyes wide, Hawk's cheeks puffed when he blew out. "That was close."

"It still is," Gracie said.

The shouts and screams moved away from the hut. They ran towards the area of the plaza where Gracie and the others had entered.

"Maybe they've found our boards?" Artan said. "Maybe that's what's got them all riled up."

Gracie flicked her head in the mob's direction. "It sounds like they're going the other way."

Artan got to his feet and turned a full circle. He dropped again.

"See anything?" Hawk said.

Artan shook his head. "The houses are too close to one another. The alleys look like cracks on a baked desert. I can't see into any of them."

Matilda pressed her finger to her ear again. "Nick, can you see anything?"

"I can't see any drones or dogs in your area."

"What about William and Olga?"

"Just focus on you, Matilda."

"Why?" Her words quickened. "What's wrong?"

"Nothing. Nothing's changed. They're being chased, and they're trying to get away. From what I gather of your current situation, you have a plaza filled with an enraged army thirsty for blood. Focus on you."

"He's right." Gracie rested her hand on Matilda's back, and her friend flinched again. She did not want to be touched.

Artan led the way. And maybe the only one of them who could. The only one who knew William almost as well as

Matilda did. The only one who could make a choice she'd accept. He crossed the roof to the opposite side.

Just before he slid into the slightly wider street below, Gracie reached out to him. "Stop. You don't think we should go across the roofs?"

"No." Artan shook his head. "We can hide in the alleys. We're exposed on these rooftops." He slipped off the roof backwards.

Gracie followed the others back into the shadows. They moved in a line, Artan at the front and her at the rear.

The plaza's perimeter wall loomed large, the gap where they needed to exit still framing the guards' block. A mazy path of left and right turns, they drew close to their way out. More people shouted at one another, but they were far enough away. And they were still heading in the other direction.

Artan led them around another right turn and along another tight alley. Gracie's eyes stung from where she strained to see.

Click!

Artan halted, and Hawk slammed into his back. Matilda and Gracie stopped, all four of them panting from the run. Gracie's collar itched with her sweat.

Pointing in the sound's direction, Artan then pressed his finger to his lips.

Click!

Another door opened ahead of them.

Two men. They conversed in their language. Grumpy. Annoyed at being woken at this time of night. The ring of steel. A sword being drawn?

Gracie peered through the window of the house beside them. A small splash of moonlight peered in with her. It cut a silver beam across the room. Across the empty table and bed.

The disgruntled men's steps drew closer.

Click! Gracie opened the hut's door.

Matilda scowled at Gracie, but they had no time for discussion. She pulled the door wide and slipped into the hut.

Hawk followed her. Artan and Matilda next.

Pushing the door to, but not closing it completely, Gracie pressed her back to the wall beside it. If someone burst in, she'd be on them before they had time to react. Sweating from their run, her throat dry, she balled her fists and watched the door through stinging and unblinking eyes.

The men walked past. They didn't have the zeal of some of the other soldiers. They took their time. But regardless of their actions, the fact remained; this community was on high alert. They knew they had intruders, and they needed to weed them out.

Her face to the window, dirty net curtains between her and the cold pane, Gracie waited for the men to vanish before she turned back to the room and a grinning Artan.

Standing between the single table and unmade bed, he gripped a machete in each hand. Matilda had a club with nails hammered into it, and Hawk held a metal baton.

"At least we can defend ourselves." Artan handed Gracie a machete.

The weapon fitted her grip, the blade slightly top-heavy, begging to be swung. It had been made with a clear purpose in mind. "We use these as a last resort, okay?"

"What?" Artan said. "You on their side or something?"

"Kinda."

"*Kinda?*"

"See it from their perspective. For all they know, we're the enemy. And now we're bringing dogs and drones to their homes while they're sleeping. Dogs, drones, and stolen vehicles. What would happen to them if the guards found the abandoned boards? We're a threat to them and their families.

Why wouldn't they be pissed off? So this"—she waved her machete—"has to be a last resort."

Hawk opened the door, cutting off Artan's reply. He led them back out into the dark alley.

They took three more turns to reach the plaza's exit. The shouting soldiers had gone the other way.

"Looks like we won't get to use them after all," Artan said as they left the plaza.

Gracie exited last. Back in the roads, the tall walls once again blocked their line of sight to the guards' block. The moon hung in the sky on their right. Keep it there and they'd remain roughly on course. For now at least.

"Shit!"

The snap of the end of Artan's word stuck Gracie with a frigid blast. That one syllable said so much.

Like a horde of diseased, they appeared and blocked the road ahead. Men, women, and even children. All of them armed. At least two hundred in total. Gracie turned around.

"Shit!"

The same the other way. Both options blocked off. While the army remained still, Gracie slowly led them back the way they'd come. They could lose them in tight alleys. But she froze at the plaza's entrance. Three times the number of soldiers compared to those in the roads. They were still a few hundred feet away, but they closed in. They blocked every route through their home. As one, they raised their weapons and loosed a booming roar. Those in the streets echoed their cries.

Artan slumped beside her. "Shit!"

CHAPTER 4

"Joni's better than this." The wind in her face, the open prison ahead of her. What good is freedom when it comes at such a cost? "Better to go down surrounded by friends than to survive alone. So long alone. What freedom is that? Different when it was Joni's only choice. When it was to get away from him. But what kind of person turns their backs on her friends? That's no way to be. That's the kind of thing he'd do. And Joni's not like him."

Still at full speed on her hoverboard. Still racing away from her friends. Joni leaned into her acceleration. Her brow cold from the headwind. The moon on her, a spotlight on the coward with the tail between her legs. "No. She won't be like him. She can't. Goes against everything she stands for."

The board's high-pitched whine eased when she adjusted her weight. She blinked repeatedly to clear the tears in her sore eyes. The chilly wind had turned them bone dry. "Bone dry, don't cry. Joni should have worn her helmet. Would have made everything easier. Hidden her face. Protected her eyes. No cries."

Joni slowed and pulled her scanner from her pocket. Five

of them. Made up of both dogs and drones. The red dots raced through the tight streets back where Joni had left them. They had to be on their tail. Chasing hoverboards. Trying to kill Joni's friends. "Is Joni already too late? No. They're still running. There are still people to chase. Still people to save. To protect. But what if the drones and dogs see her and then show him back in the observation room? She's still here. In his prison. She's the one messing with him. Has been for over twenty years. It will all make sense. Of course it was her. Who else would it be? Fucking with him. Trying to break him. Hurt him. But he deserves it. Deserves it and more. And she will give him more. But what if he sees her? She's had the element of surprise in her back pocket for over twenty years. Will she be forced to play her hand?"

The pack of five remained a tight cluster of red dots on her glowing screen. They chased something. Joni slammed her knuckles against the side of her head. "Gotta go now. Can find a way to save them and remain hidden. Joni doesn't have to blow her cover. She can still sneak into his room and cut his throat whenever she pleases. Like she planned. Or take him to the oubliette. Hang him from the roof of his precious block. Make an example of him. Humiliate him. Revenge will be sweet, and it will be hers. And her friends will be free. She'll be inconspicuous. She's done it this long. Helmet or not, she has to help. Do what he wouldn't. Don't let his poison in. Mama Bird has to help her chicks."

A press with her right foot spun the hoverboard one hundred and eighty degrees. Joni shot back the way she'd come from. After her friends. "She's not like him and never will be. She'll do what's right. Mama Bird's coming, little chicks. Hold on. Mama will save you."

Screams and yells somewhere nearby. Hundreds of voices. The residents from the plaza she'd gone through. But the dogs and drones were chasing her friends on the other side. The shouting people had nothing to do with them.

Joni leaned back when she rounded the bend, bringing her hoverboard to a halt. The rowdy mob vanished from sight. Weapons held aloft. An enraged battle cry. On a charge towards the plaza. But not after the dogs and drones. The cluster of five red dots in the streets on the other side of the square. "Far away from this lot. This mob has nothing to do with the little chicks. Don't get distracted, Joni. Don't get dragged into their drama. They're chasing something else."

Her finger to her ear, hovering over the earbud's power button. "No." Joni lowered her hand. "Can't let any more voices in. Chopped Liver is to help *them*, not to jibber-jabber straight into Joni's brain. Can't let him in. Won't let him in. Already had someone in there before. Not again. Not now. Never. No. Go after the dogs and drones. They're the threat. They're chasing the little chicks on their hoverboards. At this time of night, the machines are like Joni. They have their sensors, and she has her scanner. They can move without daylight. The little chicks can't. She has to help them before they're roasted. Filled with lead."

Joni's scanner gave her a route around the plaza. She took it at full speed. Her dry eyes still sore, she blinked repeatedly. Tears ran from her temples into her hairline. The tracks cold in the headwind. Screams in the plaza. Thank the heavens she'd avoided that. Can't go into that. Chaos. Madness. Whatever they're doing.

The industrial plaza's perimeter wall on her left, Joni burst onto the road she'd crossed earlier. The road where she'd left her friends. "What kind of person does that? Someone like him. And she's not like him." She shot into a narrower road on the other side.

The tightest road she'd been on so far. The darkness complete. The walls cast inky black shadows. But, like the dogs and drones had their sensors, she had her scanner. She could save her friends.

The backlit glow shone in the darkness. The prison mapped out on the screen. At full speed, blind to what lay ahead and dazzled by her scanner, Joni trusted the recreation on her device and threw a hard left.

Her board's motor whined. Pushed to the limit. Joni fixed on the screen with unblinking eyes. Burning eyes.

Left.

Right.

Left.

Left again.

She gained on the dogs and drones. Five red dots.

Right.

She'd never chased them before.

Left.

She slammed into a wall. Fire in her right shoulder. She wobbled, but stayed on.

Right.

Fork left.

Thawp! Joni whipped past the sharp point of steel from where the wall appeared in the centre of her path, splitting it in two. The leading edge thin enough to slice her like chopped liver. And it hadn't been on her screen. How could she now trust what she saw?

Joni eased off. "If that's not on Joni's device, what else has she missed? She can't—"

Thwip!

Thwip!

Two hoverboards and two riders shot past the end of the alley.

Clack-clack!

Clack-clack!

Drones and dogs on their tail. Three dogs. Two drones.

Whomp! A fireball. Much closer and they'd be roasting the little chicks.

Joni leaned into her acceleration. She had to head them off. Get the little chicks away from the machines.

Out of the end of the alley, Joni turned a hard right just as the last drone turned left up ahead and vanished from sight again.

At full speed, Joni blinked; her vision blurred. The map on her screen offered no answer. "How can Joni cut them off if she doesn't know where they're going? How can she predict what the little chicks are doing? They probably don't know themselves."

She turned left after the drones and dogs. She raised her finger to her earpiece. "But what good would it do to have him jabbering in her ear? How can he coordinate this? He doesn't know where they're going. Another voice to contend with. It'll just confuse Joni. Spin her out."

The machines vanished around another left turn.

"Joni needs to head them off, but how? Where?"

Another fireball glow. Joni shot around the bend, the reek of burned metal in her nostrils. How soon before one of those fireballs caught up to them? Lit up their clothes? Cremated them on the boards. Burned metal turned to charred pork.

The map on Joni's device had given her a heads-up. She now had the lights from the drones and dogs ahead.

Gatling guns whirred. Their bullets hit the steel walls, playing a tinging symphony.

Joni turned into the next alley just in time to catch the final drone going right up ahead.

She pressed on her board, her toes aching. But the pressure didn't make her any faster.

Around the next bend. The little chicks were silhouettes in the shadows. The machines had gained on them. "Fuck it."

She didn't have time to head them off. If she didn't show herself to him, her friends would die.

"Years in this place. Over twenty. And she's going to blow it all." Joni cupped her mouth with her hands. Filled her lungs. She yelled, "Oi!" It hurt her throat. "Oi!"

The drone at the back spun around. A bright headlight for a nose. It shone at her. Looked at her. On camera now. Decision made. No going back. She flipped it the bird. Flipped him the bird. "Fuck you and your shitty prison." She pointed at it. "Know that I'm coming for you."

The second drone turned and one dog.

Joni threw her slim arms wide. "Come on, you dumb shits. Come and get it."

The lead dog, the one closest to the little chicks, turned so quickly it stumbled and fell on its side. It slammed against the wall with a clattering crash. It jumped back to its feet. Re-righted itself. She had them now. All five.

Joni spun around and raced away.

Clack-clack!

Clack-clack!

The machines gave chase.

Whomp!

A fireball. The heady gasoline reek filled the air as if they were one spark away from worldwide cremation.

Her screen as her guide, Joni pressed down on her board. The vibration from the rough road ran through her legs. Hurt her shins. Stung her kneecaps.

Left.

Right.

Right.

Right.

Clack-clack!

Clack-clack!

The machines remained on her tail. And they weren't giving up.

Around the next left and out of their line of sight, Joni stopped. Panting, she jumped from her board. She swallowed an arid gulp. Device in hand. The red dots drew closer.

Clack-clack!

The hum of the drones. The drones in the lead. They were always faster.

Just feet away.

Joni slipped her device into her back pocket.

"Yeargh!" She jumped from cover. Met them head-on.

She grabbed the first drone at full speed, her legs dragging away from her as it carried her with its progress.

Bullets sprayed the walls, but she hung on. A wild pendulum. Chaos' metronome. Her weight dragged it one way and then the other. It continued shooting. Sent out a spray of bullets. Danger detected. It needed to be eradicated. But it couldn't hit her. She was a monkey on its back. A rope around its neck. An anchor on its hull.

Joni kicked the wall on her right and spun the drone around. The indiscriminate spray of bullets cut into its flying friend.

Splash!

The headlight shattered.

Clunk!

Its heavy body hit the ground.

One drone down.

Whomp!

The first of the dogs joined the battle.

She kicked the wall again, fighting against the drone. It tried to turn so she had her back to the flames, but she overpowered it. The drone's bullets chewed into the ground. They ran a line up the front of one dog and turned it limp.

Whomp!

Another fireball.

The drone fought Joni. Tried to turn her back to the flames again. "Not this time, drone."

Joni's already sore legs ached. But she kicked the wall away and reversed the direction of their spin again. Several bullets shot into the night sky. An attack on the moon.

Another kick, Joni forced its nose down.

Dog number two fell. One to go.

Joni braced for another fight, but the drone changed its tactic. It shot towards the dog. The bullets stopped.

"Shit!"

Joni tucked in her legs. The fire ran beneath her as they shot over the dog at full speed. She let go of her grip before the drone could execute the final part of its plan.

Clang!

The drone slammed into a steel wall and fell to the ground. Without her.

Joni lifted it. It took both hands to raise the heavy metal body above her head. She charged at the dog. Its mouth open wide. The glint of a camera lens. A dragon's rumble of flames in its chest.

"Yeargh!" Joni slammed the drone into the dog and snapped its jaws closed with a *clop!*

It blocked the camera's view. "Screw you!"

Crash! She hit the dog again, snapping its neck and knocking it into the alley with her hoverboard. "If you can still hear me, I'm coming for you. I'm going to cut your throat in your sleep. I'm going to gouge your fucking eyes out."

Crash! She hit the dog again. Its chest rumbled.

Joni slid the drone's body towards it and ran. She tripped and fell forwards, fire tearing into her palms from where she used her hands to cushion her fall. She crawled away from the alley's entrance just in time.

Whomp!

The dog ignited, and flames burst from the end of the alley.

Joni rolled over and lay on her back. She panted at the moon. Her ears rang. Her head spun. Her tears cut rivers down her cheeks.

"Wow!"

Joni wiped her eyes. She sniffed against her running nose. The pocket rocket stood over her.

"You really are formidable."

"Sorry." Joni wiped her eyes again. "Joni's so sorry she left you. Should never have left you. Should have been here to help. It doesn't matter what he sees. He's done for anyway. She should have been a better friend. Joni should have helped. Put your friendship first."

"Well, you did. And that's all that matters," William the leader said. "But we need to go."

"Where?"

"The residential plaza. Our friends are in danger. Where's your board?"

Joni sat up and pointed back to where the dog had exploded.

"Shit!" William crouched down and held his hands out behind him. "Get on my back. Now!"

CHAPTER 5

William's hoverboard bowed under the strain of his and Joni's combined weight. The ache in his back spoke of a similar pressure on his spine. Joni clung on while Nick jabbered in his ear.

"William! Olga! The others need you in the residential plaza. Now!"

Riding at their side, Olga pressed her finger to her earpiece. "Tell them we're coming as quickly as we can."

Joni's weight shifted when she turned towards Olga, and William wobbled, his board snapping left and right as if following a miniature chicane.

"Who are you talking to?"

William had a hold of Joni's thin legs. She'd wrapped them around him when she'd clung to his neck with a double headlock. "Can you hold still?"

"Sorry." And back to Olga. "Are you speaking to Nick? What's happening to the others?"

Another wobble. William dug his fingers into Joni's thin thighs. She yelped. "Hold still, will ya? And aren't you talking to Nick too?"

"No. Too many voices. Turned him off. Little birds cheeping in my brain stop me thinking straight."

"You think straight?"

Joni tensed and tightened her grip. He could have been more polite, but at least it had shut her up.

The hum of William's tyres deepened in the left wheel when he leaned into his turn. Joni's weight made him less mobile, and he swung wide on his entrance. He came close to slamming into one of the many small houses.

The path ahead narrowed on both sides, funnelling into a rat run of alleys streaking through the heavily urbanised area. William slowed to a halt. "Shit!"

There were prisoners everywhere.

And they were all armed.

Even the children.

Machetes …

Bats with spikes …

Chains …

Clubs …

Because they were yet to enter the tight streets, and were a foot taller on the hoverboard, they had a view over the small houses' roofs. Packed so closely together, they formed a plateau about eight feet from the ground. Gracie, Hawk, Matilda, and Artan stood on a roof on the opposite side of the plaza, watched by every prisoner in the place. They stood with their backs to one another. They too carried crude weapons, which they used to keep about fifteen prisoners at bay.

"Shit," Olga said.

Nick's metallic crackle tickled William's ear. "What's happening?"

"They're screwed." Olga sighed. "There must be five hundred prisoners here."

"You have to do something!"

"Great. You got any suggestions?"

"I can't see what's happening, can I?"

"But you see fit to issue demands?"

"All right." William waved at the red-faced Olga. "There mus—"

A woman with a spear charged at Artan. She held her weapon towards him tip first.

Machete in hand, Artan widened his stance. An unblinking glare, locked brow, and his weapon raised. He met her war cry with one of his own, threw a backhanded swipe with his long blade, and batted the spear from her grip.

Despite the hundreds of people, the clatter of wood against the hut's flat steel roof rattled around the plaza.

Crack!

Matilda caught the now unarmed woman with a clean cross to the chin.

A collective drawing of breath hissed across the square.

The second the woman fell, Matilda weighed in on her. She kicked her in the head, turning her rigid form flaccid.

Artan raised his machete.

"No!" Gracie held an open palm at him. "She's unconscious. That's enough."

Another prisoner crawled close to Artan, cowering when he raised his machete and bared his teeth. He grabbed the woman's ankles and dragged her away.

Thwip! Artan cut a slice of air with his massive blade. "I'll cut you up if you come close to me again!" *Thwip!* Every prisoner on the roof moved back a step.

Nick's metallic crackle. "What's going on?"

"A stalemate." Olga spoke with a whisper. "Matilda, Artan, Gracie, and Hawk are stuck on a roof. They're holding the prisoners back."

"For now." William shrugged to shift Joni's weight on his back. "They're outnumbered by about five hundred to four."

"Shit!"

"Yeah, shit."

"What can we do?"

The prisoners still watched Matilda and the others on the roof. They were yet to notice William, Olga, and Joni.

"*We?*" Olga said.

Nick's voice cracked. "I'm trying."

Olga flinched when William touched her arm. "Give him a break, yeah? Nick, can you patch us through so we're all talking to one another?"

"Yeah."

A slight click of connection in William's ear. He shouted, "Argh!" and leaned forward on his board. Joni on his back, he hurtled towards the prisoners. They had surprise on their side. The only advantage in their current situation.

Matilda came through to him. "William? What are you doing?" She turned his way, and a prisoner charged at her from her right.

"Matil—"

But Artan had her covered. He broke from their formation and slapped the prisoner's face with the broad side of his machete. *Crack!* It whipped around the plaza and drove the prisoner back.

William's hoverboard whined under his and Joni's weight. The prisoners were still tens of feet away, but they now faced him. Hundreds of them. Where did he expect this to go?

"Stop!" Joni squeezed her thighs.

"What?"

"Stop. Now."

"What for?"

"Just stop!"

William had halved the distance between him and the prisoners. Halved the distance without much of a plan. He halted, and Joni jumped from his back. She ran to the closest house and scrambled up onto the roof. She stood with the confidence of someone ten times her size. "What's she doing?"

Olga shrugged.

Some of the prisoners on the roof with Matilda and the others ran towards Joni. More climbed up and joined them, jumping the narrow alleys. A pack of wild monkeys. They closed in on her. But she stood there like she had the winning hand.

Olga rode closer to William. "What's she doing?"

Prisoners burst from alleys. They closed in on William and Olga from every angle like floodwater. William leaned back and rolled away from them. Natural instinct. But how would that help the others? He halted again. Held his ground.

Joni raised her hand in the air.

It halted the prisoners' charge. Both on the ground and on the roofs.

She held a small device with a red button. Her blonde hair blew in the wind. Joni faced the prisoners who'd come towards her. "William, Olga, get closer to me."

William rolled towards Joni, Olga following him over. He jumped from his board, ran down the alley alongside the house Joni stood on, kicked from the opposite wall, and boosted himself towards the roof. He caught the rough steel and dragged himself, belly-first, onto the cold flat surface. Reaching down for Olga, he pulled her up beside him.

A stalemate. Like Olga had said. Joni had her button raised. The prisoners remained still and kept their distance.

"No!" Gracie in their earpieces. "No way. Can she hear me?"

William pressed his finger to his ear. "No. She doesn't have the headset turned on. Says it confuses her."

"You have to stop her, William."

"But she's the only one who can stop the prisoners. You

think we have any other control in this situation?"

"Have you seen what those buttons do?"

"No. But I'm guessing it's effective."

Five hundred people in the plaza, nearly every one of them silent. All of them fixed on Joni.

Gracie's voice carried the entire way. Over the tops of the houses, but much clearer in William's ear. "Tell him, Matilda."

"She's right, William. We've seen what it does. There must be another way. She can't use that button on these people. They don't deserve it."

"They're trying to kill you, Tilly!"

"Still."

"Still?" William shook his head. "Still what? I'd see all of them slaughtered to save you."

Matilda sighed.

Joni held the button towards William. "Take it from me if you think I'm in the wrong."

William glanced across at the others. Gracie urged him to grab the button, but Matilda stood still. Her pale face reflected the moon's glow. She frowned at him.

"But"—Joni lifted the button a little higher—"if you do, then know I can't help you. I'm fresh out of ideas on how to get us away from here."

Gracie threw her arms up. "How can she even carry one of those? I didn't think she'd stoop so low."

Olga stood several feet away, her arms crossed. William turned to her. "What do you think?"

She shrugged.

"Helpful. Thanks."

"I don't know what it does."

While they'd been talking, some prisoners had stepped farther away.

"Do you know what you're doing?" William said.

Joni nodded. Several times. Too many times. "Yes."

"Can I trust you?"

"She's fucking mental, William. Of course you can't trust her." Gracie stamped her foot. Several prisoners jumped from the *crack* of her boot against the steel roof.

"Yes." Joni nodded again. And again.

"Olga, you have to do something."

"Look, Gracie." Olga pressed her finger to her ear. "I don't know what that button does, but it looks like it's the thin line between life and death. Right now, we're outnumbered, but Joni's in control. Why should we give that up?"

William stepped away from Joni. "Whatever you decide, I'm backing you."

The button in the air, Joni stepped towards Matilda and the others. The prisoners on the surrounding roofs retreated with Joni's progress.

William and Olga followed her. They stepped over the narrow alleys between the buildings, moving closer to their friends.

Gracie, Matilda, and Hawk all watched the button in Joni's hand. Wide-eyed like the prisoners had been. They'd seen what it could do. Artan wore a confused frown.

The prisoners exited the plaza like ants fleeing a burning colony.

"What's happening?" Nick said.

Gracie sneered. "She's shown us who she really is."

Olga tutted. "It looks to me like she's saving your arse, Gracie."

"That button's evil."

"When used." Joni wagged her finger at Gracie. "But Joni's not pressed it yet, has she?"

The last of the prisoners left the square. William grinned at Gracie. "She has a point."

"Never mind what that button does!" Artan stepped across an alley towards Joni. He pointed his machete at her.

"You left us, you snake. You showed us your true colours. You're spineless. You just told William he can trust you, but how do you expect us to trust you when you run at the first sign of trouble?" He stepped over another alley, just one roof between him and Joni.

Olga ran around and stood between them. She shoved Artan back when he stepped from the next alley. His white-knuckled grip tightened on his machete.

"Olga's right," William said. "And she's doing you a favour."

Artan spun towards William, his broad shoulders hunched. "What?"

"You start something with Joni, and she'll kick your arse."

Artan scoffed.

"It's true." Olga folded her arms. "We just watched her take down two drones and three dogs on her own. With her bare hands. She'd break you."

The left side of Artan's top lip rose in a snarl. Olga shoved him back again. "She came back for us. We all make mistakes. Fortunately for us, she realised hers before anyone die—" Olga coughed to clear her throat. "Before anything serious happened."

"Leave her be, Art," Nick said.

Artan relaxed his grip and pressed his finger to his ear. His thick jaw widened with his tight clench. He spoke through gritted teeth. "But you know what she did to us."

"As unconventional as it was, she saved us. I'm better. You're alive. How would we have fared on our own in the prison? Separated from the others, and with the state I was in … You might not agree with her methods, but they were effective. You need to let it go."

"Joni's sorry she left you." The button still in her hand, Joni lowered it and stared at the ground. "She made an awful choice. She got it wrong. She got scared. She's been hiding from him for so long, and now he knows she's here. To save you meant Joni had to reveal herself to him. Now he knows she's here. That's the one thing Joni wanted to protect. That's all she had, and now it's gone."

The tension left Artan's jaw. He shook his head. "I don't know what you're talking about."

Gracie, Matilda, and Hawk joined them. William reached out and took Matilda's warm hand. "You okay?"

Matilda shrugged, her attention flitting from William to the button in Joni's hand.

Olga pointed at it. "What is that thing, anyway? How can a button be so effective against an army?"

"It's the master's manacles." Gracie damn near spat the words. "To carry that makes her one of them."

"To *use* it makes Joni one of them." She waved the button in the air. "But she didn't use it, did she?"

"Where are your hoverboards?" William said.

Matilda squeezed his hand. "We abandoned them. One of them lost power, so we moved on foot." She pointed back across the square. "We can get them?"

"No good." Joni shook her head. "Leave them in a place like this and they'll vanish."

"Where's yours?" Matilda looked Joni up and down. "You came in clinging to William's back."

Olga laughed. "An exploding dog blew it up."

Gracie relaxed a little. "She really took down the drones and dogs?"

"Yeah."

The plaza now clear of prisoners, they stood alone, bathed in the moon's light.

"We need to go," Joni said. "On foot, it's going to take us the rest of the night to get home. This place gets much busier during the day. When it's light, the prisoners will be the least of our worries."

CHAPTER 6

Sore eyes, sore limbs, her weary body clumsy. But Joni smiled as she dragged the hatch across and closed herself in her home with her new friends. They'd made it. They'd walked until dawn to get back here, avoiding many threats, from drones to dogs to guards, and they'd made it. Safe. "Safe and sound. Round pound. Feet on the ground."

Little Chick Artan beneath her. He stepped off the ladder first and ran to Chopped Liver. The two boys hugged and shared a kiss before embracing again.

"I'm so pleased you're okay." Chopped Liver. Nick. Not so chopped liver now. Thanks to her. He pulled back and stroked the side of Artan's face. And then to the rest of the room: "All of you. I'm so glad you're all okay."

The beauty queen, Matilda, rested a hand on Chopped Liver's back. She smiled. Bags beneath her eyes, her greasy skin shone in the weak light. But still beautiful. Always beautiful. Not that her beauty defined her. The warrior. The climber. The runner. And humble, almost to a fault. Almost. Perfect in every way. "Hey!"

Everyone in the room looked at Joni. She stepped back into the shadows.

Chopped Liver let go of Artan. "How was the walk back?"

"We spoke to you the entire way."

"But I couldn't see much." He pointed at Joni's seat in front of the screens. "Sure, there's a lot going on, but none of it makes any sense."

Little Chick took Joni's seat. And he could. At some point, she'd expect to sit in it again, but her guests deserved the best comfort she had to offer. He leaned back and crossed one leg over the other. "It was a long walk back."

The pocket rocket, Olga, grabbed Joni's arm and pulled her back into the light. "Thankfully Joni had her scanner to detect the dogs and drones."

"And when she saw them, she didn't run this time."

"That's enough, Artan." Matilda smiled at Joni.

"Joni didn't need to run at that point." Her hair fell across her face, and she left it there. "Joni's already shown him she's in the prison. Over twenty years of hiding, and now Joni's exposed herself. And all you do, Little Chick, is complain."

"I'm not a fucking chick."

"Complaining chick. Not fucking chick."

Olga pressed the back of her hand to her nose and snorted a laugh. "I think it suits you, Little Chick."

The left side of Little Chick's face bulged from where he pressed his tongue into his cheek. He flipped Olga the bird. The chick.

Most of the others smirked, including Chopped Liver, who spoke before anyone else could. "And guards? Did you see many of them?"

"We avoided them." Joni raised her right index finger. "But they're a unique proposition. Unlike the drones and the dogs, we can't track them. Guards have privacy in this place. No trackers. No cameras in their homes. And there will be more of them than ever before. Because of what Joni's done. Attacking the dogs and drones is a no go. The prison will be on high alert. Flashing red lights on the white lines. Every guard and his dog searching for us. He'll punish people today. Nasty little man, he'll punish people for sure. Wants blood, and will get it. A flood of blood. But Joni's keeping her life essence to herself, thank you very much. He won't get a drop. No siree." Joni walked in circles to spend the adrenaline dump. She knocked her fists together and shook her head, more hair falling across her face. "Joni will get him first. Fit to burst. Show him the worst. Show him she's out for blood. His name through the mud." Her shouts echoed in the room. "Just you wait and see!"

"Uh, Joni?" Olga Pocket Rocket stepped between Joni and Little Chick. "You said you'd tell us about what that button does when we got back here?"

Joni jumped when Gracie appeared on her right. "Why are you carrying it around with you in the first place?"

"This button"—Joni waved it at Gracie—"saved the angry Little Chick and Chopped Liver when they were about to be killed."

"I'm not a fucking chick!"

"With it, Mama Bird dispersed the crowd. She brought them back here to safety."

"Imprisonment!"

"Without this button, angry Little Chick would be dead. Chopped Liver would have bled out like he had an implant. And now it's saved you lot. Besides"—Joni tucked her long hair behind each ear—"Joni didn't use it. She can't."

"Huh?" Matilda this time.

Several presses of the button. Joni held it towards Gracie.

"What are you doing? Stop that!"

"There are no prisoners nearby. And it wouldn't matter, anyway. It's deactivated. No matter how many times I press it, it doesn't work. And it doesn't need to. They've used them against them so many times that just the sight of it makes them scatter. Clatter. Batter. Natter."

"What?" Gracie said.

"It's a prop. Nothing more. Joni wouldn't use one of these things. No way. Not my play. Rather die today. Okay?"

Gracie's lips shrivelled, and she stepped back. Back into the shadows where Joni wanted to be.

"Uh, we're still in the dark here." Olga Pocket Rocket looked from Joni to Gracie. "What does the button do?"

Separate from the group, Gracie leaned against a stone wall and spoke beneath her breath. "When it works, it's pure evil."

"Joni can show them what it does. Joni has video footage." Joni dropped down by one of her many small storage boxes. A wooden chest about three feet wide, two feet tall, and two feet deep. She'd stolen it from him. Dark wood. Immaculate when she brought it here. Highly polished. It shone so brightly you could see your face in it. Although, why he wanted to see his face ... To stare at his own piggy little eyes. His vicious little smirk. She'd scratched it good and proper. Cut deep gouges into it. Banished the memory of his reflection. Destroyed his prize possession. Precious to him, a functional piece of junk to her. The laptop charging in the chest, she disconnected the cable, retrieved the laptop, and closed the chest. The laptop's screen lit their side of the room.

"What's that thing?" William leaned over Joni's shoulder and scowled at the screen.

"A computer. It's a laptop."

"A what top?"

"A laptop. Watch this." She stretched her right hand so her fingers splayed. The sensation settled her rampaging heart. The stretch of her digits a physical comfort that gave her peace. She couldn't tell why. She'd put the laptop in the chest for a reason. Like a Ouija board that couldn't be destroyed. Its presence, an evil in her home. But necessary. Footage that needed to be seen. She double-clicked on a file.

Now on the other side of the room to the rest of them, Gracie tutted. "I can't watch it. Whatever it is."

His face sent a shiver through Joni. His long forehead that went on forever. It ran from the top of his nose over to the top of his neck. He sat on the back of a buggy while a guard drove. The guard wore a helmet. Hid behind their anonymity. The faceless cowards enforcing his will. A dictator's army. But he grinned for the camera. Didn't give a shit who saw him. He had the certainty of a psychopath. He did what the world needed. What others were too afraid to do. Classical music played from a speaker on the back of the buggy.

"What's making that sound?" Matilda said.

"He is." Joni nodded at her screen. "He has a penchant for the dramatic."

"Wait!" Matilda stood next to William and leaned closer. "Hawk, have you seen this?"

The scarred warrior joined the other two. "It's him."

"Louis!" Joni said.

"Oh, shit." Olga came closer. "William, we've seen him too."

"You all know him?"

"I don't." Little Chick remained in Joni's chair.

"We saw him on our way over here," William said. "In the rat run. As a massive floating head."

Artan sat up in Joni's seat. "What?"

"Yeah." Matilda nodded. "Us too."

A drone followed the man on the back of the buggy. Recording him. "That's him. Louis." Joni pointed at the screen with a shaking finger. "And he now knows Joni's here. He might think he's in charge, but Joni will make him pay for everything he's done. Everything! She'll cut his throat in his sleep. Or drag him into the oubliette and leave him to rot. To be forgot."

Her blood still cold, Joni's skin crawled when Louis turned to the camera again. "So, how many do you think we'll get? You've still got time to guess."

"Guess what?" Little Chick said.

"Get ready." The driver's helmet muffled his voice. He turned them into a residential plaza.

Louis held the button aloft and cackled wild laughter.

Screams lit up the plaza. The prisoners scattered. A flock of spooked birds.

"Shit!" Hawk said. "Don't tell me he's—"

"What the …?" Little Chick joined the others, his face slack.

On the screen, scores of prisoners fell while they fled. Many flat on their fronts. Many to their knees. They face-planted. They leaked blood.

"What's he doing to them?" Little Chick said. "What's happening?"

The cackling laughter had morphed into a maniacal titter. Louis yipped and whistled. He leaned towards a group of children. About fifteen in total. From the ages of about four to about twelve. "Want some sweeties, kiddies?" He pressed the button.

Some children screamed. Some coughed blood into the air. They all fell.

The first plaza behind them. Half the prisoners slaughtered. The only thing working in their favour. A guarantee he wouldn't return. He couldn't afford to kill any more. Production must continue. Needed to keep some prisoners who knew how to run the machines.

"Why?" Matilda spoke breathy words. "Why's he doing that?"

"They attacked him first. He's getting payback."

"You think that justifies it?" Gracie said.

Joni shook her head. "No."

"Sounds to me like you agree with him."

Joni sprang towards Gracie, knocking the others aside. She led with a pointing finger. "Don't you dare say that." Olga and William grabbed her and pulled her back. She twisted and writhed. Spat when she shouted, "Don't you dare."

Olga and William turned Joni back towards the screen. She rocked with her hard breaths. She ground her teeth. "Don't you dare."

The buggy entered another plaza, the wobbly drone footage on its tail. Hawk sighed. "Oh, shit. Not again."

The button back in the air in his outstretched hand. Louis laughed again. Different people, same shit, they scattered like the ones before. But he didn't press the button. Not yet.

An old couple stepped from their home and blocked the path. Both were in their seventies. Joni had seen this too many times already. The poor couple were bent and broken from their hard life. Who knew how long they'd been his prisoners. Joni's stomach twisted like the fingers on the old woman's halting hand.

The buggy slowed. The rest of the prisoners continued to scatter.

"What are those old people doing?"

Louis turned to the camera again. "Looks like we have a couple of heroes." His grin damn near reached his ears. Nasty bastard. "Poof!" He pressed the button. The camera zoomed in on the old couple's faces. They cried blood. Claret spilled from their noses. They coughed and spluttered. They dropped to the ground.

The camera pulled out for a wide shot. Louis jumped from the back of his bike, kneeled down in front of the fallen pair, smiled, and gave a thumbs up. A trophy hunter with his prize. "Such a shame. I was going to spare the prisoners in this plaza. They should have stayed indoors."

"Jeez! Power trip, much?" Artan spat his words. "He's a nasty little rat."

"Evil." Joni punched her open palm. "Pure evil."

Louis jumped on the back of the bike again, and they left the plaza.

"We've seen enough," Gracie said.

Joni closed the laptop's lid.

Gracie frowned at her. "Why do you have that footage?"

"Because he's not released it."

"Huh?"

"Joni's hacked into his cameras." She pointed at the twenty screens and her now empty chair. "She sees what he sees. She sees *everything*. Sees and records. He might decide some of the footage is too cruel for general consumption. It might fail to meet even his low standards."

"And you don't?"

"Joni has it all stored. Joni sees what the drones and dogs see. Joni has the full, uncensored experience. And the world, or at least our part of the world, will see it all at some point. See that he has no limits. No morals. Nasty little man. The world needs to know. Once that's done, so is he. Then she can cut his throat."

"You said they attacked him," Matilda said.

Joni nodded.

"*Who* attacked him?"

"The child army. The secret army. The hidden soldiers. The invisibles. The unregistered. Whatever you want to call them."

"That doesn't answer my question."

"The child army are made up of children born inside the prison's walls. They should be registered and given an implant."

"An implant?"

Joni ran a finger along the back of her neck. "Those who have an implant have a small scar."

Matilda turned to Gracie and then Hawk. "Like the ones we met."

"*Most* prisoners have an implant."

"And that's why they bleed when he presses the button?"

"When the implant is triggered, it releases highly concentrated acid that turns their insides to liquid. Like a frog in a blender."

"Which is why they haemorrhage?" Matilda said.

"From every orifice."

"The button can do that to anyone?"

"Anyone within about ten to twenty feet. And for anyone who crosses the white lines—"

"Which is how they contain the prisoners?"

"Precisely."

"But not the hidden army."

"They don't have the implants. They can move through this place like you or I."

Matilda raised her eyebrows at Hawk and Gracie. "And that's why some prisoners can cross the white line. That makes sense now."

"The dogs and drones have scanners," Joni said. "They can tell who has an implant and who doesn't. But they have to see them first. They can't sniff them out."

Olga Pocket Rocket took over. "Which is why we brought ourselves to his attention? Crossing the line in the rat run showed him we didn't have an implant?"

"And us in the warehouse?" Hawk said.

"Yep, and yep."

William said, "That must have been what those kids in the stable were about, Olga."

"Kids in the stable?" Matilda looked up at William.

"When we were running from the dogs and drones, we got pulled into a hiding spot by a group of kids. We waited with them until the machines passed. We wondered what they were doing there. They seemed well practiced. What's their purpose?"

"When they're old enough, and they have enough of them, they form an army and attack the guards' block every few years."

"Why?" William said.

"To get control of this place."

"How can they possibly win?"

"They can't."

"So they send their kids to be slaughtered?"

"They're desperate. They have nothing else."

"This is all a nice distraction," Little Chick said.

Olga Pocket Rocket frowned at him. "It's fucking awful. And a distraction from what?"

Little Chick held his fingers in a pinch. A small gap between the tips. "Let's not forget she was this close to leaving us on our own."

"Nearly." Joni slipped the laptop back into the scratched wooden chest. "Joni *nearly* left you alone. But she came back. You shouldn't underestimate what that means, Little Chick. What it means for Joni to expose herself like she did. For over twenty years, she's been in hiding. Been able to move around this place as she pleases. To get food. To go into the guards' block. To torment him when he sleeps. But that's all gone. In one action. And all because you and your friends were too slow."

William rested a hand on Hawk's back, but Hawk shrugged it off.

"Torment the man we just saw?" Olga said. "Why haven't you killed him if he's so evil?"

"They'd find someone else to replace him. And Joni knows this devil. Joni knows him well."

Olga spoke with a soft voice. "We get it was a big decision to reveal yourself after such a long time—"

"Over twenty years."

"Over twenty years." Olga nodded. "Why?"

Joni's fingers splayed and bent back. She batted her palms together. It kept her grounded. "You don't want to know what Joni's been through." She walked in small circles. "What he's done to her."

Joni flinched at Olga's touch. "You can tell us."

"The south is a hard place to live."

William snorted. "So's the north."

"No meal is guaranteed. And for someone like Joni, when you have no one else—"

"No mum and dad?" Olga said.

Joni shook her head. "Mum done, had a dad. Joni was on her own and needed to eat. Something to eat. Somewhere to sleep."

"And that's where working in the prison comes in?"

"Check out the big brain on Pocket Rocket. The prison's a job for life with guaranteed bed and board. That's not to be sniffed at." She dragged in a wet sniff. The damp air clogged her nose.

"Which is why you stayed here after you left the prison?" Matilda said. "Better than returning south? At least you can steal from him."

"I *could* steal from him. Not anymore. Because of what the prison offers, he has a lot of power. You take the job, you give him control of your life. For most people, that's not a problem. Especially the people who come with their partners. He mostly leaves them alone."

"Mostly?" William said.

"He's a snake. Will fuck over anyone to get what he wants. But Joni came here by herself. On her tod. Her Jack Jones. And" —Joni ran her hands up and down her body—"Joni didn't always look this way. She came here as a grade A beaut. If she says so herself. He took a shine to her. A shine she couldn't scuff. And it was flattering. Joni warmed to the attention. After being a street rat for so long. Invisible and unimportant, she suddenly had someone who noticed her. Who saw her and paid her the right kind of attention. He was kind. In the beginning, anyway."

Joni rubbed her itching eyes. Her view of the others blurred. "But then things changed. *He* changed. Or maybe didn't change. Maybe just revealed himself. A moth coming from what I thought was a butterfly's cocoon. A horrible brown moth with glowing red eyes. Hungry little eyes that had to have what they desired."

Warm hands fed into Joni's. Olga's warm hands. "You don't have to say anything else if you don't want to."

Nodding more than most people needed to, Joni dragged in a clogged wet sniff. She pulled back from Olga, releasing her grip.

"Happy now?" Olga Pocket Rocket threw a backhanded slap into the front of Artan's shoulder. "Convinced she's on our side?"

"Yeah." Little Chick stepped back and looked at the ground. "Sorry."

"Well, I think we can all agree—" William clapped, and Joni jumped from the crack of his hands "—this place is awful. The sooner we get away from here, the better."

His chin stretched to the sky, Hawk scratched the fresh scar on his neck. "And if the training for the south nearly killed us, I say we might as well just take our chances with the real thing."

"It won't be easy," Joni said.

"And that was?"

"No. I don't suppose it was."

William again. "I agree with Hawk. The part with the booby traps is only about ten percent of the prison, right?"

"Right."

"And at least there are no prisoners in that final bit."

"That's true."

"Uh." Gracie stepped forwards. From the shadows. From where she'd separated herself from the group. "I don't think you're going to like this. Any of you."

William turned his palms to the ceiling. "Just say it."

Gracie's eyes flitted from one of her friends to the next. Her skin flushed. She bit on her fingernails. Her hand in front of her face muffled her words. "I can't leave this place until I've freed the prisoners. Now I've seen how they're living and being treated, I can't walk away without helping them."

The hum from the bank of twenty monitors filled the silence.

Artan's cheeks puffed out with his exhale. He sat back down in Joni's chair. Deflated into it.

Gracie said, "If you don't want to help, I understand. You do what you need to do. But I'm going to do all I can to help the prisoners. If I don't, I'll never be able to live with myself."

CHAPTER 7

While she'd chosen to remain in the shadows, Gracie couldn't avoid the stark glare of everyone's attention. She squirmed where she stood, twisting back against the cold and damp wall. Artan remained in the chair, illuminated by the glow of twenty screens. The others gathered around Joni and the scratched wooden chest to which she'd returned her laptop.

A distant drip pierced the silence. It came from somewhere in their dank hideout. The oubliette? Some other corner in Joni's squalid home?

Drip!

Drip!

"Someone say something."

"You just said you want to free them …" Olga turned her palms to the ceiling. "But where will they go? They hate the south, and the south hate them."

"Then we'll send them north. They have communities there who will help them."

The echo from William's derisive snort whipped around the underground space. "The north is hardly paradise."

"Paradise is a high benchmark in a world like this, William. An excuse for inaction. We can't give them paradise, so why bother?"

"Then what are you trying to do, Gracie?"

"Give them freedom. Improve their lives, even if it's only incrementally. Give them choices. Choices in a shitty world is a vast improvement from no choice in an even shittier world."

The distant drip played its damp metronome.

"Why go to war for these people?" William said.

"You really need to ask that? After what you've just seen? Joni, do you have any more footage? Apparently William still needs convincing."

"And you're going to hide away from it again, are you? Stand over there and avoid the reality of the situation? Because that footage will show you what we're up against. The scale of the task at hand. I feel for the prisoners, of course I do, but what can we do against an army of guards? With their weapons and numbers, they'll tear us to shreds. They have control of thousands of prisoners. Hundreds of thousands of prisoners. And you think a band of seven, eight if Joni joins us, can somehow get the better of them?"

Gracie pushed off from the damp and cold wall. She joined the others, and they gathered around Joni, who removed her laptop for a second time.

"Now!" Joni licked her lips and stroked her blonde hair flat against the sides of her head. "Let me be clear ... When Joni met Louis. When she had a thing ..." She shuddered. "If she could even call it that. Joni didn't know what he was like. She saw he was a creep, but nothing like this. Oh no." She wagged a long finger at those around her. "Nothing like this. Otherwise, Joni would have kept her distance from the very start. Minded her own. Even run a mile if a mile needed to be run. She hated him before she found all this out, so you can only imagine what this has done for her feelings towards him." She turned her back on them and hunched over her laptop. "And Joni will still cut his throat. He knows she's in the prison, but she'll still slit him. Hurt him. Kill him."

Gracie joined the others in moving back a step from the nutty woman as she grew more animated and unpredictable. William's attention seared the side of her face. Waiting for her to look away. To return to the shadows. To avoid facing the very real threat of what going to war with the guards meant. "I know this won't be easy, William."

"You think?"

"But how can we walk away with what's being done to these people?"

"On the button! On the nose." Joni pointed at Gracie. "She has it on the nose. Spot on. Send them north. That's where the prisoners would choose to go, so that's where they need to be sent. Paradise? No, certainly not. But better. Much better." She hit a button on the laptop with her right index finger, and footage played.

The gates opened. Gracie had seen this countless times. She'd watched from the top of the hill as prisoners made a bid for freedom into the waiting arms of the furious diseased. But she'd never seen it from inside the prison. They watched through an elevated camera. It hovered over the heads of the crowd. It looked out towards the diseased meadow. About five hundred people gathered, waiting to run. She rocked with them. Anxious butterflies danced in her stomach. A line of dogs and drones in the foreground. Between the camera and the five hundred. They formed a barrier. None shall pass. No prisoners or diseased were getting back into the prison.

The siren wailed. It called to the diseased.

Clunk!

The gap in the gates grew.

The dogs and drones stepped forward, driving the crowd on from behind.

Gracie turned her body from the screen, but kept watching. Wild activity at the open gap. More diseased shoving to get through than could make it. "They've got no chance."

The diseased blocked their exit.

The dogs and drones pressed from the back.

The prisoners at the front grew more animated.

Wild.

Frenzied.

They fought.

They turned.

The new diseased turned on their friends behind. The frenzy that had started at the gap in the gates spread out and ripped through the crowd.

Bleeding eyes.

Snapping jaws.

Wild limbs.

Olga slumped. "They've got no chance."

As if they'd heard her, the prisoners turned towards the line of drones and dogs. A gap of about ten feet between them and the machines. The diseased now a greater threat, they ran at the guards' enforcers.

The footage glowed with an explosion of flames.

The stutter of bullet fire came through the tinny speakers.

The prisoners closest to the camera, the ones who hadn't turned, either fell to the bullets or burned from the fire. The machines then moved forward and wiped out the diseased, both those from the prison and those from the meadow.

The entire thing lasted a minute at the most.

"See!" William pointed at the screen. "That's what we're up against."

Olga ran a hand through her hair, sweeping it over the top of her head. "I can see why they didn't release this footage. The south seem like bloodthirsty savages with a high tolerance for the suffering of their enemy, but even this is a step too far."

"Oh." Joni laughed. "They showed this. This is prime-time viewing. Those in the south lap this up."

"You're shitting me?" Olga said.

"I shit you not, Pocket Rocket."

Gracie frowned. Why had this nutty woman given some of them nicknames? Although, her assessment of Olga hit the mark.

"This is perfect for those in the south," Joni said. "It shows them the prison guards are in control. It allays any fears they might have of the creatures storming the prison. Half their island is overrun with diseased, but the monsters are staying put. The diseased will never get through. No way, José. No chance. The house always wins. The rest of the footage shows most of the diseased chasing after the prisoners who broke free."

"Some broke free?" Gracie said.

"Sure they did. Some prisoners always get free. It wouldn't be entertaining if they all died. This is the bit that got cut." Joni clicked another button.

Gracie and William shared a glance. The footage had clearly diluted his rage.

The scene played out from a different camera angle. Farther back than the first. The same siren wail. The same gap opening in the gates. The same carnage. The same man Gracie had seen in the arena and warehouse. "Louis?"

Joni spat on the floor. "Soon to be dead Louis. Will cut his throat."

He had wild ginger hair, a similar colour to Gracie's. Bald on top, it clung to the sides and back of his head. He wore a goatee as if the scruffy beard would make up for what he lacked. A guard knelt before him. The man cried, his hands pressed together in prayer.

Crack! Louis slammed the butt of his gun into the side of the man's head and sent him sprawling.

Gracie twisted away again, but kept her attention on the screen. William thought she didn't have the stomach for it. What did he know? She'd stomached worse. Seen worse happen to people she cared for. Both through Dout's cameras and in the flesh. She could stomach it all day long. Even if every beat of her heart twisted with a sharp pang.

The guard scrambled to his feet and wiped his bleeding nose with the back of his sleeve. Louis rested his gun's stock into his shoulder and looked at the man down the barrel. His laugh, tittering and loud. The same laugh that had been the soundtrack for the previous piece of footage.

A dog walked up and stood on either side of Louis. He shot the ground in front of the guard's feet.

The guard stepped back, but pressed his hands together again.

Louis shot the ground a second time.

The guard turned and ran. Through the line of dogs and drones into the onrushing prisoners fleeing the diseased spilling through the opening gates.

"Jeez." Nick walked away when the dogs burned the guard.

"Why didn't we see that from the other angle?" William said.

"Edited it out." Joni tapped her laptop. "It's why it's on here. He doesn't want anyone to see it. To know what working for Louis really means. The guards are heroes. Especially him. King Louis. Don't want to shatter the illusion. But Joni sees the truth. Joni will shatter it into a million little pieces. She'll shatter him."

"W-wha …" Gracie cleared her throat. "What did the guard do?"

"Who knows?"

Olga stepped back from the others. "Does he often kill the guards?"

"Not often. No. But he's not above it. You have to really screw him over to get this treatment. Or have something he wants. Imagine what he's going to do to Joni if he ever gets a hold of her." She clasped her hands in front of her chest. "But imagine what Joni will do to him first!"

Artan stood up from Joni's seat and rested a hand on her shoulder. "I'm sorry."

Silence fell in the room. Joni paused the footage.

Swallowing as if he had something stuck in his throat, Artan said, "I didn't appreciate what it meant to expose yourself to him. And I see you were trying to help me and Nick. And you helped us. In your own way."

"Mama Bird has her own special way."

Artan half-smiled. It fell almost instantly. "I'm seeing that now. Gracie?"

Gracie flicked her head in Artan's direction.

"I'm with you. Whatever you need to do. Whatever it takes."

"Me too." Olga walked away from Joni's laptop. "I've seen enough."

"So all this"—William waved his hand in the laptop's direction—"is to show the south they're in control of the prisoners?"

"Partly, yes. But not the main reason. They also make a killing from it."

Gracie's friends frowned with her. The drip called to them from the other side of Joni's home.

"Bad choice of words." Joni knocked on the side of her

head. "Not the right choice. No. Not good. Killing, living, winnings." She clicked her fingers and pointed at William. "Winnings! The people in the south love to gamble. They put bets on the prisoners. On which one will die first. Who will escape? Who will get taken down by the machines? The prison takes a cut on all bets. It's how they fund the place. What, you think they get state funding? Ha! Like the shining metropolis would find credits to help anyone but them and their own." Joni rolled back and folded her arms across her stomach as if she'd laughed harder than she actually had. "Can you imagine it? No, of course you can't. No state funding here. Privatisation! Sort yourself out. However you see fit. They see fit to use the prisoners as tools for gambling."

Her stomach in knots, Gracie's tight throat restricted her words. "But they're betting on people's lives."

"Not people to those in the south. The enemy. Savages. Most people know someone who's died at their hands, or at the hands of people like them. Why would they have any feelings for them other than abject hatred?"

Nick joined Artan and Olga in stepping away from the laptop. Matilda remained at William's side. Gracie stepped closer. She'd watch it for longer than him. She had the stomach and then some. "Joni, what else do they bet on?"

"The arena. They bet on the winner. How long it will take them to win. How they'll win. The warehouse. Who will press the button first? How many people will try to press the button. How many will choose to leave if they open the doors. How long will it take for the entire warehouse to turn into diseased. How long it will take for all the diseased to leave. To cross the lines and die within feet of the place. They never get away, which the south always see. They know Louis is cautious. It only takes one, you know. They also bet on the rat run."

William raised an eyebrow. "So they would have seen Olga and me running through it?"

"And bet on it, yeah. You showed him you didn't have a chip and that you spoke English. He would have pretended to the rest of the world that you made the right choice of exit and would have muted your voices. Got to keep the narrative alive. He's in control."

"Matilda told me about the arena and the warehouse. Why does he put people in the warehouse?"

"To punish them when they've wronged him."

Matilda's features buckled. Her weak voice lifted no louder than a whisper. "How did the most recent lot wrong him? They played his game in the arena. They won fair and square."

"Fair and square? He doesn't care. Wronged him. That's all that matters. Wrong him and he'll wrong you. He'll see you and raise the stakes. Harder and more violent. Someone had to pay for the child army's attack." Joni pressed a button on her laptop.

Gracie reached towards Joni, but stopped. She had the stomach for it. Whatever Joni wanted to show her. Turn away now and it would give William the chance to refuse to help the prisoners. She could last longer than him.

A group of children and young adults stood in front of the guards' block. The window shutters were down. Dogs and drones charged at them from behind. An encroaching line of death. They stretched from one side of the wide main road to the other. The kids were armed with nothing more than bats, clubs, and blades. Gunfire. Flashes from small gaps in the guards' block. The kids at the front fell. The drones and dogs attacked from behind. A wall of flames. Gatling guns whirred. They tore through the small bodies. Dropped them faster than those who'd tried to leave via the gates.

ESCAPE: BOOK TWELVE OF BEYOND THESE WALLS

"That army took years to amass." Joni sighed. "Whenever a child army attacks, he attacks back. Someone has to be punished. The districts fight in the arena for their chance at freedom. For a chance to head north. This time, he took that away from the winners. Because he could. Like with the button in the residential areas. He can't prevent the armies of unregistered kids, but he can remind the prisoners who's in control."

Gracie flinched at the next piece of footage. A close-up of a child's burned face. A streak of livid pink flesh exposed by the charred and cracked skin. Burned like volcanic rock. The kid's white teeth stood in stark contrast to the blackened destruction. William's cheeks puffed out.

The drone rose, the shot widening. Several guards exited the block. "His own special team." Joni pointed at them. "All men. His inside men. Fellow sadists. The slaughter isn't punishment enough for them. They need to twist the knife they've stuck in."

One guard kicked the head clean off a charred body. Armed with guns and machetes, they picked their way through the fallen army. They nudged the children's corpses. Checked for signs of life. A few men shoved spikes into the ground. Pointed on top. Dirty with either rust or dried blood. The footage made it hard to be sure. Although, what did it matter? Gracie had seen the result. Even if they weren't slick with blood now ...

A guard pointed down at one body. He used his long machete to identify the boy. Gracie lost her breath. The boy with the birthmark on his face. "He's still alive?"

Hawk stepped away while shaking his head.

Matilda stared at the ground and also turned her back on the screen. Away from the footage and away from William. Gracie took her place beside him. She'd stand there all day. She had the stomach and then some.

Louis took his guard's machete. He flicked it up and made the boy stand. The boy who'd led them to freedom.

Louis encouraged him forwards and made him kneel.

The boy complied. He knew his fate. He leaned forwards. Showed Louis the back of his neck.

A smirk painted Louis' face when he raised the machete above his head. He brought it down with a hard swing.

William whimpered, but Gracie held her ground. She folded her arms across her chest and blinked against her stinging eyes.

The first cut deep, but not deep enough to behead him.

Louis swung again, blood spraying from the wound. The second strike sank deeper still. But still not deep enough.

"You had enough yet, William? You ready to bring a stop to this?"

The strength left William's voice. "But look at what they're doing. How can we beat them?"

"Maybe we don't need to. We just need to free the prisoners. There are enough in here for a revolution."

"What if we fail and the guards catch us?"

Thud! The boy's head hit the ground as if in answer to William's question. Louis kicked it across the blood-soaked concrete.

The footage changed again. The guards lifted the heads they'd severed and impaled them on the spikes. One after the other, they raised them high, gripping their ears like handles. They slammed them down, the steel spikes punching through the tops of the children's heads like they were skewering pumpkins.

Tears ran freely down Gracie's cheeks. But she remained at William's side. "I hated these prisoners for so long. When I lived in Dout, I believed they were the enemy. And maybe they were then, but they're not now. All I've known my entire life is war with these people. I've lost family and friends to it. As I'm sure many of those have too. It's too late for those who have gone, but maybe we can change things for the future. Maybe we can act with compassion and send these prisoners north, knowing that not everyone who sounds like their oppressor is their oppressor. I see how nasty these guards are. Louis especially. But we have a chance to help thousands upon thousands of people. And maybe the guards will be too busy panicking about what's happening with them to notice us."

"Okay." William nodded. "I'm with you." He turned to Matilda. "She's right. We can't walk away from this."

"I know." Matilda nodded. "I know."

Deflating with a hard sigh, William stared at the ground for a few seconds before he lifted his head. "I want to go south. I can't hide that, and I won't try. But I wanted the same when we were in Dout, and I pushed it. I didn't think about the group. Max especially. I couldn't see his point of view. Or maybe I didn't respect it. I'm sorry, Olga."

Olga remained in the shadows and spoke in a monotone. "We all played our part in what happened to Max."

"I can see we need to do this. We need to try to help because we can. When we do finally go south, we either do it as a team, or we don't do it at all."

CHAPTER 8

The tighter streets were dark at this time of night. Hell, they were even dark on an overcast day. And most days were overcast here. As if the sky acted as a mirror and simply offered a reflection of the dull and monotonous prison. But, on those days, at least the promise of a storm swirled within the roiling clouds. No such promise existed on the ground inside the prison's walls. Monotony. Restriction. Apathy. Hopelessness. Not that it dulled Joni's heart. Oh no. She had enough fight for every prisoner in this place. She'd help get them out of there, and then she'd take her rusty blade and plunge it between his ribs. The handle lay against the base of her spine. The knife sheathed down the back of her trousers.

The road too narrow and the walls too tall. Unless they were directly beneath the moon, they had no chance of using its light. But Joni had her scanner. The others gasped and huffed behind her from where she kept them running. She held up the glowing screen for them to see. "Joni knows the way, so don't you worry. No dogs and drones around, and the guards won't come out at this time of night. Maybe one or two, but why would they be so close to their block? A block filled with guards. They're in control of this place, so they don't need to patrol its perimeter."

The leader, William, ran closest to her. "Don't you ever get lost?"

"Not anymore. Joni knows this place back to front and inside out. She could run it blindfolded."

"How large is the prison?"

"Coast to coast. East to west and miles deep. The UK's waistband."

The beauty queen quickened her pace. His lover. And what a pair they were. "And when will we be—"

Joni pointed at the sky, slowed her pace, and slipped her scanner back into her pocket. "Hide the screen. Don't want to stand out in the darkness."

The next opening on the left spilled out into the plaza in which the guards' block stood. They'd taken a long route to get here. Just in case anyone watched on. They didn't need to see where Joni lived. "Joni's already revealed herself to them. She doesn't need to reveal her home too. Also, coming this way round has landed us much closer to the block with less open space to cross." Joni peered at the block and laughed.

"What's so funny?" The angry little chick's familiar scowl had returned. He'd left his lover back at Joni's. In front of the screens. Talking to them through the earpieces.

The guards' block stretched at least one thousand five hundred feet wide and stood over one hundred and fifty feet tall. Taller than most walls, but not the main walls. Nothing stood taller than the prison's perimeter. They usually had the solar panel flaps at an angle conducive to drawing power from the sky, but they were closed, covering every window like when a child army attacked. "They've gone into lockdown."

Angry Artan raised an eyebrow. "They don't do this every night?"

"No. Oh no. Why go into lockdown if you don't feel threatened?"

"Them feeling threatened is a good thing?"

Unable to suppress her grin, Joni instead covered her mouth with her hand and nodded. "Oh yes! It means they're scared. It's an acceptance that they're not as in control as they thought they were. Fear leads to mistakes. Headless chickens when their pulses quickens."

"Huh?" Artan said.

Joni tutted. "This lot don't know what they're doing. They don't know what it means to fight an actual war."

Gracie stood a few feet back. "But we're not going to war with the guards. If we free the prisoners, they'll overrun this place. We'll be the last thing the guards think about when that happens."

"Yes, yes." The base of Joni's skull hurt from her vigorous nodding. "Of course. Sneak into their house. Quiet as a mouse. When all's said and done, Joni will cut his throat. But a war is still coming to them, even if it's not a war with us. His time has come. Yes, yes. A time of reckoning."

Joni grinned at the group again. Slack horror met her joy. Wrong crowd. "You have the weapons Joni gave you?"

The guns were clear to see. Like the one she carried, they all wore them across their fronts. Hanging from their straps. Each one read two hundred bullets on the small LED screens. Each one fitted with a laser sight. "Put the red dot on your target and pull the trigger. Simple! Damn, they make killing so easy. Even a moronic guard can do it. Make it too hard and the enforcers in this place would end up shooting themselves in the foot." Laser targeting and very little recoil. And they had ammo for days in William's and Gracie's backpacks. "All standard guard issue, you know? Joni's taken it from them over the years." They all had grenades strapped to their belts. Nearly everything she'd given them. "Where are your buttons?"

The leader, William, pulled his from his pocket. One by one, they showed them to Joni. "Now be careful, these work. Not like the one Joni usually carries."

Gracie scoffed. "I still say it's a waste of time. Why give us these buttons when none of us plan on using them?"

"Better to have them than not," Joni said. "There are two hundred thousand prisoners in this place. We can neutralise almost every one of them at the press of a button."

Gracie threw her long arms out to the sides. "That's not a good thing."

"It is when two hundred thousand of them are baying for your blood. Just hold onto them. Even if you don't plan on using them. It will make Joni very happy."

A snort this time, Gracie shoved her button back into her pocket, burying it deep.

"Nick!" Angry Artan pressed his finger to his ear. "Can you see anything of concern?"

"No."

Joni winced at the tinny intrusion. The unwelcome guest in her ear.

"But I can only see what the dogs and drones look at."

Her back tense, her heart slamming in her chest, Joni held her breath and waited for the fly to buzz in her ear again. A few seconds passed, so she said, "We ready?"

They all stared at her.

Joni stepped out into the plaza and pressed her back against the cold and rough steel wall. The vast guards' block in front of her. Just a few hundred feet away.

"What are you laughing at?" William said.

"Joni was laughing?"

"Uhh …" He looked at Matilda, who nodded back at him. "Yeah. You just did."

"Well, if Joni had to find anything funny, this would be it. Look at it. Locked down like it will make a difference. They're rattled. He's rattled. He would have made the choice to have the block like this. And I can guarantee you every guard is inside tonight. They're too scared to do the night shift. But locked block or not, Joni's like a gas. She'll sneak into his home and kill him in his sleep no matter what he does. Carbon monoxide. She's in control, not him. Also, I wouldn't mind betting all the guards are in there with him. All holed up in Hell's hotel."

"What?"

"It's what I call the place. Hell, because of, well …" Joni spun around with her palms turned to the sky. "And I think the hotel part's obvious."

The scarred warrior said little, but he clearly spoke for the group at that moment. "What's a hotel?"

"They don't have them in the north?"

A line of blank faces met her question.

"It's like a huge guesthouse where hundreds of people can stay. Many of them look like this place, but prettier. Much prettier."

"This is all well and good," William said, "but can you get in?"

"Does a diseased shit its pants when it turns?"

"Huh?"

"Yes!" Joni knocked the side of her head, her attack on her own skull so vigorous it stung. "Of course Joni can get in. Joni can shit her pants. And she can cut his throat later. She's here for whatever you need. You're her number one priority. You, and the moment when Joni gets to see his face when he realises the prisoners are running free. Their escape will hurt him more than any wound ever could."

Silence.

"See the garage doors over there?" Joni pointed across at the large block. Hell's hotel.

The beauty queen nodded. "The locked ones."

"Watch them. They won't be locked for long. Joni's the best hacker in this place. She'll get into the controls and open them so you can get in and out. You've already been in there when we got the hoverboards. Quads are the best. Battery life for days. Nick?"

"Yeah?"

The metallic tinny hiss sent a needle into Joni's ear. "You have the directions still?"

"Yeah."

"Good." Back to the others. Joni licked her lips and swallowed a dry gulp. "Okay, we're all good to go. Joni will open the doors, and Nick will take you to the quads. Just watch the doors, okay?"

Just as Joni set off, Olga grabbed her arm with such a tight grip it stung. "Ow!"

"I'm coming with you."

"What?" William, the tall leader, shook his head. "No, Olga."

"She might need help. I'm going with her."

"Don't you trust Joni?"

"Quite the opposite, in fact. I trust you with my life, which is why I'm prepared to follow you."

Joni smiled with her entire body. From the tip of her toes to the top of her head.

"I want to help you should you need it. Everyone else has someone watching their back. You don't. And you're risking a lot for us." She reached out and held Joni's hands, her grip warm. "I won't slow you down. I promise. I just want to make sure you're okay."

A lump swelled in Joni's throat. It made her voice tight.

"You." She pointed at William. She rubbed her stinging eyes. "You watch the shutters, okay?"

William nodded.

Matilda rested a hand on Olga. "Are you sure you want to do this?"

"Of course."

"Also," Joni continued, pointing at William, "watch the path I take. They have no cameras here. Respecting privacy and all that. But they have eyes. We need to remain in the shadows for as long as possible. Only expose yourself when you have to, okay?"

"Okay."

Joni ran in the shadows. Just an inch of space between her right shoulder and the tall steel wall. Olga behind her. She moved like a ninja. Maybe Joni did need her.

As close to Hell's hotel as they could get, Joni scanned the windows. She couldn't see anyone looking out. They had to take the risk. She broke from cover and ran across the plaza.

Joni slammed, back first, against the block's steel wall. The same cold gunmetal grey steel as everywhere else. Back in the shadows. Olga at her side. She pointed up at a three-foot-square steel vent attached to the wall. About five feet from the ground. "The best way to access the maintenance and ventilation shafts is through the garage. But when they go into lockdown, we can use these." She reached up and ripped the steel grate clear and placed it on the ground beside her. It gave them access to her network of tunnels. "Carbon monoxide. Joni moves through this place like a gas."

Her hands out in front of her, Joni jumped up and dived into the shaft. She slapped her hands to either side of the tight tunnel, braced to hold herself in place, and dragged herself in. She turned around to find the silent ninja behind her. "Wow. You're quiet!"

Olga smiled.

Like the roads in the prison, the maintenance shafts all looked the same. Hundreds of feet of brushed steel with grates looking down on the rooms below. The fluorescent glow from the garage punched up through the openings as dazzling bursts in the gloom. They passed several grates, each one looking down on a different vehicle or machine. Tanks. Dogs and drones. Cylindrical chain bikes. Quads.

"Joni knows this place inside out and back to front." She stopped at the next grate and pressed hard. It swung open and swayed on squeaking hinges. Just before she dropped into the garage, Joni paused. "Can you hold Joni's legs so she can hang down?"

Olga shrugged and grabbed Joni's ankles.

Easing out of the gap until she hung into the garage, bent at the waist, Joni reached for the garage's control panel in the ceiling. Retrieving a small screwdriver from her pocket, Joni undid the tiny screws on each corner of the panel and pulled the cover free. She placed the cover and screwdriver in the maintenance hatch and pulled out her tiny computer. She plugged it into the port. It had three red lights in a line. Each one turned green, one after the other.

Thunk!

The garage doors all unlocked in unison.

"And there we have it, ladies and gents." Joni grabbed the small control panel cover and screwed it back into place. "The marvellous Joni Muldoon strikes again."

CHAPTER 9

The garage shutters slowly rose, the fluorescent glow spilling out into the dark plaza around the block's base. Open mouths that both invited William and the others in and showed them they could close again as easily. Their lives depended on the trust they invested in Joni the lunatic inside Hell's hotel.

"You ready?" Matilda tugged at William's hand.

"Yeah." He nodded, but didn't move. "Yeah."

Artan shoved William forwards.

Like Joni and Olga before them, William ran alongside the wall in the shadows. The shutters lifted higher, and more of the fluorescent glow shone out. In the dark night, the illuminated entrance ramps came close to appealing. But not as appealing as heading south. Shame no one else shared his desire.

At the point where Joni and Olga had crossed, the whir of the garage doors still opening, William kicked off from the steel barrier, forced himself away from the protection of its shadow, and sprinted towards the closest opening door. Artan and Matilda followed a step behind.

"We'll wait here for you." A tinny version of Gracie's voice in his ear. "Just let us know if you need our help."

"Will do." The change from night to the stark artificial glare in the steel basement blinded William, and he slowed his pace when he hit the entrance ramp leading down into the garage. They'd already been down here once, but the place looked far from familiar. There were vehicles everywhere. They must have recalled everyone in the prison for the building to go into lockdown. All the charging points were in use. Their lights showed the status of the batteries. Some were green. Some red. Some pulsed amber.

Their steps echoed through the underground space. Every surface made from cold, hard steel. Artan's voice joined the resonating chorus. "Nick, can you guide us to the quads?"

They passed several tanks parked nose to nose. Each had six wheels, three on either side. They were nearly as tall as William and wrapped with chunky tyres.

"Yep." Nick came through. "You need to head r—"

Fzzt!

William pressed his earpiece. "Nick?"

Fzzt!

They stopped.

Artan's stamp whipped around the garage. "Shit! We've lost contact with him."

"What do we do?" Matilda said.

The garage was large enough to hold all the guards' vehicles. According to Joni, they had more than they could ever use. She'd said they had over one hundred tanks. Three hundred wheeled boards. Fifty quads. Familiar eyes would see the order in this place. William only saw chaos. He turned on the spot. "We have to find them on our own."

Matilda shrugged. "How hard can it be?"

Artan pointed back the way they'd come from. "One of us

could stand by the door and contact Nick again?"

Matilda walked in the opposite direction to where her brother had pointed.

"Tilly?" William's voice ran away from him. "Where are y—"

"Here they are."

William and Artan ran over to Matilda. She stood in front of a cluster of quad bikes. At least thirty, if not more. But they were surrounded. Penned in by the other vehicles. Hoverboards, wheeled boards like Joni's, the massive cylindrical circular bikes with the chain wheels.

They went to work. The hoverboards were the easiest of the lot to move. They lifted them one at a time and laid them down in the pathway.

They grabbed the wheeled boards similar to Joni's next. Again, they pulled them aside, clearing a path to get just three quads out of there. Impossible to be silent in a place where the environment amplified a gnat's heartbeat. They could be noisy and slow, or noisier and fast. William rolled his shoulders to make his backpack more comfortable and tossed the next wheeled board into the pile.

Crash!

"What are you doing?" Artan held a board identical to the one William had thrown.

"We're making noise anyway. We might as well do this as quickly as possible."

Artan tossed his wheeled board aside. He grabbed the next one and did the same. They needed to first clear a space so they could move the cylindrical chain bikes. Once they were out of the way, they could get the quads free. "I just hope it's worth it. I hope the batteries are as good in these quads as she says they are." Artan threw another wheeled board onto the pile.

Crash!

CHAPTER 10

Crash!

Gracie squinted as if narrowing her eyes would somehow help her see through steel and concrete. The others had gone into the garage and vanished from sight. "What are they doing in there?"

Crash!

Hawk looked back into the dark road they'd emerged from. "Who knows?"

Like those before her, Gracie ran alongside the wall on her right. A well-trodden and well-hidden path.

Crash!

Hawk caught up with her. "I guess they've given up on being quiet."

Crash!

"But why?" Gracie scanned the side of the dark and ugly building. The solar panels shone in the moonlight. The side of Hell's hotel now another flat wall in a maze filled with flat walls. If anyone looked out, they had no way of knowing. And with all the noise in the garage, chances are someone would be looking out. "And what can we do to hel—"

"Oh damn!" Hawk pointed at the garage doors. The shutters were closing.

"Damn."

Crash!

"You think they know?"

"With the noise they're making?" Hawk shook his head. "Doubt it."

"Nick?" Gracie pressed her finger to her earpiece. "I need you to tell William and the others the garage doors are closing."

"Can't." The tinny reply tickled Gracie's ear.

"What?"

"I've lost contact with them. Them, and Olga and Joni."

"And you didn't think to tell us?"

"I didn't see the point in stressing you out. I figured they'd find the quads and be back out again."

Crash!

The shutters slowly closed.

Like those before her, Gracie broke from the cover of the wall's shadow and ran towards the ugly block. Hawk followed just a few feet behind.

The fluorescent strip lights in the ceiling dazzled Gracie when she passed beneath the closing barrier and looked up. She stumbled, the incline sharper than she'd remembered.

Crash!

A wall of hoverboards blocked their path. She halted and cupped her mouth with her hands. "Artan!"

Artan had been pushing one of the huge cylindrical bikes with the chain tracks. He paused, his face glistening with sweat.

Gracie pointed behind her. "The shutters are closing. We have to get out of here now."

Hawk ran past Gracie and joined the others. He took another wheeled bike from Matilda and grunted with the effort of rolling it into the wall of vehicles already there. "They've nearly got them free, Gracie."

"Shit." Bouncing on her toes, Gracie turned back towards the closing door. "Will they be quick enough?"

"I think so."

Gracie ran for one of the wheeled bikes and jumped into the seat. The magazines in her rucksack pressed into her back.

"What are you doing?" Artan said.

"Just keep going." She pressed the green button by the handlebars and turned the throttle.

Crash!

She slammed into a nearby wall. The impact threw her from the seat against the inside of the circular track.

"What are you doing?" Artan called at her again as he threw down another circular bike.

A twinge twisted between Gracie's shoulder blades, but she clenched her jaw and pushed through the sharp ache. She returned to the seat, pointed the handlebars where she wanted to go, and twisted the throttle again.

The bike took off for a second time. She wobbled as she hurtled along the path towards the ramp out of there.

Gracie did a sharp turn onto the exit ramp. The bike swung wide. She dragged her right leg across so she didn't lose it in the pinch between vehicle and wall. The screech of steel against steel. Sparks flew. She shot up the exit ramp and out into the night.

"No!" Gracie shook her head. "No. Shit!"

"Gracie?" Nick's tinny voice. "Are you okay?"

"No. Really not."

"What's happening?"

Another turn of the handlebars. The chains sang with their contact against the concrete. Gracie turned a wide half-circle and shot back towards the garage. She should have learned how to stop this damn thing before she rode it.

The wind in her hair, her teeth clenched, she flew at the garage door. She should have learned how to stop it.

Krang!

Gracie hit the wall beside the closing shutter. The sudden halt catapulted her into the bike's inner steel ring for a second time.

"Gracie?" Nick in her now ringing ears.

"Gracie, what's happening?"

A coppery flow of blood ran down the back of Gracie's throat. She stood on weak legs.

The garage shutter closed. Unrelenting. Determined.

Gracie yelled with the effort of rolling the now buckled bike. Sweat burned her eyes, and her head throbbed.

The bike nearly too tall, Gracie forced it beneath the shutter just in time for the steel barrier to pinch it in place. Creaking and groaning, the bike wobbled beneath the strain of the unrelenting shutter. But it held. For now.

Still dizzy, her legs still weak, Gracie spat blood as she ran back down the entrance ramp. She reached the bottom in time for Artan to appear on the first quad, Hawk on the back.

Gracie waved her arms.

Artan rode the quad like he'd done it thousands of times before. He hurtled towards Gracie and took a sharp turn out of there.

Hawk nodded at her on their way past.

The squeak and churn of twisting metal. The cylindrical bike buckled beneath the force of the closing shutter.

Matilda appeared next. Like her brother, she rode the quad with ease, turned hard up the ramp, and left the garage, ducking the shutter on her way out.

Thunk!

The cylindrical bike buckled another notch. The shutter

pressed down on top of it. It had dropped by about a foot. The cylindrical bike's groan grew more laboured as if in warning of how little resistance it had left. The prelude to the inevitable structural failure.

"Come on, Wil—"

William appeared and followed the same path as the others, but he stopped at the bottom of the ramp for Gracie.

She threw her leg over the back, gripped the bar behind her with both hands, and leaned forward with him, both of them wearing their ammo-filled rucksacks like shells.

Thunk!

The shutter dropped like a guillotine as they passed beneath it. A second later and they would have been crushed.

Outside again. The wind in her ears.

Nick rabbited through the earpiece, "What's happening? Someone speak to me."

"We're all right, Nick." Artan laughed. "Everyone's all right."

William reached back and patted the side of Gracie's thigh. "Thanks to Gracie."

"Yeah, but now we need to talk to Olga and Joni. We might get to those gates, but if we can't tell them to open them, we're screwed."

The quad kicked with William's acceleration. "Let's get there first and worry about communication later. With the noise we've just made, I think this is the absolute last place we need to be right now. We've already stretched our luck paper thin."

CHAPTER 11

The skin on Joni's elbows had hardened from where she'd crawled through these tunnels so many times. She lived in these maintenance shafts. She owned them. Not him. "No, never him."

The swishing of her and Olga's clothes filled the tight space, punctuated by the occasional *thunk* when Olga's gun slipped from her back and hit the brushed steel. But not Joni's gun. She could balance it on her back and crawl through these tunnels all day long without it slipping off. All day and all night.

The thunks were never loud enough to be a problem. Olga caught her gun each time before it made too much noise. They wouldn't prevent Joni from showing Olga around. Showing her how many shafts they had the run of. After all, it had to be seen to be believed. They could get anywhere in this place unnoticed. And the vertical shafts gave them access to every floor. Silent and deadly Joni. Carbon monoxide. Kill him in his sleep. But no, not his sleep. Not anymore. The rusty knife down the back of her trousers. He'd see that blade before it took his life. She'd make sure she loaded his blood with fear before she opened up his neck and decorated his walls.

Swish! Swish! Swish!

They passed over grates looking down on corridors. An empty kitchen. The recreational room. Too late at night for there to be any guards in any of them. Most of them would be asleep somewhere. Definitely not out patrolling the prison. Lazy bastards at the best of times. Cowards at the worst. They'd put Hell's hotel on lockdown because none of them had the stones to venture out into the wider prison and look for Joni and her new friends in the shadows.

Swish! Swish! Swish!

Just Joni and her thoughts. Her thoughts and her quiet friend.

Thunk!

Mostly quiet. The company she needed after so many years on her own. Someone there, but not jabbering in her ear like an annoying child.

"Shit!"

Olga Pocket Rocket's words snapped through Joni, and she halted mid-crawl. Her heart rate quickened. Raced towards panic. Her chest tightened. She pressed her cheek against the cold steel of the maintenance shaft. The cool grounding settled her pulse. She filled her lungs.

"Nick?" Olga said.

The whispers smothered Joni like icy water. "Nick?" She pulled her face from the cold steel and peered back at her friend. "Why are you saying that?"

"We've lost contact with him."

No jibber-jabber in her ear. Joni pressed her finger to the earpiece. "Nick? Can you hear us?" If she said it much louder, she'd alert the guards. She shrugged and lowered her voice. "At least it gives us peace."

So long on her own had left Joni unable to read the

nuance in people's gestures. Maybe Olga knew that and made sure she had no ambiguity in her hard scowl. Joni flinched in anticipation of the blast to come.

But Olga breathed in. Her entire body rose with her expanding ribcage. Her features softened, and she shook her head. "I don't think you understand, Joni. If we don't have contact with Nick, we don't have contact with the others. How will we know when to deactivate the white lines? What if we do it when they're not ready and we cause them more problems? What if they're out there right now needing our help, but they can't ask for it? What if they've not even made it out of the garage?"

"A lot of what-ifs!"

"Exactly."

"Exactly." Joni copied her friend. It took a few seconds for comprehension to smother her. Molasses poured on her head. It covered her crown and ran down her face. She poked out her tongue and discovered the sweet taste of realisation. "Oh damn!"

Olga's eyes widened, and she nodded along.

"Joni hadn't thought about that. What do we do?"

"I was hoping you'd know?"

"Yes, of course. We're in Joni's playground now. Not his. No, not his. Joni's the one in control here. She knows what to do." She wagged a finger at Olga. "Don't you worry, Joni knows just what to do."

"Uh …?"

"What?"

Olga winced. "So, what will you do? You're not moving."

"Of course. Of course. Elementary, my dear Pocket Rocket."

"Ele-what?"

"A blocker! A signal jammer. That's all it is. Something to

prevent comms in Hell's hotel between anyone other than those authorised to communicate."

"So what do we do about it?"

"Like with everything else in this place. We find it and destroy it. We break it beyond repair."

"You know where the jammer is?"

"Of course. You're in Joni's playground. Joni knows where everything is. We go to it, we frazzle it so it won't work again anytime soon, and Bob's Fanny's."

"Bob's what now?"

"Uncle and aunt. Come on." Joni waved Olga on. "This way."

The swish of their progress hissed through the tunnels like a gas. Carbon monoxide. In his sleep. Cut him off. Stop his heart. Take her gun, shove the barrel down his throat, and unload every one of the two hundred bullets.

The grates revealed more empty rooms and empty hallways. A bump in the road about every twenty feet. They passed over one after the other. Nothing to see here. They carried on. Over them again and again. Until ...

Joni raised her right ear. Music called through the tunnels. From the room up ahead. Love songs. Ballads from her past. Her skin prickled with gooseflesh. The music came from the observation room. She sped up, her movements drowned out by the warbling voices and sickly-sweet melodies. She reached the grate and peered down. A jolt snapped through her like she'd had a cattle prod shoved into the base of her back.

Olga panted behind her and tapped the soles of her shoes. "Is this the comms room?"

Sweat dripped from the end of Joni's nose and landed on the grey brushed steel.

"Joni!"

Her jaw tight, she spoke through gritted teeth. "The observation room. The screens. It's the eyes of this prison. The dogs. The drones." She stared down at his bald head. The wild ginger hair around the sides and the back. Not beautiful like Gracie's. No. Coarse. Wiry. Greasy. She could fall from the ceiling like a spider. Stinger first. Rusty knife first. Use the momentum of her fall to drive it into the top of his skull. Plunge the tip so deep she sheathed it in his throat. Turn his lights off. End it now.

"Then why have we stopped?"

"Joni's been in this room before." She kept her voice low, his love songs masking her words. A romantic at heart. "He brought her here to work with him." She snorted a laugh. "Not work at all. She did nothing after a while. Surplus to requirements. Hidden away and kept like a trinket. Separated from everyone else in the place. She became his possession."

Joni reached down and placed a hand on her stomach. Sick to her stomach. Stick a knife in his stomach. Cut him. Scar him. Fuck him up.

"Joni." Olga tapped her shoes again. "We need to keep moving. We need to get to the comms room, remember?"

"You don't know what it's like for Joni. You've not lived her life. Here he is. In the flesh. Ready to be stabbed. Oh, Joni's had this chance countless times before, but that was Joni in the shadows. Carbon monoxide Joni. The silent and invisible killer. The Joni who had control. Who took it back from him. But she's not invisible anymore. No. She's out in the open. And she won't be silent. She'll cackle in his face as she cuts his throat. She'll—"

Joni flinched when Olga grabbed her again. "Think of the others. We need to make sure we're in contact with them for this plan to work. Come on, Joni, let's get to the signal jammer. Let's get these prisoners out. That will hurt him more than anything."

What does Pocket Rocket know? The chance to end this

right beneath her. Maybe she should end Pocket Rocket? Shut her up. She didn't need voices in her ear. Thinking they could tell her what to do. Where did she get off? Joni owns the space above the guards. She does what she damn well pleases. One rusty knife, two kills. A blade coated in Pocket Rocket's blood. Drive that into his brain. Sheathe it in his throat. End them both. Turn down the noise. The interference. End it all.

Olga grabbed her again.

"Will you stop touching me?"

"Please, Joni. We need to keep going."

A kind face. A good person. She didn't deserve to die. She'd come with Joni so she could help her. Like Mama Bird helped her little chicks. "Yes, a good person with a kind face. Come on. Joni will show you where the comms room is. Joni will destroy the jammer so we can have jibber-jabber. Chopped Liver. Do you deliver?"

Swish! Swish! Swish!

They left the ballads behind. Louis getting romantic with himself. The only person he loved. Even when he'd kept Joni as his little pet. She'd served his whim. There for his own amusement. He'd controlled her. "Joni thought he was all right at first. Joni didn't fancy him. Oh no. But he might have been a grower. In the beginning he was kind to Joni. Treated her right. Few people treated Joni like that before. Few people cared. It flattered Joni. Blinded her."

Swish! Swish! Thunk! Olga followed behind.

"But when Joni opened her heart to him, his charm left. It held hands with his kindness and his compassion, and all three of them skipped from her life and from her relationship. Getting Joni was a game. Joni made it too easy. Before long, he had total control over her. Chose where she worked and when she worked. Kept her isolated, so he became her only contact. That's when shit got really bad."

"I'm sorry to hear that, Joni. I really am."

Hot beneath her colour, she shook, and her vision blurred. She clenched her teeth so hard her gums ached. "That's when shit got really bad. But Joni will get him back. She'll repay every ounce of pain she's suffered at his hands."

CHAPTER 12

Mocked by the echo of her own panting breaths and her collar itching with sweat, Gracie paused on the spiral stairs and lifted her face to the cool breeze coming down on them. The fresh air smelled of hope. An end to the long spiral staircase. She adjusted her backpack's straps. Just her and Hawk on the stairs, but she carried half the group's ammo. William and the others had dropped them off and left on their quads. Little point in all of them waiting here. Part way up the climb, they'd lost contact with them and Nick. The radio waves couldn't get through to them in their thick steel cocoon.

"Keep going." Hawk took several deep breaths. "We're nearly there."

"Yeah." Gracie nodded and pushed on, her thighs on fire, her lungs tight.

Gracie stepped out into the fresh night air and flung her arms wide. She turned on the spot, the strong wind cooling her sweating skin. "Hello?" She pressed her finger to her ear. "Can anyone hear us?"

"Yep." Nick's voice came through. "Are you okay? You sound out of breath."

"So would you if you'd just climbed the stairs we have."

Matilda came through. "We're staying on the ground. Just tell us if you need anything."

Hawk watched Gracie with his eyebrows raised.

Silence from Olga and Joni.

He slumped and muttered, "Shit!"

"I know. It's been at least half an hour since we left Hell's hotel. Do you think Joni even knows we've been cut off?"

"Or if she even cares? Being cut off is her preference, right?"

"Surely Olga will have noticed by now."

The open space about one hundred feet square. A mini plaza in the sky. The outer edge surrounded by a low wall, Gracie walked to it, rested her hot palms against the cold top, and peered over. Her stomach lurched, and she pulled back. "How many people have—" she made air quotes with her fingers "—fallen from here?"

"No!" Hawk pulled back too. "You think?"

"Joni didn't have many nice things to say about the person running this place."

"Jeez."

From their current spot, they had a view over a vast section of the prison, the moon providing the light. It revealed the maddening routes made up from streets of varying widths. Sentry guns studded every wall. They stood as a silent threat. A reminder that the prisoners had no control here. The white lines. Hundreds upon hundreds of white lines. And many more they couldn't see, the prison stretching away left, right, and ahead. Joni had called it the UK's waistband. Coast to coast and miles deep.

Gracie's heart thumped. It beat harder than it had on her climb up the stairs. The arena's roof had been vast when they were on the ground. From here, it represented only a patch amongst the chaos. The plazas were the same. They broke up the dizzying routes designed to confuse and disorientate. One plaza sat bathed in the unflinching glow of floodlights. "There's fewer of them than I thought."

"Fewer of what?"

"Plazas." Gracie nodded out over the prison. "From the number of prisoners we bumped into, I would have expected them to need more residential spaces."

Hawk stretched his chin to the moon and ran his fingernails along his scars. "But when you think about it, Joni said there are about two hundred communities in this place, each containing about a thousand prisoners. One hundred on this side of the guards' block, and another hundred to the south. That's not many for somewhere this vast."

"It's a shitload when you're thinking about getting them all out."

"All of them?"

Gracie shrugged. "Go big or go home, right?"

"I suppose."

The main road ran straight through the prison. The only order in the chaos. A major artery flowing directly to the dark heart that was the locked-down guards' tower. Hell's hotel.

"Maybe we will go home?"

"Huh?" The cool wind burned Gracie's eyes.

"I mean, if we have no contact with Olga and Joni, how can we orchestrate a prison break? Are you having any more luck than us, Nick?"

"No. Not yet."

"Shit!"

Leading the way, Gracie crossed the elevated plaza. Two hundred feet from the ground, every step flipped her stomach. Away from the sheer drop to either side, and solid steel beneath her feet. But none of that mattered. "No person should be up this high."

"Huh?"

Gracie shook her head. "Nothing." Diseased ran through the meadow. Dark and canted silhouettes. Twitching movements and snarling rage. Groans of pain and discontent. "It's still strange seeing it from this side." The hill several hundred feet away. The hill Olga had thrown herself down when she had a horde on her tail. The hill Gracie had stood on many a time. She'd been called to it like a diseased responding to the siren's wail. She'd watched the gates open and the prisoners run for their lives. She'd watched most of them fall. "If only I'd known then what I know now."

"You wouldn't have come here?" Hawk said.

"I would have helped the prisoners escape. When I stood on the other side of that wall, I only saw my enemy. I only saw what made us different."

"Well, if we get in contact with Olga and Joni, maybe you can make up for it tonight. There aren't a massive amount of diseased out there. And with no siren going off, I'd say it's as good a night as any for a prison break."

"What if we screw up, Hawk?"

"Let the diseased into the prison?"

"Yeah."

"It's a risk."

"One we should roll the dice on?"

"What other choice do we have?"

Two diseased squabbled in the meadow. Fury ran through their veins. The loud argument flared and died in seconds. Gracie scratched her head. "Like you said, there won't be a siren, but there will be thousands of prisoners leaving this place. Hundreds of thousands if all goes according to plan. Maybe this is a huge mistake? Life was so much simpler in Dout. Sure, we were at war, but we knew the enemy. Looking back now, I can see there was a strange comfort in that."

"So you think we should leave? Head north?"

"You'd come?"

"From what I've seen so far, this entire world is shit." Hawk scratched his neck again. "No matter where you go, someone is fighting to have dominance over someone else. From the asylum and Grandfather Jacks' palace, to Dout—"

"Dout wasn't that bad."

"Did you meet Aus?"

Gracie caught the surge that flared up in her. She dropped her head. "Okay, fair enough."

"And then this."

"Same shit, different day?"

"If you like. So I've decided that I want to be wherever my friends are. That's the only part of this life I have any control over."

Maybe he had a point. Maybe Gracie being with her friends should be enough.

"But that's not you," Hawk said.

"Huh?"

"You need to do this. And I want to stand by you. This is important. You can't walk away and leave thousands of people suffering. I could, but you're better than me. Much better. And I won't let you give up on that. And we won't let the diseased in here. We'll keep it outside so the prisoners have a fair crack at freedom. We just need to watch the gates and make sure we close them whenever we feel threatened. It'll be fi—"

"Jammer slammer Alabama."

"Joni?" Gracie pressed her finger to her ear.

"Gracie?"

"Olga?"

"Yeah."

"You reconnected."

"Joni did, yeah. Sorry it took a while. But we should be okay now. We fried the thing that jammed our communications. We also cut off all the comms in the guards' block while we were at it. So we can now talk to one another, but they can't. That should slow down their realisation as to what's happening to them."

"Could have done it sooner. Like when we were getting locked in the garage."

"William?" Olga said.

"If Gracie hadn't come in and helped us out, we wouldn't have stood a chance."

Gracie hugged herself for warmth. "Let's move on, yeah? It wasn't their fault our radios got jammed. And it's fixed now. Joni, how long before you deactivate the white lines?"

"Already deactivated, the cats have mated. Plated. Sated."

"Olga?"

"We've done it already."

"You what?"

"We found the control panel for the implants and deactivated it."

"Proper fucked it," Joni said. "That and the comms. Joni one, Louis nil."

"It won't be coming back online soon," Olga said. "And we've turned most of the lights white so the prisoners know they can cross the lines. We're turning the lights in the south, far west, and far east amber."

"Why?" Gracie said.

"To drive the prisoners towards the open gates. They'll eventually turn red. Joni thinks it's the best way to help them realise they can leave. Shepherd them towards their freedom."

Gracie took off across the elevated plaza, back to the side overlooking the prison. She slapped her hands down on the top of the small steel wall, her stomach turning somersaults. Several hundred prisoners ran along the main road towards the gates.

The slap of Hawk's palms hit the wall beside Gracie. His face pale, he pressed against his earpiece. "How long before you get the gates open?"

Thunk! The vibration of the freeing lock snapped through the entire wall. It rang the massive steel structure like a god striking a vast bell.

"Okay!" Gracie nodded repeatedly as if it would go some way towards settling her rampaging heart. "This might just work ou—"

Whomp!

A fireball slammed into the prisoners on their right side. It set about twenty of them ablaze.

"Shit!" Hawk slammed both hands down on the wall. "Shit!"

"William? Matilda?" Gracie said. "We need help. There are dogs and drones on the main road. The prisoners are about to get slaughtered."

CHAPTER 13

The flames lit up the night. They swelled through the main road as a screaming ball of fire. The prisoners burned alive and howled at the moon. The fire's bright glare reflected off the brushed steel surroundings. A shimmering and shifting glow like the walls were lava.

William brought his quad bike to a halt, close enough to the heat for it to pull sweat from every pore on his body. His throat dry, he squinted at the dazzling white-hot fury. The blinding glare spared him the massacre's gruesome details.

A small form burst from the flames. A child. They waved their tiny arms. Their mouth stretched wide on their blackened face in a silent scream. Or maybe a scream William couldn't hear, their mewling death throes buried by the cacophony of suffering behind them. Their clothes burned like everything around them. After three or four steps, their skinny legs failed them, and they slammed, face first, against the ground. The back of their head blackened and hairless. A girl? A boy? Who knew? What did it matter? They were dead. Now just one of many corpses.

The fire subsided enough to reveal the drones zipping

through the sky. Their Gatling guns spun; the stuttered burst of bullet fire tore into the prisoners who'd somehow evaded the flames.

His stomach in knots, William turned his quad bike around so he faced the other way. Both Artan and Matilda watched the slaughter, the reflection of the flames in Matilda's wide brown eyes. "We need to make them follow us."

Artan scoffed. "Are you mad?"

"We have to help. Why else are we down here?" William slapped his bike's metal tank. "We can outrun them."

His scowl still fierce, but Artan followed his sister in turning his bike around so he had his back to the devastation. "This will get their attention." He pointed his gun at the carnage and looked down the barrel.

William reached over and pushed it down. "What are you doing? You'll kill the prisoners if you do that. Shoot the wall."

The boy had an ego, but he could accept when he'd made a bad choice. Artan lifted his gun again. This time, he aimed it at the wall close to the drones and dogs. The red dot of his laser target danced on the steel surface. A sputter of bullet fire to match the drones' Gatling guns, he made the wall sing.

The machines stopped.

William lost his breath. His pulse throbbed through his skull.

Three dogs and four drones ran at them.

"Shit!"

"What do you mean, *shit?*" Matilda took off. "This was your plan."

Artan accelerated after his sister, and William took up the rear.

Looking back, Artan's eyes widened. "Are you sure this was a good idea, William?"

He didn't need to see what Artan had. They needed to move forward, not look back. "Would it matter if I changed my mind?" William followed them around the first bend into a tighter road. "Just keep going."

Clack-clack! Clack-clack!

The drones and dogs followed their mazy path through the tight streets. The fifty-foot-tall walls on either side loomed over them, reminding them their survival hinged on just one thing; they had to be faster than the seven machines because they wouldn't get out of this prison any other way.

Clack-clack! Clack-clack!

But they weren't faster.

"Shit!"

Tilly's words were softer than her brother's. They whispered to William through his earpiece. "What's wrong?"

William's tight grip on his handlebars sent aches streaking up the backs of his hands. His right twitched, but if he turned the throttle any more, he wouldn't get around the bends. He followed the path laid down before him. He took the next right too fast, and two wheels lifted from the ground.

Clack-clack!

William shifted his weight, his bike crashing down to four tyres again.

"William," Matilda said, "what's up?"

Clack-clack! Clack-clack! The drones' hum joined the dogs' rattling steps.

"They're gaining on us, Tilly."

"Shit!"

Artan overtook his sister and pulled out onto a wider road. "We need to move faster. They're clearly nimbler than us. Hopefully, we have the beating of them for pace."

On the long and straight road, behind Artan and Tilly, William fully opened his throttle. The bike hummed with the acceleration. The chunky rubber tyres played a single and continuous base note against the rough concrete.

William crossed a thick line. White lights atop the walls on either side. They told the prisoners they could move through the prison. They invited them to run into a massacre. Their half-baked plan had done this to innocent people.

The wind in his face, William flinched at the sharp sting on his right cheek. A fly, but it hit him like a bullet. An inch higher and it would have blinded him on that side. He should have taken a helmet when he took the quad.

Clack-clack! Clack-clack! The machines burst onto the wider road, the three dogs at the front in a V formation. The four drones formed a line above and behind them. William faced forwards again. "It's not working."

"What do you mean?"

"It's pretty simple, Art. They're faster than us. What was I thinking? We can't outrun these things."

"Shit."

The whine of spinning Gatling guns locked William's back tight. They'd fill him with lead. And the first he'd know of the flames would be when they fused him to his vehicle. Turned his entire body to black wax like the back of that child's head. He swerved left.

The drone's bullets shot past him. They missed Tilly and Artan. He turned right, snapping into a snaking path down the main road.

Matilda and Artan continued straight and pulled away from him. Matilda looked back. "What are you doing?"

The wheels of William's bike lifted at the sharpest point of each left and right turn. But it worked. The dogs and drones tracked him. "I'm slowing them down."

Bullets whipped past William. Sparks burst from the darkness when they hit the walls.

Whomp!

William left a fireball behind with another right turn. The

heat made his back itch. "They might be fast, but they're not very smart. Now, think of something while I keep them busy."

Matilda slowed down.

Left. Right. Left. Right. A snapping and snaking path. Bullets shot past him. Flames crashed against the steel walls. "What are you doing, Tilly? Giving them two targets to hit won't help anyone."

The drones' bullets whistled through the air. William grabbed his gun with one hand and fired back. A wild spray of bullets, many of them tinged off the walls. But several hit a drone. It fell from the sky with a *crash!*

William grabbed his handlebars and wrestled his quad back under control. "Three dogs and three drones."

"Well done, William," Artan said. "I have a plan. Follow me." He threw a hard right up ahead.

Matilda followed him.

A good few hundred feet from the turn, William continued his snaking path. His head spun, his balance threatening to abandon him. The bullets came closer. The fire hotter.

Liberating a grenade from his belt, William bit down on the metal pin and pulled it free with his teeth.

Five.

Four.

Three.

Two.

He dropped it.

Whomp! An explosion to match any fireball. Black smoke engulfed the machines.

A drone shot from the smoke.

"Shit!"

Two more flanked it.

Clack-clack! A dog on the ground.

The smoke cleared, revealing the twisted corpses of two robotic canines. "One dog and three drones left." William turned right after Artan and Matilda.

Another industrial plaza like many they'd seen before. Five workshops sat in the moon's glow. The place was abandoned. "Artan? Tilly? Where are you?"

Clack-clack! Clack-clack!

The machines entered the plaza. The drones flew above the dog. Their Gatling guns sang. William pulled to the right around a workshop.

More bullet fire joined the Gatling guns.

William drove around the workshop and came out on the other side. He faced the entrance. Artan had gotten off his bike. He gripped his gun and continued firing at the downed drones and dogs. They were all inactive, yet he kept his trigger pulled. Their steel corpses jumped and hopped on the ground. Animated by his attack.

Another drone burst into the square. It shot past Artan and Matilda and headed directly at William.

William raised his gun with shaking hands, filled his lungs to steady his aim, put the red dot on the front of the drone, and pulled his trigger. A pulse of four or five bullets. Every one of them sank into the drone's shell. It continued towards him as it fell from the sky, slammed to the ground, slid, and came to rest when it hit the front of his quad. Dead like the others.

Exhaling so hard his cheeks puffed, William watched the drone like it might move again. "Well, that was close."

Artan unclipped his spent magazine, threw it to the ground, and slapped another one in.

"You did the whole lot?" William said.

"Yeah."

"Two hundred bullets?"

Artan shrugged. "When I last checked, that's what the whole lot was."

Nick, a tinny hiss in William's ear: "What did he do?"

"Unloaded two hundred bullets into four machines."

Nick laughed. "Gotta make sure, innit, Art?"

Such a serious boy most of the time, Artan lost his stoicism when one side of his mouth lifted in a smile.

"We did it, Gracie." Matilda kicked what remained of the machines. "We took them down."

"Uhhhhhhh ..."

The single syllable plummeted through William, taking his stomach with it. "Why don't I like the sound of that?"

"You did really well, but that was a handful of drones and dogs in a prison filled with them."

"But it's cleared the main road at least, right? Helped out some of the prisoners?"

"Uhhhhhhh ..."

"Shit!"

"They're *everywhere*, William. What do you want me to say?"

"Damn."

"Can you lead some more away?"

"And still be alive at the end of it?" William shook his head. "I doubt it."

"So what then?"

The tinny quality of the earpiece added to Joni's haunting voice. It ran a chill down William's spine. Fingernails against a blackboard. A squeaking door hinge in a haunted house. "Eeee-M-pee. Eeee-M-pee."

Tilly and Artan frowned.

William pressed his earpiece. "What?"

Matilda shrugged.

"They have them here. Joni's seen them. EMPs. They have them in abundance."

Artan tutted. "You're not making any sense, Joni. What are EMPs?"

"Micro EMPs."

"Thanks for clearing that one up."

"Patience, Little Chick. Let Mama Bird explain. Micro EMPs are like buttons for the machines. Will drop them like a popping implant drops a person. Stops. Drops. Flops."

Some of Artan's frustration left him. He spoke in a softer tone. "It disables the drones and dogs?"

"That's what Joni said. You need to listen better, Little Chick. Clean out those dirty little ears of yours."

"Well, it's not really what y—"

"Can you get them?" William said.

"Of course. Joni runs this place, not him. Can do what she wants when she wants. No problem at all."

"Gracie!" William pressed a finger to his earpiece. "We need to head back to the guards' block to pick up these buttons."

"That's going to take time."

"It will, but it's the best chance we have. And I think it will work. Unless you have a better idea?"

"No."

"We'll be as quick as we can."

"I know."

William turned his throttle, ran over the drone he'd shot from the sky, and led the other two back onto the road they'd just left. He accelerated and flinched when another fly stung his forehead. They needed to get back to the main road. The quickest way to Hell's hotel. Not ideal to be so visible, but at least they had a plan to disable the dogs and drones. They couldn't save every prisoner, but hopefully they could be quick enough to make a difference.

CHAPTER 14

Even as she said it, Joni winced from the impending aural intrusion. "How far away are you?" She leaned from the maintenance shaft she'd used to enter the guards' block. Olga had already climbed out and hid in the building's shadow below.

"We're close."

William's voice screeched in her ear from where he'd shouted over his hurtling momentum. The tinny invasion burrowed into her brain. Joni slipped her gun from her back and laid it beside her in the steel shaft. She pulled three micro EMP buttons from her back pocket and handed them down to Olga, one after the other. "These will screw them over. Stop them dead." Once Olga had taken the third and final button, Joni held up her right index finger. "Wait!"

In her other back pocket, large enough to need a back pocket all of its own, she pulled out her scanner and passed it down to Olga.

"You won't need it?"

"Not as much as they do right now."

"What?" Little Chick squawked in Joni's ear.

"Turn it down. The frown of a clown. New to town."

"What are you talking about?"

"Give her a moment, Artan." Olga rolled her eyes.

"Yes, a moment. And keep quiet, Little Chick. Quit your chirping in Joni's ear. Turn down the volume. Scanner planner. Olga has Joni's scanner. That way, Little Chick and his friends can find the dogs and drones and get to them before they get to you. No surprises here. We'll leave them by the entrance to the side road we came into the guards' plaza from. You know where that is?"

"Yep!" William the leader said. He finally got it. As few syllables as possible. Each one a crashing symbol in Joni's brain. She needed to think straight to help them.

"Will you be okay on your own for a moment?"

Joni scowled at Olga. "Of course. Joni's been okay for years. Why won't she be okay now? Of course she'll be okay."

"You're a survivor, Joni. I get it. But are *you* okay?"

"Y—" Joni coughed to clear her throat. "It's been a long time since someone asked Joni that. Yes, thank you, Pocket Rocket. Joni's okay. Thank you."

Olga smiled, nodded, spun around and tore across the plaza to the wall they'd walked alongside when they came in.

A cylindrical bike lay crumpled by a garage door close to Joni. The angry leader had complained about being locked in the garage. Well, they were clearly resourceful enough to get out again.

Olga reached the wall on the other side of the plaza and pulled into the relative safety of the shadows. No more than a silhouette, she ran towards the narrow entrance they'd used to get to the guards' block. "Hidden from sight. Very good."

The darkness buried the small pile Olga made by the entrance. Three buttons and one scanner. But they'd find it. They'd left it exactly where they'd told them it would be.

While Olga ran back alongside the wall, the three amigos appeared. Little Chick, Beauty Queen, and their leader. The quads' quiet hum accompanied them, closing in on the spot Olga had just vacated.

Little Chick jumped from his bike and handed buttons to the other two. He handed the scanner to their leader. William took it and waved at Olga. He clearly couldn't see Joni inside the maintenance shaft. How Joni liked it. She moved like a silent killer. Carbon monoxide. But even carbon monoxide made a sound when it escaped. Joni spoke with a low hiss. "Now be free, little birds." They left via the small side road. "You take down those cursed machines, and Joni will take care of him." Her gun lay beside her, but she kept the rusty blade sheathed down the back of her trousers. "Never part with it. Not now she'd brought it out. She'd cut him open. Slit him. No, Joni will never part with it."

Nick hissed another assault in her ear. "Won't taking down the drones and dogs kill my sight from here?"

"Yes, Chopped Liver. That's exactly what it will do."

"Huh?"

Even the single syllables jarred. "That's the goal. Making you blind will be a success."

Olga remained on the other side of the plaza with her back pressed against the wall. She gripped her gun with both hands, and even in the darkness, her wide eyes stood out.

"Come over here." Joni beckoned her across.

But Olga shook her head.

"What's wrong?"

Olga pointed across the plaza.

Joni leaned from the hatch and gasped.

"What?" Nick Chopped Liver said. "What is it?"

"Shh!" Joni slapped the side of her own head. "Let Joni think."

Olga's words were slow and measured, the only ones that

didn't stab knives into Joni's eardrums. "Some prisoners have come here instead of going to the gates. And I'm still outside the block."

"What?"

"Turn it down, yeah?" Joni whacked the side of her head and her earpiece.

Nick whispered, "Sorry, Joni. Olga, how many are there?"

"An army. Hundreds. They're here for the guards' block. If I move now, they'll see me."

"Damn!"

"Uh …" Gracie said. "We also have a problem with the prisoners. The white lights have clearly worked, but maybe a little too well. They're coming towards the open gates in droves. If we don't close the prison soon, we might be overrun with diseased."

CHAPTER 15

"There are too many of them." Gracie stood beside Hawk, overlooking the prison. Hundreds more prisoners filled the main road and were heading towards them. They were about a mile away and closing in on the gates quickly. "We need to shut this place before the diseased work out what's going on."

"For us and the prisoners." Hawk's glazed stare widened. "They'll get massacred, and we have no chance of heading south if this place is filled with diseased. They're bad enough when you come across them in the open, but penned in with them somewhere like this ... we won't last two minutes."

"So what do we do? I'm not sure Joni can help us right now." Gracie turned from the prisoners on the main road and headed to the other side of the wall. No shelter from the sharp and chilly wind. Her nose and ears tingled on their way to turning numb.

Hawk nodded out over the meadow. "At least they're still none the wiser. Yet."

The number of diseased outside remained about the same as the last time they'd checked. A sprawl of canted silhouettes mostly minding their own business until they got close enough to one another to squabble. Some wandered. Some stood still, swaying. Just remaining on their feet took a great will. "Why do you think they wait here?" Gracie said. "It's like they know, on some kind of instinctual level, that they'll get rewarded with more prisoners."

"Maybe." Hawk scratched his neck. "But I don't like to give them that much credit. Besides, where else have they got to be? They're reactive. They see something worth chasing and they chase it. Otherwise, they wait."

"And they're going to get something worth chasing in a minute." Gracie pressed her earpiece, but let her hand fall again. What good would it do? Joni knew the deal. She didn't need hassling.

Screams from inside the prison snapped through Gracie. Several diseased heads turned towards the gates, but none of them ran over.

Hawk held his bottom lip in a pinch. "They can't see them. The siren used to call them close, but they still had to see something before they attacked." He pulled on Gracie's arm. "Come on." He ran back across to the other side.

"Where have they gone?" Gracie rested on the small steel wall, her palms cold. The main road was now clear where prisoners had filled it. The only bodies were those from the previous slaughter. Burned corpses, scorch marks up the walls on either side. Even the ones who were shot got burned. Just to be sure. The dark paths branching off either side of the main road were too dark to see into.

"Look." Hawk pointed farther down the main road towards the guards' block. Drones and dogs. About five or six of each. "They must have seen them in time to get away."

"William. Matilda. Artan." Gracie pressed her finger to her earpiece. It helped her hear them better. "We have some machines on the main road."

William's voice came through. "Do we need to come? We're already on the trail of some down here. Did you just say the prisoners have gone?"

Of course Gracie wanted them to come, but how could she decide if she had the greater need?

"Actually, no." Hawk shook his head. "Not right now. The prisoners have made themselves scarce because of the machines. I can't see anyone in immediate danger."

"We'll monitor things and let you know," Gracie said. She continued leaning on the cold wall, the side roads too dark to see into. Hawk beside her scratched his neck again. "Do they hurt? Your scars?"

"Not often, no." He continued scratching. "Sometimes, when it's cold, but no."

"You scratch them a lot."

Hawk pulled his hand down and rested on the wall beside her. "I wish I'd killed him, you know? When I was a kid."

"Grandfather Jacks?"

"Yeah. Think about all the suffering I could have prevented. And I had plenty of opportunities. Plenty of times when we were alone …" He coughed to clear his throat and scratched his neck again, harder this time, his hand shaking. "I should have done more. I could have ended him."

Gracie flinched at Artan's voice in her ear.

"That comes at a heavy cost. It's a burden no kid should bear."

"Look!" Gracie pointed down into the prison. A group of twenty to thirty prisoners reached the end of a side street leading onto the main road. They checked back towards the tower at the dogs and drones. They were several hundred feet away. They broke from cover and ran towards the main gates. "They must have split up and taken different routes. Come on." She tugged on Hawk's arm. "Let's see how they do."

Gracie's head spun when she leaned over the wall on the other side. Her stomach turned backflips like a performing seal. The group of prisoners exited through the gates. The shadows were their friend. They remained close to the main wall and stayed hidden from the diseased. And the diseased seemed none the wiser. Shambling. Stumbling. Squabbling. Oblivious to the twenty to thirty escapees.

Another group of prisoners followed them out a minute or two later. They ran in the opposite direction to the first lot. "You know—" Gracie snorted a laugh "—if they continue to leave the prison in small numbers like this, they might just be okay. We might be able to leave the gates open after all."

CHAPTER 16

William glanced at Joni's scanner while they rode. It offered an accurate layout of the prison ahead. It depicted the walls as dark blue bars and the roads in light green. No wonder she'd been faster than them when they were chased by the machines in the darkness. If only one of them had had a micro EMP then. It would have saved her fighting the things with her bare hands. He smiled. But then he wouldn't have seen her fight.

A cluster of pulsing dots ahead, William eased off his throttle. Matilda and Artan slowed with him. He turned the device towards them. "Am I reading this right? We're still a few turns away, but it looks like there are some dogs and drones close by."

"It looks that way." Artan took the device and angled it so the image on the screen lined up with the road in front of them. He pointed. "Take that next left and right, and there they are."

"Can you tell how many?"

"No. But it's not like they move in huge packs. It can't be any more than five or ten."

Matilda rolled her eyes. "That's all right, then. For a moment I was worried we might be outnumbered."

Artan poked his tongue out. "I say we go for it. The fewer of them in this place, the better, and if we're going to take them down, we might as well start now." He drove down the road on their left, away from the drones and dogs.

"Where are you going?" William continued their conversation through their earpieces.

"Bring them back to me, and I'll stop them. Much like we did in the plaza. I'll jump out and take them down. Just let me scout ahead and see what the prison looks like. I need to plan my route in case it turns into a chase."

"You're prepared to do this on your own?" Matilda said.

"I need you to lead them to me."

"What if the buttons don't work?"

Artan raised his gun in the air while he drove away from them. "I'll have this. But the buttons will work. I trust what Joni's telling us."

"Really?" Matilda said. "You didn't trust a word she said a few hours ago."

"She's led us true so far. Her methods might be a bit on the kooky side, but she knows what she's talking about. I'll be down here. Bring the machines this way, and I'll fry them."

William sat on his bike and waited. Not his call.

Matilda shrugged. "Okay. Tell us when you're ready, and we'll bring them to you."

"Will do."

William led them slowly away while Matilda stared in the direction Artan had gone. "I'm not convinced, but if Artan is, then what can I do?"

His attention divided between the screen and the road ahead, William shrugged. "We're here for Artan if he needs us. He won't be doing this on his own."

"You know, I'm pleased Gracie said what she did about the prisoners."

"Really?"

"Yeah. She's right. We need to help them get out of here. We saw some awful things while we were out here trying to get to the guards' tower. How was it for you?"

"Scary. Especially in the rat run."

"We saw what the guards did to the prisoners. How they punish and control them. How they used that damn implant against them."

William took the first left. The pulsing dots of the machines around the next right. He eased off, turned his bike to face back the way they came, and halted. A steel wall blocked the machines' line of sight. The drones' hum resonated in the tight street beside them. An aural reminder of just how close they were. Pressing his lips tight, he raised his eyebrows at Matilda. They needed to wait for Artan's signal.

Clack-clack!

William snapped rigid. The drones had dogs with them. And they were on the move.

Clack-clack!

Slow steps. They drew closer. The machines had nothing to chase. Yet. That could change soon. They needed Artan's signal.

Clack-clack!

Matilda chewed the inside of her mouth.

Clack-clack!

William whispered, "You ready, Art?"

The dogs stopped. The drones' hum remained.

Clack-clack! Clack-clack!

"Shit!" William accelerated, Matilda beside him. "You'd best be ready, Art. They've seen us."

Clack-clack! Clack-clack!

The dogs and drones appeared as William drove back onto the road they'd used to get there. His grip on his throttle ached. Twist it much harder and he'd snap it.

Clack-clack! Clack-clack!

His back tensed as he waited for a fireball's heat. For the whir of Gatling guns. But William turned right before that happened. Matilda followed him into the road Artan had ridden down.

Joni's voice came through to them. She spoke with a haunting whine. "Not on your bike still, are you, Little Chick?"

"What?" Artan said. "Of course I am."

"No." Joni laughed. "No, no, no, no. Micro EMPs kill machines. Drones. Dogs. Bikes. Guns. Why Joni hadn't used them until now. Can't ride and use micro EMPs."

"You're telling him that now?" Matilda said.

"Little Chick didn't ask before."

William cut in before Matilda. An argument wouldn't get them anywhere. "Artan, we'll let them follow us."

"You don't have time," Artan said. "They're faster than you. We already know that."

The quads whined with William's and Matilda's acceleration.

Clack-clack! Clack-clack!

The dogs and drones gained on them. Nine in total. Five dogs. The drones opened fire.

The bullets hit the walls and ground. William ducked as if that would help. He moved from side to side. Made himself harder to hit.

"Come on then, you bastards!" Artan ran from a road William and Matilda had just passed on their right. He appeared between them and the machines, held his gun with both hands, and opened fire. Before the machines could return his attack, he ran back down the road he'd emerged from.

Matilda slowed and looked back. "What are you doing, Artan? You can't outrun them."

But Artan had already gone, and the machines had followed him.

The tinny speaker in William's ear carried Artan's voice. "I'll be okay. I've got this. I—"

Whomp!

Matilda pressed her finger to her earpiece. "Artan? Artan?" She turned the handlebars hard, changed course, and rode in Artan's direction. "Hold on, Artan. We're coming."

CHAPTER 17

"She's done this a thousand times before. It's what Joni does. She moves from one level of Hell's hotel to the other like it's nothing. Because it isn't. Then why does she have sweaty Betty palms today? It's because Joni doesn't usually have anyone relying on her. Maybe a little chick needing a little snack, but she's never had life hanging in the balance like it is now. No coming back tomorrow for another try. Tomorrow will never come if Joni gets this wrong. A whole gaggle of little chicks to care for. Close the gates for some. Get rid of the army for the others. And they tweet, tweet, tweet in her ear the whole time."

Her hands and feet braced against either side of the vertical tunnel. About ten feet up. Slip now and she'd make a lot of noise. "Probably hurt herself. Fall down on some guards. Blow her cover." Sweat ran into her eyes. Joni blinked against the sting.

Bracing with her hands, Joni lifted her feet and pressed them to either side. The shaft's walls popped and creaked under the strain of her pressure. But she remained in place and reached higher. "Steady progress to the next level, even if she sweated more today than usual."

Joni reached the top of the shaft. The next level stretched away. She slipped her gun's strap over her head and slid it down the tunnel ahead of her. The rusty knife remained down the back of her trousers. "Keep it there. Not doing anyone any harm. Only harm for him." Nearly for Olga. "No." Joni crawled along the shaft after her gun. "No, Joni wouldn't have done that. No matter how angry. No."

A shaft like the others. "A level higher. A level lower. What did it matter?" She could get anywhere, and she had a mental map of the place. A maze within a maze. "Only a maze to the uninitiated." Her first stop has to be the control room. Olga Pocket Rocket can look after herself for now. The shadows are her friend. The shadows are always your friend in this place. Live in the shadows. Move in the darkness. Silent and invisible. Carbon monoxide. "Also, Olga had a gun across her front and a button in her pocket. A rocket in her pocket. Should the shadows fail her, she can keep the prisoners back." But she has to close the gates. Let the diseased into this place and it's game over. "Game over, white cliffs of Dover."

Joni's swishing movement ran ahead of her in the tunnel. No need for stealth. Guards fired their guns beneath her. "Guards in every hallway. At every slot near every window. Every one of them armed and firing on the prisoners below. Soldiers killing prisoners. Nothing to see here. Normal service resumed."

The next grate cold against the side of her face, Joni angled her head. Two soldiers, like many others. They were by a slit beneath one window. They lay on their fronts, the ends of their guns pointing down at the crowd below. They shot them for fun. What guard didn't like a good massacre?

One sat up and ejected the magazine from his gun. He

tossed it aside. "Why didn't they send this lot with the unregistered army that's just attacked us?" He inserted another magazine and slapped the bottom to lock it in. "You think they would have felt better with more numbers. How does it benefit them to send them in two waves? It just makes them easier to kill."

He lay down again. Back at the slot, his gun barking its murderous report. The guards continued their conversation. Too much noise to hear their words. Firing guns. Screaming prisoners. Cackling laughter. Too much noise below. Too much noise in Joni's ear. She slapped the side of her head. "Too much twittering." The twittering turned into a single and continuous tone. She slapped her head again and again. Each contact sent a bass drum thud through her brain.

"Just keep moving. Mama Bird has a job to do. Gotta leave the guards be. But Mama's not been on the inside when they're shooting prisoners. They deserve to have their guns turned on them. A massacre in the hallways. Teach them a lesson they need to learn. But she has a job to do. A job much bigger than this. Take all the prisoners away from them. From him. Yes, Joni needs to keep her eye on the prize."

The chaos grew louder.

Gunfire.

Laughing guards.

Twittering.

Gunfire.

Laughing guards.

Tw—

"Twinkle, twinkle, little star."

Everything else stopped. The twittering halted.

Joni crawled on her stomach towards the control room. "How I wonder what you are." Her heart slowed. Even the gunfire became a background noise.

"Up above the clouds so high."

There were multiple routes to the control room. "Joni knows them all. From every angle. Backwards, and with her eyes closed. This is her home. She's the Minotaur of this labyrinth. The tomcat." She knew many routes that didn't cross over the observation room. Some that would get her to the control room quicker, too, but she needed to check on him. "Always has to know where he is. Slippery little fucker can vanish quicker than a fart in the wind. Need to know where he is and what he's doing. How quickly she can get to him to cut his throat."

The music was louder than before. He leaned back in his comfy chair with his eyes closed. A man at peace. His heart calmed by the killings outside the block's walls. The cold and hard plastic chair nearby. "The one he made Joni sit in when he brought her here." She rubbed her flat stomach. Sometimes he kept Joni locked in their bedroom for weeks. Sometimes this small room would be the only change of scenery for Joni for months on end. "Sit on the chair like a good little girl and keep quiet." And she'd be grateful. "But don't look at anyone they passed on the way. Especially with that black eye you got when you fell. Don't talk to anyone unless etiquette requires it of you. Don't arouse suspicion. Don't let anyone know what's happening. Everything's fine. Smile and wave. But it's not fucking fine. The bruises hurt, and the chair has no padding. Joni needs help. A doctor." And help existed on the other side of that door. But a few feet or a few miles, what did it matter? He kept it locked. The world beyond might as well be another dimension. "Joni won't get there. No chance. No way. And when he locked the door, that's when he started picking on her. Going at her. Goading her. Dirty Joni. Stinky Joni. Stupid Joni. She'd be nothing without him. And the door always stayed locked."

He sat in the glow from the bank of twenty screens. Joni had copied the layout in her own home. The one the twittering little chick sat in front of right now, watching the same footage. But they need to blind them both. Chopped Liver and him. "Yes." She nodded. "Blind him. Cut his fucking eyes out with a rusty blade. Come down from the ceiling like a black widow and break him. Payback."

Joni jumped when he burst into song. His deep voice delivered words his spirit hadn't earned. "What does he know about love? She should cut his tongue from his mouth and shove it down his throat. Choke him on his own deceit." He rested his hands on his paunch. A paunch he'd had over twenty years ago. It had only grown larger with the passing of time. The fluorescent ceiling lights shone on his scalp. Liver spots on his head. The largest of the lot where she should plunge the knife. "X marks the spot."

Joni shifted over the observation room's door. She pulled her screwdriver from her pocket and slotted it into the screw beside the lock. An electronically operated door, but she could manually override it. She bit down on her bottom lip and turned the screw. The door locked. She pressed the tip of her screwdriver against the power cable. A thin wire. She pressed hard and broke the cable. Cut the power. Killed the lock.

"That'll keep him in there. Locked away. Joni's little project. Her pet. Now *she* controls *him*. Joni will say when he can and can't leave. Unless he gets into the shafts with Joni. Into the labyrinth with the Minotaur. And then it's game on. She'll hunt him down like a rat in the sewers. She's the tomcat up here. Not him. Tomcat versus fat rat. What do you think about that?"

The twittering jabbed into Joni's ear again. She had to move on. People needed her help. He can wait. Locked in his room. She'll be back for him in her own time. And why rush what she can savour later? She'll skin him alive. Starting with that paunch of his. "Cut it off and smother him. Suffocate him with his own skin like it's a plastic bag."

The control room was close to the observation room. Like the observation room, it had one door in and out. Joni locked it like she had his door. She cut the power to the lock and crawled to the grate overlooking the room. Lying on her back, she kicked down.

Crash!

The grate swung open into a room unlike any other in this place.

Joni slid from the hatch, hung down, and dropped to the floor. A circular space about twenty feet in diameter. Someone had painted this room like a rainbow. Seven equal strips of colour from floor to ceiling. Six of them housed a computer terminal. The final colour, the red stripe, had the locked door. The slightest smile lifted the side of Joni's mouth. "And how can she not be happy in a place like this? Surrounded by colours and computers. Screens. Keyboards. Machines to control everything. The lights, which she'd already changed. The trigger for the implant, which she'd already disabled. And now the gates. Open, close. Open, close. Now they want Joni to close."

All the while, the twittering and shouting had been jabbering in her ear. White noise. Chaos. Until it stopped.

At the terminal in the green-painted section, the three lights on Joni's small computer turned green. The monitor blinked on. "And she's in." Joni typed on the keyboard. Still nothing in her ear. She pressed a finger to her earpiece. "H-hello?"

"Joni?"

The soft voice. The only one she could hear. "Olga Pocket Rocket? Are you okay?"

"Yes. For now. Have you closed the gates yet?"

"Jeez, give a girl a chance, will ya?"

"Good. Don't close them."

"What? But she asked me to. Gracie said close the gates. Keep the diseased out."

"That's changed. Some dogs and drones have dispersed the prisoners. Slowed down the flow of those leaving. It's working for now. The prisoners are escaping, and the diseased are staying away. Can you do anything to disperse the prisoners from the guards' block?"

"Are you in danger?"

"No, but they're being slaughtered out here. The guards are mowing them down, and they're not leaving."

"Slaughtered. Daughter. Oughta." Joni tapped her pursed lips. "Yes, Joni can clear them. Disperse. Reverse."

The yellow computer controlled the lights. Joni had already hacked into it to direct the flow of prisoners. She brought up the prison's map on the screen and used her finger to draw a line around Hell's hotel and most of the main road. With that area selected, she tapped a button. "Is it working?"

"Yes! What did you do?"

"Turned the lights amber around the guards' block and on the main road. A warning. They need to get away before they turn red and trigger the implants. Which won't happen, but they don't know that. Also, it'll keep them away from the main road. Slow down the flow of prisoners exiting the gates."

"Well done, Joni." Gracie's screech cut into her, and she winced.

"Turn the volume down," Olga said.

"Sorry. Well done, Joni."

"Not so well done, Joni. Joni's clearing the prisoners from the plaza and the main road. Controlling them with the lights like so many other prisoners. Like those in the south, east, and west. A slow and steady flow towards the gates and out of here. And hopefully the diseased continue to mind their own."

"So what's the problem?"

"The guards will see the prisoners run because the lights have changed colour. They didn't notice the lights from inside their block when Joni turned them white, but they will now. Impossible to ignore. Now the guards know these are prisoners. Not the unregistered army. That they're implanted and running free. They'll know something's up. That they've lost control of the prison. They'll want to take that back."

"Shit! Can you do anything to hinder them?"

"Yes!" Joni smiled at her reflection on the screen's monitor. She ran to the blue computer. She crouched down and pulled the panel by her knees free. She plugged in her small hacking device. The lights changed from red to green. One. Two. Three. Joni tapped the keyboard, and the screen illuminated. "Several taps. Clickety-click. Joni's just forced this block to remain in lockdown. She's the jailer now. She'll keep them all like him. As her pets. Lock down the block. Keep the shutters shut. Prevent them from leaving unless she says so. Or unless they take to the shafts. But she's the tomcat in the shafts. They're juicy rats. However, Joni won't be able to occupy them forever. She'll do her best. She'll bring chaos down on them. Keep them busy for as long as she can. But she can't do it forever. Olga, I'm coming back to get you."

"Don't worry, Joni, I'll get back in soon. The prisoners are clearing out quickly."

"Good. We need to keep the guards busy. Are you ready to help Joni turn this place into a hotel of fun? Hell's hotel of chaos."

"Sure thing. Let's do it."

CHAPTER 18

"Tilly, wait up!"

Maybe she'd heard him, and maybe she hadn't. Either way, Matilda continued at full throttle and vanished down the road Artan had led the machines into.

Tighter than the road they'd been on, William entered it in time for Matilda to fly into a right turn up ahead. All the while, Joni continued in his ear. A constant murmuring where he only made sense of the occasional word. That and the entirety of 'Twinkle, Twinkle, Little Star'. But sometimes it was better not to ask.

Matilda's scream reached William before he caught sight of her again. Her shrill distress speared his heart. He tore around the next bend and eased off.

Matilda had stopped next to Artan's quad bike. Her own gun hung across her front from the strap. She held Artan's in William's direction and shook it. "Why didn't he take this?"

Damn near deafened by his own raging heartbeat, and with Joni, Gracie, and Olga chattering in his ear, William strained to listen to the prison. No bullet fire. No flames in the distance. "I'm sure he's okay."

"That's the best you've got?"

"What's going on, Matilda?" The tinny Nick added to earpiece chaos. "I can hear how many of you are talking, and I'm trying to only speak when I'm spoken to. The last thing you need is me in your ear, right? But where's Artan? What's happened?"

"I du—"

Matilda spoke over William. "He's gone, Nick. I don't know where. Or what's happening, but he's gone. Vanished. The dogs and drones. They must have taken him somewhere."

"Taken him?" Nick said. "Do they do that?"

Joni's haunting voice next. "Why would they take him? They have nowhere to take him. Just kill him. Anything else is a waste of time and energy."

Matilda threw up a sharp shrug and raised her eyebrows at William. But what could he say? No one could tame Joni. "We've not heard any shooting or flames, so maybe he's okay." He winced at Matilda. "Maybe they have taken him?"

"Got him to hand over his gun and marched him away from here?"

"I dunno." The red numbers on Artan's gun showed he had about eighty-three bullets left. "Maybe they had nothing to do with him leaving his gun here?"

"Huh?"

"Maybe he threw it down? Maybe he left it with his bike? Follow me."

William rode his bike slowly so Matilda could get back on hers and catch up. After two turns, he halted again.

"Artan?" Matilda's shrill voice speared William's eardrum. "What are you doing? Why didn't you come back?"

Nine machines lay on the ground. Five dogs and four drones. Artan moved among them. Poking and prodding. He flipped over a dog and then looked back at his sister. "These things are fascinating."

"What the ..." Matilda turned her palms to the night sky. "Why didn't you come back?"

"I figured you'd be here in a minute. And I wanted to check out these machines. They're quite amazing. When else will we be able to get close to them?"

"We lost contact with you!"

"Of course." Artan held up the micro EMP. "That's what these little buttons do. They kill electrics. I feel like an idiot for not realising sooner. I should have left my earpiece back with my bike and gun."

Nick joined the conversation again. "Is he okay?"

"He's fine, Nick. The micro EMP killed his earpiece, which is why you can't reach him."

"But it also killed the dogs and the drones. Tell him that, William."

Nine machines. All of them broken on the ground. So destructive when they were active. Scrap metal when they weren't. "He's taken down the dogs and drones."

"Well done, Art."

"Nick said well done. So we clearly have a method that works. Lead the dogs and drones somewhere far enough from the bikes and guns, and then press the buttons. At some point soon, Joni will have to close the main gates. Until then, we can make it easier for the prisoners to leave by taking down as many machines as we can."

"Blind him!" Joni said. "Blind him in his little room. Lock him in and blind him."

"I am here, you know," Nick said.

"No, not you, Chopped Liver. Although, to blind him is to blind you. Blind him in his control room in Hell's hotel. Stop him seeing his prison. Kill the machines. Blind him. Cut his fucking eyes out."

"And there it is." William directed his words at Artan. "Our plan is to kill every one of Nick's screens. If we kill all the machines, Nick can't see the prison. If Nick can't see the prison, the guards can't see the prison. Gracie, how are you getting on at the wall?"

"Fine. They're leaving in dribs and drabs. The diseased are none the wiser."

"Yet," Hawk added.

Gracie said, "We'll let you know if anything changes."

"Olga?" William said. "Everything okay?"

"Yeah, we're fine for now."

"Nick?"

"Of course. I'm still doing nothing, and I'll do even less when I can't see."

"You're keeping us all in contact. Okay." William showed Matilda and Artan Joni's scanner. "Let's go hunting."

CHAPTER 19

"Joni can create chaos. Yes. She's been looking for the opportunity for a long time." Joni lay on her back and kicked down on the hatch.

Crash!

The grate swung into the room below. The familiar creaking of rusty hinges. Like a shop sign in the wind.

"Joni's going to take control." She flipped onto her front again, slid her gun so it rested on her back, and slithered from the hatch feet-first. She could do it blind. She'd done it a thousand times before. She landed on the steel prep table flat-footed.

Thunk!

She twisted as she walked, grinding the soles of her shoes into the tabletop with each step. "Contaminate their food-prep area. Poison the bastards." She hopped off at the end, landing on the ground.

Thunk!

The sound echoed around the large kitchen. A vast space with more steel than any other room in the block. Steel tables. Steel work surfaces. Steel fridges and freezers …

Olga's legs hung down from the hatch and swung as they searched for purchase in the air.

"Just drop, Pocket Rocket. Nothing for those little feet to stand on. But the table will support you."

Thunk!

Olga landed on the main prep table in the centre of the room. She too still wore her gun. And a good job too. They might need them.

"Joni's owned this place via the maintenance shafts for the longest time. She's ruined both his sleep and where he sleeps. She's made him move more times than she can remember. She waits for him to settle in his new place of rest, and then she starts all over again." She clapped her hands, the *crack* amplified by the room. "Always pulling the rug from beneath him. She's helped herself to his things. His food. His supplies. His weapons. But she's never taken control of the entire block." She spun on the spot. Several full circles, her long blonde hair whipping away from her. "Not like this." She stumbled to one side, rested against a nearby fridge and thew her arm in a wide arc, addressing an imagined crowd. "Now, ladies, gents, boys, and girls. Diseased and those ill at ease. Joni's here, and she brings with her a dose of disorder. A mandate of madness. A cacophony of chaos."

The ambient sounds fought for Joni's attention. The echoes of her words. The jibber-jabber in her ear. She shouted louder and pointed at the line of industrial ovens. "Olga, my dear, I want you over there."

Olga ran to the ovens.

"Now, open the doors and place everything I pass to you inside."

Joni turned pirouettes around the room, crossing from the fridge to a set of drawers. She pulled out the first one, removed an apron, and snapped it open with a *thwip!* It had a cartoon body of a woman in a sexy maid's outfit. Holding it up to herself, Joni snorted a fake laugh. "Well, aren't we a hoot? Will you look at this? It's funny because the person wearing it isn't a maid." Her face fell slack. "How droll." She scrunched it into a ball and threw it. "Catch."

A stack of about ten tea towels. Joni held them in the palm of her left hand and, with her right, threw one at a time across the room to Olga. The colours of the rainbow, each one opened and spread wide, mid-flight.

Olga ran around and gathered them up. As instructed by Joni, she stuffed them into the oven.

Another prep area close to the drawers. A fruit bowl filled with apples rested on the side. "Hungry?"

Olga shrugged.

Joni tossed her three apples, one after the other. Underarm throws. She didn't want to hurt Pocket Rocket.

Catching all three, Olga pocketed two and ate one.

About twenty apples remained in the bowl. Joni bit into the first one and held it up while she chewed. "Well, that's tart." She wound back and pitched the apple at the opposite wall.

Boom! It shattered on impact.

Nineteen apples remained. Joni went through the lot. She took a bite and threw. Took a bite and threw. Took a bite ...

She reached into the empty bowl. "None left." She turned it upside down. "Still none left." She lifted the large ceramic bowl an—

"Joni! No!"

Crash! The bowl shattered against the wall.

"You say no, but this is Joni's place now. She's running things. She's making the choices. She needs to keep the guards busy on the inside so they can do what needs to be done on the outside."

The clinical glow from the fluorescent lighting stung Joni's tired eyes. She opened a cupboard filled with plates and mugs. She reached in with one hand and hooked out the entire stack of white plates. They smashed on the ground. The sharp shards kicked back and stung her shins, but her thick trousers prevented any cuts. A selection of mugs. Some matched the plates, and some didn't. Although Joni made them all part of the same shattered mess. "Oh, will you look at this." Joni held a mug in Olga's direction. White with black writing. *Chef!* "What, these people need a mug to tell them their fucking job?" Joni tossed it over her shoulder, and it hit the steel floor with yet another ringing *crash!*

Even after she'd broken everything, the ringing continued in Joni's ears. A tinnitus whine. She slapped the side of her head with her earbud.

Ingredients in the next cupboard. A pot of flour. Joni removed the lid and sniffed too hard. "Achoo!" She sneezed into the pot, forcing the contents into the air. It covered her face. Her hair. The ground. Joni upended the pot over her head and then tossed it aside.

"Ah!" A small glass jar filled with white granules. "This is what Joni wanted." She ripped off the lid, licked her finger, plunged it in, and pulled it out again. It shone with its new coating, the granules catching the bright light. She sucked her finger.

"Ewww!" Joni spat. "Salt. Bloody salt!" She shook with the force of her words. "Why don't they label things? What kind of place is this? How is anyone supposed to know what— argh!" Joni launched the pot at the door.

Crash! It shattered on impact.

"Uh ... Joni." Olga remained hunched down by the open oven doors. "How much longer do you want to stay here?"

"You getting bored, Pocket Rocket?"

"We want attention, right?"

"Right."

"And I think you're doing a grand job of getting it, but

surely someone has to walk in here soon. We want attention, but we don't want to get caught."

The next glass jar filled with white granules. Joni popped the lid again and discarded it. A little more cautious than before, she licked the tip of her pinky and poked it in. Just the smallest taste. "And there it is." She grinned. "Sugar."

Joni ran across the kitchen to Olga at the ovens. "What recipe is complete without a pinch of sugar?" She thrust the open jar towards the open oven, tossing the granules in with the towels.

Olga looked from Joni to the door and back to Joni again. "Can we move on now?"

"Darling, you should never rush an artiste while they're working. Don't you know that? This recipe is far from complete, my impatient friend."

Joni ran to another drawer filled with wooden spoons. She pulled them out one after the other and tossed them towards Olga. They clattered against the steel floor and slid close to Pocket Rocket, several of them coming to a halt when they hit her feet.

Olga ducked one. "Jeez! Be a bit more careful, will ya?"

Her hands filled with wooden spoons, Joni dropped them all with a clatter. "Sorry." She shook her head and paced small circles. "A bit overzealous. Sorry, Pocket Rocket. Will be gentler next time."

"We really need to get going, Joni. We—no! Put them down." Olga reached towards Joni, her hand outstretched. "Do not throw them. I repeat, *do not* throw them."

The block of knives beneath her arm, Joni tutted and crossed towards Olga. "Are you crazy, woman? Of course Joni wouldn't throw them. They're knives. Why would she throw knives?" She held the block in Olga's direction. "Handle first, right?"

"Why are we burning these?"

"Handle first."

"I get that." Olga continued to take them handle first and shove them in the ovens. "But why use these?"

"Handle first, plastic first. Quench my thirst. Burning plastic fantastic. Smoke like a chimney. Quite thick. Toxic. Gotta loc—"

"Hey!"

The shout from outside halted Joni mid-flow. Someone in the hallway. "Shi—"

"I told you." Olga slammed the oven door. "We've taken too long."

Steps closed in on the kitchen. Joni spun all the dials along the front of the stuffed ovens. Lights on. Heat on. Ready to cause chaos. "Now hide!"

Joni ran to the main prep table in the centre of the room and crouched behind it. It hid her from the door's line of sight.

Olga hid behind some shelves closer to the ovens and farther away from the action. And who could blame her? Who knew what would come into that room at any moment? But Joni had control now.

Whoosh! The door opened.

"What the …?" A woman's voice.

"What's happened to this place?" another woman replied.

"First the comms go down. Then the place goes into a lockdown we can't control. The prisoners are running wild. No one can find Louis, and now this. What—"

"Get the fuck down, motherfuckers!" Joni jumped from behind the prep table and pointed her gun at the two women. She coughed, black smoke billowing from the oven doors. "Get down! Now."

The two guards raised their hands above their heads and dropped to their knees. Joni kept the stock of her gun wedged in her shoulder and stepped closer to them, her finger on the trigger. "Joni doesn't want to kill you, but she will if you push her. Guards aren't people too. Especially not him. But he will get his. Just you wait and see. Oh, yes. He will get his."

Joni flipped her gun around and slammed the butt against the right side of each guard's head. *Crack! Crack!*

Both fell on their sides. Limp on the ground.

"Whoa!" Joni jumped when she turned around to find Olga close to her. Her hands on her hips. "What's up, Pocket Rocket?"

More black smoke spewed from the ovens.

"We need to put them outside." Olga Pocket Rocket pointed at the guards. "They'll suffocate in here. We need to give them a chance to be found and rescued."

"But we have a mandate of madness. We're here to cause chaos. To unleash the beast. Fuck shit up!"

"And you're doing a good job of that. But that doesn't mean killing guards."

"It means killing him. Just you wait and see. Joni's waited too long to not kill him. He will get his. Just you see if he doesn't."

"But these two women aren't him." Olga bent down and grabbed one guard's ankles. She dragged her towards the door and slapped the control button.

Whoosh!

Joni followed Olga out with the other woman. She dropped her feet, and they hit the corridor's steel floor. Two dead weights. *Thunk. Thunk.*

"Right! We need to burn more things. Set fire to this place." The smoke joined Joni and Olga out in the hall.

Olga grabbed Joni's hands. "We need to move on."

Tears blurred Joni's vision. Two warm hands in her own. A human contact she hadn't had for such a long time. Someone who cared. Someone who stood by her. They didn't need to burn anything else. They'd already set fire to enough. "Okay. Follow Joni."

Back in the large kitchen, half the room filled with thick black smoke. The hatch they'd used to get into the room hung open, most of it buried inside the noxious cloud.

"Hear that?" Olga said.

"What?"

"Footsteps."

Several guards raced towards them. More than before. "Damn. We can't go back the way we came. Mama Bird's dropped the ball. Gonna fall. Two feet tall."

"Slow down, Joni. Is there another way out of here?"

The guards' thunderous approach closed in on them. Hard to tell how many. The steel walls turned the echoes into echoes of echoes. "Egg nose."

Joni filled her lungs and jumped up onto the prep table. The smoke burned her already tired eyes. Like giving herself a facial with chopped onions. Joni swung for the hatch blind and missed. She swung for it again, caught it, and slammed it shut.

Thud! Landing two-footed beside Olga, Joni motioned for her to follow. "Let's go."

A wall of smoke near the ovens, Joni held her breath and ran blind.

She hit the steel door sooner than she expected, slamming into it with her left knee. Suppressing her scream by biting down on her bottom lip, she slapped the wall in several spots before she hit the button.

Crack!

Whoosh!

The door opened out into another corridor.

Whoosh!

"What the ...?" Guards' voices entered the kitchen on the other side of the wall of smoke.

Followed out of the room by the dark and toxic cloud, Joni ran through the dining hall, the taste of burned plastic lining her throat. Tables everywhere, she jumped up onto them and crossed from one to the next.

Olga kept pace with her, but ran on the ground between the tables.

The next gap from one tabletop to another stretched by several feet. Joni launched herself, her arms windmilling as she sailed through the air. She landed two-footed. The last table in the room. Olga waited for her on the ground. Joni jumped down and turned back to the door they'd just come through. The smoke followed them, but the guards didn't. "That fire should keep them busy. We need to find a way back into the maintenance shafts. Joni's labyrinth. She's the tomcat now."

Crack! She hit the button for the next door.

Whoosh!

Out in the corridor. Olga behind her. Joni crossed to the door on the other side and hit the next button. *Crack!*

Whoosh!

She ran into the massive room, stopped, and bent over double. Joni fell to her knees and clutched her stomach.

"What is it?" Olga's voice echoed in the cavernous hall. "What's wrong?" She held her hand down. "Get up, come on."

Joni took her friend's hand and stood, but she still held her stomach. A vast empty hall. She'd seen it from above plenty of times. Nothing to see here. A sports hall. Nothing more. Mostly unused. "But not a sports hall. No. A meeting room."

"Have you been in this room before?"

"Joni's seen it lots of times before, but it's always better from up there." She pointed at the maintenance shafts. "That's where Joni belongs. Joni's world. Where she's in control."

"What happened the last time you were in here?"

"No." One arm still across her stomach, Joni rocked where she stood. "No, we need to move on. Need to keep running."

Olga glanced over Joni's shoulder at the door. "I'll keep an eye on the door. This is important. What happened?"

Joni pointed across to the other side of the hall with a trembling finger. "He had a stage there. A stage on which he sat. Seats spread out all across the room. All facing him. Him and Joni sat on the stage with him. But she can't remember it all. Something in the water. Something in the food."

"He drugged you?"

"And then some, yes. Memories hazy. What's real and what's not?" Joni shrugged. "Who knows? Who cares?"

"I care."

"You d …" Joni coughed to clear her throat. "You do?"

"Of course. Now, why were you on the stage with him?"

"Someone got fired. He made a big song and dance about it. Said they were going home. Back south. But that was a lie." Joni's hair fell across her face when she shook her head. "No, not back south. He didn't go home."

"Who was he?"

"A guard. A guard who didn't listen."

"What did he do?"

"Talk to Joni."

"That's all?"

"That was enough. And it was Joni's fault because she talked back. Led him on. Made him think she wanted something more. Like him. He wanted something more. But Joni wanted nothing more. By that point, Joni already had her hands full. Why would she want more?"

"So he killed someone for talking to you?"

"Because Joni spoke to them. It was all Joni's fault."

"That's insane!"

Joni stepped back. She kept her right hand pressed against her stomach.

"Not you, Joni. I'm not saying you're insane. I'm saying that kind of behaviour is insane."

"But Joni's insane too. Can't be trusted. Can't be relied upon. Joni should be locked away. That's what he did after that day. The last time Joni saw her fellow guards. She needed to be locked away for her own good. Kept away from people where she can't do any harm or cause any trouble. She's trouble with a capital T-rubble. A grade A hindrance to harmony. An agent of chaos."

"Did he drug you often?"

"Always. After that day. Always. Looking back on memories from that time is like finding the hatch to a maintenance shaft in a fire. Sometimes Joni feels the edges of the steel grate, but mostly it's too hot to hold even if she gets its location. So she lets it go. Lets it sink back into the smoke. Lost and forgotten. Like Joni. But Joni needed to be kept away. Nothing but trouble. She learned. She kept her mouth shut. She'd lie there, in her room, and listen to him next door. Listen to him with the next Joni. The one who would replace her eventually if she didn't learn to follow the rules. To keep her mouth shut."

She pushed Olga. "You should go now. Leave me. To be around Joni is to invite trouble."

But Pocket Rocket remained rooted to the spot. "*We* should go. *We* need to get out of here."

Screaming and shouting outside. Maybe Joni should wait for them? Hand herself in. Let them take her away and put her where she needed to be. Out of the way. Not underneath anyone's feet. T-rubble.

But Olga pulled Joni's free hand. She dragged her away from that spot. From the memory of him. The day she said goodbye to a guard she didn't know but has thought about every moment since. The day she said goodbye to her agency. Even now, the only way she's leaving that room is with someone else's help. How far has she really come?

Crack! Olga hit the door's button.

Whoosh!

She dragged her out of the sports hall and away from the fire.

They'd wanted chaos, and Joni brought it. Inside and out. Chaos personified. The centre of the storm. T-rubble.

CHAPTER 20

Another sharp sting from where a fly struck William in the centre of his forehead. He frowned against the headwind, his nose running from the cold. He and Matilda weaved from side to side on the wide road. She went one way, and he went the other. They crossed in the centre each time.

Bullets flew past them, but their distance from the drones and their movement helped them avoid being hit. A deep scar ran across the back left of William's quad from where a bullet had grazed the bodywork on their last run. They'd done this three times already. Taken down twenty-two machines in total. They couldn't afford to be complacent, but they were getting good. With enough time, they'd disable every drone and dog in the place.

They had more machines on their tail than before. Twelve in total. The whine of Gatling guns. The dogs' uneven clacking gait. William snapped left when he came close to the right wall and snapped right when he closed in on the left.

Matilda, slightly ahead of him, checked back before swinging into the next turn on their left.

Close to the right wall, William turned hard and followed her in. Away from the machines. The *clack-clack* of the running dogs died.

Clack!

Clack!

Clack!

Clack!

The drones' steel bodies hit the ground.

William turned around first and led the way back out onto the road they'd just left. Artan stood amongst the fallen machines, micro EMP in hand. He waved it in the air and danced around the metallic corpses.

"That's thirty-four in total now. Nick"—William pressed his finger to his ear—"how many screens are out?"

"Two of the twenty. Well done. How's Artan?"

"He looks quite happy right now." Matilda shook her head and smirked. "How are you doing?"

"Wishing I could be more helpful than sitting on my arse in a damp dungeon. But other than that, I'm doing all right, thanks."

"Gracie? Hawk?" Matilda said.

A strong wind accompanied Gracie's reply. William shuddered. Bad enough on the ground in the middle of the night, but it must have been chilly up on that wall. He squinted like it would help him hear better over the loud flapping. "Good job, you three. We're doing okay. Joni's using the lights to herd the prisoners towards the gates and keep them off the main road. It seems to be working for now. We're getting a steady flow, and they obviously know the risks outside the gates. They're doing what they can to avoid the diseased and, as much as I'm reluctant to say this, so far so good. The stupid creatures are just wandering around in the darkness."

William pressed his finger to his earpiece. "How many prisoners have already left?"

"Ten thousand. Maybe more."

He rolled his eyes at Matilda. "Only one hundred and ninety thousand to go."

"It's a start. We're doing all right for the moment. We'll let you know if we have any issues."

"And Olga?" William said. "Are you both okay?"

"Yeah, we're fine for now. Keeping the guards occupied."

"Oka—" William eased off on his bike's throttle. "Damn!"

Artan still focused on William and Matilda. He still danced around the machines' corpses. His hands in the air, he shuffled one way and then the other. A victory dance. And a well-earned one at that. But he hadn't yet turned around. Hadn't seen the several hundred prisoners who had emerged from a side road. They were about two hundred feet from him. William and Matilda were twice that distance away.

Matilda matched William's slower pace, her words falling from her mouth. "Why on earth have we slowed down?"

"We need to take it steady."

"Steady? Artan's in danger."

The prisoners at the front of the pack halted while the road filled behind them. All of them stared their way. "Any sudden movements and they'll rush him and us. We need to get as close as we can before we make our move." The quads' motors hummed. The steady bass note of rubber against road had quietened. "Especially as we're riding the vehicles of their oppressors, and we're carrying the guns they use against them."

Matilda jabbed a finger in Artan's direction. She spoke from the side of her mouth, too quiet for him to hear. For them to hear. "Turn around!"

His hands already in the air, Artan waved them higher. He

pretended to swim, two steps one way and two steps the other.

The prisoners stepped closer.

Matilda cupped her mouth with one hand. "Art—"

"Stop! They don't yet know we speak English." William's eyes burned from where he hadn't blinked. His hand twitched on his throttle, ready to accelerate the second they made their move. "Just keep going forwards. Right now, I'd say they're more intrigued about how the dogs and drones have been taken down. Let's keep it that way until we're closer."

The crowd of prisoners swelled. A few hundred had turned into several hundred and were well on their way to over a thousand.

Artan shot finger guns at William and Matilda and spun on the spot. He halted when he faced the prisoners. His arms fell to his sides.

"Shit!" William twisted his throttle.

Artan kept his attention on the prisoners.

The prisoners stared back.

Neither made a move.

William's and Matilda's motors whined. Their tyres hummed.

Matilda beside him, William leaned towards her. "He might walk away from this if he keeps his mouth—"

"Uh, William? Matilda? A little help here."

"Fuck!" Matilda said.

The prisoners yelled. One thousand enraged voices amplified by the walls. Their stampeding feet turned into rolling thunder.

Matilda took off slightly ahead of William. Lighter than him, she moved quicker at full throttle. She stopped next to Artan, her bike facing the road he'd sprung his ambush from. He jumped on behind her, and they took off again.

William held back, gripped his gun with one hand, and aimed it at the prisoners. Little point in helping them escape if they were going to open fire on them. But if he had to choose between him and them ...

It should have been enough to slow their charge, but it galvanised the prisoners, their faces a twisted mess of hatred. He vanished into the road after the other two.

Artan leaned close to Matilda's ear so William could hear their conversation. "I should have shown them my other button."

"That's probably as dead as your earpiece."

"Shit. But they don't know that."

"Artan, we're trying to save them. If there's a chance to run, we take that first. It's the sensible choice."

Matilda slowed down near Artan's quad. He jumped from the back before she'd come to a complete halt, grabbed his gun from the seat, threw his head through his strap, and jumped on his bike. He moved off as William passed him.

"Well done, Art." The prisoners flooded into the road behind them. William accelerated with Artan. "Now let's get away from here."

Matilda led the way into the next plaza on their right. Residential, it had two large barns in the centre, facing away from one another. Much like the one William and Olga had passed through. Small residential buildings ran around the perimeter wall. It could very well be the same place. Hard to tell. The bleak monotony of their surroundings and the similarity of the layout in this plaza blinded William to any identifying nuance.

The place had already been abandoned. Hopefully they'd found their way to the gates. Before leaving the plaza, Matilda slowed. William caught up to her. She raised a finger for him to be silent.

Clack-clack! Clack-clack!

William sank in his seat. "They're coming this way?"

Matilda nodded.

The prisoners' thunderous charge closed in from behind.

Artan waved his micro EMP in the machines' direction.

William shook his head. "Use that now and we'll lose our bikes and guns."

"What other choice do we have?"

"Follow me." William rode to the side wall around the back of one of the residential huts. He jumped from his bike. Matilda and Artan pulled up so theirs were beside his, hidden from sight. They too dismounted.

"What," Artan said, "we wait here for everything to pass us by?"

William said, "Hopefully neither of them come in here."

Matilda pointed around the side of the building. She raised her eyebrows, her lips tight.

The prisoners ran into the plaza. Several hundred quickly turned into over a thousand. They made a beeline for the other side.

William moved across the back of the hut. The drones and dogs came in through the other entrance. The prisoners froze. The machines halted. One thousand against seven, but the numbers didn't matter. There'd only be one winner.

"I can't let this happen. I know I was all for heading south, but we've committed to this now. We're supposed to be helping these people." William stepped from cover and removed his micro EMP button just as the drones and dogs charged the prisoners.

The prisoners screamed.

But the machines cut a path through them without attacking. They vanished through the other side of the plaza.

"What the …?" Matilda had stepped from cover with William.

Artan came out too. "What just happened?"

"I think that question can wait." A thousand prisoners in the plaza with them. A thousand pairs of eyes. Where they'd all focused on the dogs and drones, they now focused on Artan, Matilda, and William.

CHAPTER 21

"Joni's not a child!" She tore her hand from Olga's grip, pressed a finger to one side of her nose, and sent a snot rocket clogged with flour to the floor. She did the same with the other side, sneezed three times, and wiped her nose with the back of her sleeve. "And you, Pocket Rocket, are not Joni's mum. She can lead herself around this place, excuse me very much!"

"I'm not saying you can't." Olga Pocket Rocket pressed her hands together as if praying. "But please follow me."

"Who put you in charge?"

"There's a fire back there." Pocket Rocket pointed down the long corridor. "Lots of guards are trying to get to it. We remain this close, and they'll find us. I'm trying to get us away for my and your safety. Come on." Olga tugged on Joni's hand again, and she followed her into the next corridor.

Their feet slapped against the steel floor. They passed door after door. The maintenance shaft ran along the ceiling. Joni's domain. Somewhere she belonged. "Joni can't be trusted to make any decisions. Maybe she deserves to be locked away for good. To be put in a little room and looked after like a child. She can't be trusted to do anything. Maybe he was right."

"He wasn't." A tightening of her grip, Pocket Rocket quickened their pace and turned right. Screams and shouts from behind. Calls of, "*Fire!*"

Joni smiled. "That's Joni's doing. Sweet, sweet fire. Flames flying higher. But that's all she can do. She destroys." She ripped her hand away again.

Pocket Rocket halted. "What are you doing?"

"Leave Joni be. Get away from here and leave her alone. She needs to be by herself. She only brings trouble to anyone who gets too close. Go back to your friends. Joni will wait for the guards to find her. It might be enough to stop them looking for anyone else." She sat cross-legged on the cold steel floor.

"Come on, Joni." Olga Pocket Rocket grabbed Joni's hand and pulled.

Joni fell on her side. She rolled on her back, kicked her legs in the air, and laughed. "Pull much harder and Pocket Rocket will rip Joni's arm from her socket." Her throat tightened. It shredded her words, and she growled, "Leave Joni be. Joni's useless. Joni's trouble."

"Joni." Olga crouched down in front of her. "We need you."

"You do?"

"You've done so much for us so far. Without your help, Nick and Artan would be dead. And probably more of us, too. We'd certainly be lost, wandering around this insane place, not knowing which way to go and why. We're in control because of you. You've shown the guards this block and prison are yours to command. You're the one calling the shots, and you're using that power for good. You're helping us, and you're helping thousands of innocent people."

Shouting in Joni's ear. Tweeting birds. She scowled. Gotta focus on Pocket Rocket. She slapped the side of her head, but when she tried to slap it a second time, Olga caught her wrist.

"Stop that. Stop hurting yourself. Now get up. Come on, let's g—"

Pocket Rocket looked right.

Footsteps coming from around the bend.

Guards.

"Shit." Olga Pocket Rocket ran towards the sound.

Joni remained on the floor and folded her arms. The guards drew closer, still hidden by the bend in the corridor. Pocket Rocket waited in ambush where Joni could see her. Her back to the wall. The footsteps closed in.

Two guards appeared. One and then another. They stopped. They pointed their guns at Joni. A sitting duck. Let them take her. End the madness now. What life had she lived anyway? She'd let him take control of her from a young age, and then she'd lived in the sewers like a useless rat. What kind of life? Sad, sad Joni.

Crash!

Olga kicked the guard's gun. It hit the maintenance shaft running along the ceiling and shattered a neon strip light. He covered his head with his hands, glass and white powder raining down on him. Olga slammed the butt of her gun into his nose. His legs failed him.

Holding her gun like a club, gripping the barrel with both hands, Olga swung with her entire body. She caught the next guard clean on the side of the head.

Crack!

Joni winced as the second guard went down. "He won't get up from that again in a hurry. Hurry, curry, runny, money."

"What's she talking about?"

The chirping in her ear.

"I don't know."

Another voice. Another reply. Something that made sense in the madness. Joni's madness. She said, "They need to take Joni away. Be done with it. Put her out of her misery. An old dog. A boiled frog. The temperature has gotten too hot, but she's remained in the pan. Sat on the ground. Waiting to be taken."

"Come on, Joni." Pocket Rocket's face glowed like a beacon. She thrust her hand at her. "You can't sit there all day."

"Joni's already told you to go. Leave her. She's worthless. She's a grade A liability. Save yourself."

"I can't save myself without your help."

"Are you kidding?" Joni threw her hand toward the two unconscious guards. "Joni has eyes. Pocket Rocket versus an army, and Pocket Rocket would still win. Now go. Save yourself."

Crack!

Fire exploded in Joni's cheek. Olga Pocket Rocket had slapped her so hard her head damn near spun around. "Why did you do that? Why hit Joni? She's tried to help you, and you do this? That's what *he* did to her. Beat her. Attack her for no reason." She stood up and balled her hands into fists. "How dare you!"

Joni threw several punches.

Olga blocked every attack.

Her view blurred through her tears. Joni clamped her jaw. "This won't happen again. Joni won't let someone treat her like he did. No way! Yeargh!" Punch after punch. Block after block. Until she landed one.

Olga Pocket Rocket stumbled.

Joni landed another blow.

Olga wobbled on her tired legs.

Moving in for the kill, Joni charged with her fist raised.

But Olga dodged, grabbed her punch, and used Joni's momentum to throw her over her shoulder.

"Omph!" Joni hit the ground, back-first. The hard steel floor drove the wind from her lungs. She gasped and panted at the steel ceiling. At the maintenance shaft.

Pocket Rocket stared down at her. "There she is."

"Huh?"

"Joni. The Joni I can see inside you. The one who won't take shit. The one who won't give up."

"The one who will knock you the fuck out!"

"Good." Pocket Rocket clapped her hands. "Now listen to me."

Joni fought to catch her breath and rolled as if she could squirm away from the aches streaking up her back.

Cupping her right ear with her right hand, Pocket Rocket lifted her head in the sound's direction. "Hear that?"

"Footsteps."

"Guards. *Lots* of guards. And when they get here, they're going to see Pinky and Perky over there, and they won't be best pleased."

Joni snorted a laugh.

"Now, I'd suggest we're not here when that happens. You have unfinished business with him to attend to. Let's get back into the maintenance shafts where we're in control and show these clowns what it's like to be in Joni's funhouse, yeah?"

"Yes." Joni nodded. "Yes, you're right, Pocket Rocket. You're absolutely corr—" The tweeting in her ear threw her off. Joni slapped the side of her head with the earpiece in like swatting a fly.

"Give me that." Pocket Rocket held her hand towards Joni.

Joni removed the earpiece and let go of a relieved sigh. She could do this now.

With one finger pressed into her ear, Olga Pocket Rocket dropped Joni's earpiece on the floor and stamped on it. "If you need to talk to Joni, speak to me. I've taken out her earpiece so it's easier for her to concentrate." Back to Joni, Olga gave her a thumbs up. "Okay?"

"Is Joni mad?"

"You've been through a lot. That takes time to process. But we don't have time right now. We have to keep the guards busy. What's the quickest way into the maintenance shafts?"

Joni did a backwards roll to help her get to her feet. She ran to a nearby door and slapped the button beside it.

Crack!

Whoosh!

The reek of bleach spilled from the cleaning cupboard's door. Joni ruffled her nose. The same stuff she'd taken for him. "Fill his eye sockets. Blind the fucker. Cut his eyes out. Burn them. Burn one. Look at himself in a mirror." She stumbled forwards, forced into the cupboard by Olga's shove in her back.

Enough room to walk in, access the shelves, and walk out again. The steel shelves from floor to ceiling doubled as a ladder. Joni climbed.

She knocked into a mop. The long wooden handle slammed against the ground.

Crack!

Up the side of the room like a spider. Like a black widow. Joni pushed her fingers into the grate, bit down on her bottom lip, and tugged hard. The hatch swung open. She climbed higher and slid into the shaft. A silent snake. Carbon monoxide.

Not enough room to swing a tomcat, but enough room for the Minotaur to turn around. Joni reached down and took Pocket Rocket's hands. She slithered backwards and dragged her in, waited for her to close the hatch, and turned back around again. She waved her on. "Follow me, Pocket Rocket. Back in the maintenance shafts again. Joni's the tomcat. She owns them from here. She owns them all. She'll blind him. She'll blind them. She'll blind everyone. And eye for an eye for an eye for an eye."

"Let me out!"

Joni stopped and cupped her ear. She smiled. "Hear that, Pocket Rocket? Hear him asking for help? Locked in his little room. In a room where he can see for now. Soon he'll be blind. They'll all be blind."

"He can wait, though, Joni. He's not going anywhere, is he?"

"He might come up here."

"And what happens when someone comes at Joni the tomcat in the maintenance shafts?"

"Then there's only one winner, Pocket Rocket, and it won't be him. Only one winner, winner, bald old men for dinner. You're right. Always right. Shining bright tonight. Fight or flight." Joni led them on. "Time for him later. And he will pay, Pocket Rocket."

"I know he will."

"For what he did to Joni. She was young and foolish. Let him get away with it, but he will pay. Karma's a bitch. Joni's a bitch. Joni will cut his eyes out. Blind the fucker. Blind them all."

Over the control room, the hatch was open from when Joni last visited. The chair remained in the centre beneath her. She didn't need it to get in, but she needed it to get out again. She slipped backwards from the hatch into the circular rainbow room.

The indigo section next. Joni dropped in front of the computer terminal as Olga landed behind her. She plugged in her small computer. "Green lights, one, two, three." The screen came to life. Two taps later and the white lights in the rainbow room turned red. And not just the lights in this room. She'd bathed the entire prison in the red glow of emergency lighting.

Several rooms away, his scream echoed through the maintenance shafts.

CHAPTER 22

A single syllable left William, along with a small cloud of condensation that turned silver in the moon's light. "Shit!" He held his gun in shaking hands and pointed it at the prisoners. It gave them pause. If just for a second. But what could one gun do against all of them? He might have been carrying a backpack filled with ammo, but it did little good if they jumped him while he reloaded.

Artan knocked William's right shoulder as he charged past him, his button raised. "Get back!" He waved it at the prisoners. "We all know what this button does. I'll turn your insides to liquid."

William shook his head. "What are you doing, Art? You can't use that against them."

"You said we'd use these if our lives depended on it." Artan slashed through the air with his button, and the prisoners jumped back as one. Despite the packed square, his voice carried over the near silence. "I'd say our lives depend on it right now."

Next to William, her gun raised like him, Matilda shrugged. "Unless you have a better suggestion?"

With every step Artan took forwards, the prisoners took two back. They watched Artan, many tripping over those behind them in their haste to exit the plaza.

These people didn't need to understand Artan to get his sentiment. And they wouldn't understand William, but he kept his voice low anyway. "Does your button even work? You've had it on you the entire time, right?"

"Mine might not." Artan waved his hand in the air and stamped his feet. "But yours will. Yours and Matilda's."

"There must be ano—"

Matilda pulled her button from her pocket. Some prisoners screamed.

"Well, that's our minds made up, then, is it?"

She shrugged. "Sorry, but Artan's right. And we don't have time to discuss it."

"Aren't we supposed to be helping them get out of here?"

"I don't want to press it," Matilda said.

"But we might?"

"Don't bring a weapon if you're not prepared to use it."

"What are you doing?" Gracie squawked in William's ear.

"Not now, Gracie."

"Are you using the buttons on the prisoners?"

"Not now, Gracie."

William pulled his button from his pocket, and Matilda dipped a nod at him.

The prisoners bottlenecked at the plaza's exit. They shoved and barged one another to get away.

The three of them moved forward with slow and deliberate steps. They gave the prisoners the time to get out of there. They herded them until no more than one hundred remained in the plaza. William said, "We can't leave our quad bikes here."

Artan peered over his shoulder. "Let's get on them and ride after the prisoners." He walked back past William and

Matilda. "The pace of a vehicle will encourage them to scatter even quicker. We need to get back to taking down the machines."

The few prisoners who remained at the plaza's entrance scattered when William rode from behind the hut, Artan and Matilda close behind.

The relative quiet of the prisoners' panicked escape escalated into screams, shouts, and the thunder of another stampede.

Out on the main road, just a few hundred prisoners remained. With his button in one hand, William accelerated after them. "We might as well disperse them while we're here. Give us time to get away."

A line of prisoners ran ahead of him, but they slowed, even with the three of them in pursuit.

"Uh, William…"

"What?" He turned to Artan beside him.

Artan rolled to a halt, and William stopped with him. "Look." He pointed back the way they'd just come from. William had driven the prisoners over a white line. The lights on either side of the wall flashed red, but they'd crossed them with no consequence.

"Gracie." Matilda pressed her finger to her earpiece.

"What?" Gracie's tinny reply hissed in William's ear. "Did you move the prisoners on without killing any?"

"Yep!" Matilda said.

"Good."

"Are things still looking all right by the gates?"

"For now. Why?"

"That might change."

"What's happened, Tilly?"

"We've accidentally shown a group of prisoners they can cross the lines while the lights are flashing red."

"What are you saying?"

"That we've shattered the illusion of the red lights. And that you might have a shitload of them coming your way."

CHAPTER 23

"Shit!" Gracie slid the last few feet, the toes of her boots slamming into the low wall. She stopped her momentum by slapping her hands on the wall's cold steel top. She might not have gone over the edge, but her stomach did, leaping with a forwards somersault and plummeting to the ground a few hundred feet below.

The wind in her face, her nose running and numb. Her ears hurt, and the joints in her hands were sore. They'd been up there for several hours, exposed to the elements, waiting for an organised escape to descend into chaos. Group after group of prisoners left through the open north gates like they'd done it a thousand times before. They knew the risks well enough to keep them cautious. They stuck to the shadows. Despite being close to the diseased in the overgrown meadow, most of them got away without incident. Breathing heavily from the quick sprint, she pressed her finger to her earpiece. "How are we looking back there, Hawk?"

"Fine. For now."

"Well, that fills me with confidence."

"I'm not here to fill you with confidence. I'm here to tell you what I see. And what I see is fine."

"For now."

"For now."

"What the hell were they doing sending the prisoners this way?"

William's tinny interruption. "Hey! We didn't do it on purpose. And you said it's fine where you are."

"For now," Hawk said.

"Yeah, I get it. Maybe it will stay fine."

Another group of about fifty prisoners exited through the gates. Gracie leaned over the wall, her stomach turning like a hamster wheel. No amount of time up here would get her used to the height. Or rather, the drop. Humans were stuck to the ground for a reason.

The most recent prisoners remained in the shadows, like those before them. Close to the wall, they escaped under the cover of night. All the while, the shambling diseased remained just that. Stumbling. Tripping. Slashing at the air. They sent agonised squalls at the moon. The group below halted at a particularly loud call. But their cries spoke only of their torment, not because they had a target in their sights. "Shit," Gracie said.

"What?" Hawk faced her from the other side of the plateau and turned his palms to the moon.

"This was working so well. And now we're screwed."

"You're fine for now."

"William, can you keep the channel clear unless you have something useful to say?"

"Uh, Gracie."

Gracie's stomach twisted. Hawk's tone said it all. She turned to him, but he had his back to her. He leaned on the wall and stared out over the prison. The group she'd watched leave through the gates made it to safety. Would she see another group get away from here? She ran back to Hawk. Her boots slapped against the steel floor. "Shit!" She pressed her finger to her ear. "Joni, we need help."

"What's happened?"

"William, will you please keep the channel clear?"

"Gracie, it's Olga. What's up?"

Prisoners filled the main road. A thousand or more. The crowd stretched from one wall to the other and ran tens of feet deep. They charged towards the north wall and the open gates. "We're screwed."

"What?"

"We have a thousand prisoners or more running for the gates. That many will attract the diseased's attention the second they step outside. They'll overrun this place. We need you to shut the gates. Now."

"Again?" Olga said.

"You've not done it yet."

"But you keep asking us."

"That's because I don't want this place overrun with diseased. I wasn't the one who sent a thousand fucking prisoners down the main road, was I?"

"We can't get to the control room right now. You should have asked us twenty minutes ago."

"How could we have asked you twenty minutes ago? We're not psychic, Olga."

Men, women, children. They all ran at them, their faces locked with grim determination. They'd spent their lives in this prison, and now they had a chance to leave, they weren't stopping for no one.

"How long do we have?" Olga said.

Gracie turned to Hawk, who shrugged. "A few minutes. At best."

"No good."

The earpiece hurt Gracie's eardrum from how hard she pressed it. "What do you mean *no good?*"

"We can't get there that quickly. We're on the other side of the guards' block."

"Shit! Where are the machines?"

William again. "You want them to come?"

"They broke them up last time. It's a quick fix and far from ideal, but right now, we need to sort out your mess."

"Well, fuck me for trying to save my own life. Jeez, Gracie, you'd think you cared more about these prisoners than you do your friends."

The words rocked Gracie. She swallowed a dry gulp. The prisoners continued charging forwards. "I'm sorry. You're right. I'm stressed. If you were looking at what I'm looking at, you'd understand. Do you know where the dogs and drones are?"

"No, but something strange happened. We saw them run into the group of prisoners heading your way, and they just charged straight through them as if they weren't there. They paid them no mind."

"Were the prisoners where they were supposed to be?"

"Maybe," William said. "But since that moment, I can't see any of them on Joni's scanner. There nowhere to be seen, and we've been looking."

Gracie slapped the top of the wall. Her already numb hands stung from the blow. "Shit! Joni?"

"She's taken out her earpiece, Gracie."

"Yeah, sorry. We really need some help here."

"I've already told you, we can't do anything at this moment. We'll close the gates as soon as we can."

Hawk pointed down at the prisoners. "The ones in the side roads are joining them."

"Shit. It's more than a thousand now and growing. The ones who'd been slowly making their way here have seen the prisoners on the main road. They've worked out the red lights are useless too and have joined them. If we don't get the gates closed, Olga, the second the diseased see them, it's game over. All bets are off. This place will be overrun, and there's no chance of us heading south. I don't even fancy my chances of getting down from this wall."

"We'll do what we can."

"That's it?"

"It's the best I have. We're heading to the control room now."

"Damn it!" Gracie goat-stamped on the steel floor. "What am I supposed to do, then?"

"Think of something."

The harsh wind had chilled Gracie's mum and dad's wedding rings around her neck. Cold against her palm, she spun around and ran to the spiral staircase leading to the ground.

"Gracie, what are you doing?"

She halted two steps down. Hawk's face had turned pale. "I understand if you don't want to come with me."

"What are you doing?"

"Someone has to stop that mob from running outside. Maybe I can reason with them before they alert the diseased."

"But that's suicide."

"So's letting the diseased into this prison." Gracie spun around and ran down the spiral stairs two at a time.

The *thud* of Hawk's steps joined her. Her radio crackled from where she lost service. The signal had no chance getting through the thick steel wall. She pressed her finger to her ear. "You're coming with me?"

"Yeah, why not? What could be better than getting ripped limb from limb by thousands of angry prisoners?"

CHAPTER 24

Joni's nose remained clogged with the flour she'd sniffed in the kitchen. She scrunched up her face and relaxed it as she ran, but it did little to relieve the deep itch in her sinuses. She'd probably snorted some of it into her brain. Flour brain. Power name. Hour insane.

She and Olga, bathed in the crimson glow of emergency lighting, ran side by side down the corridor. "Joni's turned the entire guards' block red. Hell's hotel. Even more fitting now. Looks like the walls are bleeding. And his scream adds to the ambiance. It makes it all worthwhile, even when Joni's too far away to hear it. Just to know he's suffering. That he's beating his pasty little hands against the side of his locked door. Let him out or else! Or else what, Louis? What can he do to Joni now? What can he take from her that he hasn't already? Back when he held all the cards. But he hasn't even got a deck now. His precious little block is too dark. Dark like his piggy little heart. What now, Louis? Where's your power now?"

The crimson bulbs cast splashes of red light in the darkness. They helped Joni lead Olga from point to point, but anything could be lurking in the shadows. A Minotaur. A tomcat. At the end of the next corridor, Joni turned back, looked down the barrel of her gun, and pulled the trigger. One bullet. The red emergency light over one hundred feet away. The splash and tinkle of shattering glass. The place fell into total darkness. Joni punched the air. "Another one bites the dust. Soon this place will be as dark as his soul. No light. No dogs and drones. Joni will cut his damn eyes out. Even when it gets light again and the machines come back online, he'll stay blind."

"Come on, Joni." Olga pulled on her arm, but Joni snapped away from her.

Pocket Rocket pointed. "We need to get back to the control room. We need to close the main gates."

"We need to blind these bastards. Take their eyes away from them. Cut his from his skull and crush them like overripe grapes. Joni has unfinished business." She ran down another corridor, reached the end, spun around, and shot another light. "One shot, one bulb. Splash. Tinkle."

Joni took off again, and Olga ran with her. She fought to get her words out. "These lights can wait, Joni. If we don't get the main gates closed, the diseased will overrun this place. We need to act fast!"

"Joni's already waited too long. Joni's waited a lifetime to take control of this place. And now Joni's here with a knife in her hand, she will put out their eyes like she's been planning. With the help of William and the others taking down the machines in the prison, and Joni taking out the lights in this block, we'll turn all the guards blind."

"But they're not taking down the dogs and drones."

"Huh?"

"You know what?" Olga threw a hand through the air, batting away her comment. "It doesn't matter. Let's just focus on us. Come on."

Joni stopped at the end of the next corridor. She looked down the barrel of her gun. "The best shot in this place, Joni can shoot the wings off a fly's back." She squeezed the trigger, but halted before she fired the bullet. Two guards appeared at the other end of the corridor. No more than silhouettes in the crimson glow. Joni shifted her aim. "Take them down." She paused. "No. They're not him." She returned her attention to the red light and pulled the trigger. One shot. *Splash!* The light shattered. Glass rained down on the steel floor. The guards ran, and Joni threw her head back with laughter. Her voice echoed in the dark corridors. "This is Joni's block now. You'd better recognise, fools."

"But you could show them this entire prison is Joni's."

Joni paused. "Go on?"

"You can show them you decide what happens around here, both inside *and* outside this block. Close the gates. Show them you're in control."

"But how many times have they said they want us to close the gates? Close the gates, leave the gates, close the gates, leave the gates ..."

"I know. And every time we've gone to do it, they've changed their minds. But that's why we're in here. To help them with what they need. They're our eyes out there."

"That's why you're in here, Pocket Rocket."

Olga frowned at her.

"Joni's here to bring chaos. To blind the entire block. Them for tonight. Him forever. Joni's here to do what she should have done over twenty years ago were she not such a coward. That's why Joni's here."

"But all it takes is for us to ignore them once, and this prison could fall. This is fun, turning all the lights off—"

"Yeah, it is."

"And when we've closed the gates, we can finish what we started." Olga dragged Joni towards a door on their left. "But for now, we need to close the gates. We need to get into the maintenance shafts again. Where Joni knows the way. You can take us to the control room from there. Come on, Joni. We all need you right now. We all need Mama Bird to step up and protect her chicks." Olga slapped the button beside the door.

Crack!

Whoosh!

She stepped inside. "Come on."

Joni ran in and halted as soon as she entered the room. Ice ran through her veins. She trembled, and the insides of her thighs turned warm with her urine. A hand on her flat stomach, Joni shook her head again and again. She rocked where she stood. "No. No." They were in the medical bay. Joni pointed at the bed in the corner. An old rusty frame with a stained mattress. Leather straps hung down. "He tied her to that bed." The place stank of bleach. "Bleach in his eyes. Blind him. Bleach to clean up the stink. From where Joni had been a bad girl. From where she couldn't hold it and soiled herself. Another mattress ruined, but he made her sleep on it anyway." She fell to her knees against the hard steel floor. *Crack!*

Olga grabbed Joni beneath her arm and tugged. Her fingers stung Joni's armpit from where they dug in. But she didn't budge.

"Come on, Joni. You can do this. Get up now. Come on."

"The bed." Joni pointed at it again. She opened her mouth so wide the skin on her cheeks itched. She released a monotone cry. A primal wail.

Olga's eyes widened, and she pulled her hair away from her face. She threw a glance at the locked door. "Come on, Joni. Someone will hear you. We need to keep moving."

"The bed." Joni pointed at it again. The frame made from the same gunmetal grey as everywhere else. The dirty mattress. The soiled mattress. "She's done it again. Bad, bad girl. And how many others have lain here? How many others have sweated into that filthy mattress like Joni did? All those months. Months and months. Sorry, Little Chick. Joni did the same to you. How awful. Tied you to a bed. Secured you in place. Forced you to remain lying down." Snot and flour ran from her nose.

"Argh!" Joni jumped up, snapped her gun into her shoulder, and opened fire on the bed. "Argh! Argh! Argh!" The bullets tore into the mattress and pinged off the steel frame.

"Joni!" Olga ran to the corner of the room and crouched down, her hands over her head. "One of those ricochets is going to kill us. We need to get out of here."

But Joni doesn't care if she dies. Why would she? She let go of the trigger and pointed the gun at the bottom of her chin.

Olga jumped up and grabbed Joni by her shoulders. A powerful grip that could crush bones. She shook her. "Snap out of it!"

Joni turned her gun on Olga. "Are you going to hit Joni again? Hit her for being sad. For what he's done to her? Months in this room. Strapped to that bed. Are you really going to hit Joni again? Well, Pocket Rocket? Wanna try?"

"If you're going to pull that trigger, then do it. I won't attack you again, Joni. You're a good person. You're kind. I don't know what's happened to you in this place, but I can see that whatever it is, it's awful."

"Joni wishes she knew." She lowered her gun and knocked on the side of her head with her knuckles. "The details are cloudy. Who knows what he's done to her? Who can remember?"

"But I know you care about people. You care about Gracie and Hawk. William, Matilda, and Artan. Little Chick. Chopped Liver. You care about Pocket Rocket."

"I care about them." Joni nodded, her hair falling across her face and sticking to her sweat and tears. She swept half of it away and tucked it behind her right ear. "Joni's kind. Not like him."

"Not like him at all." Olga shook her head. "No, not like him. So help us, Joni. Help all the poor prisoners who need it." Olga held her hand towards Joni. "Come on."

A warm hand. Joni hadn't held many warm hands over the years. Not a warm hand that wanted to hold hers. Occasionally, she'd sneak into the guards' rooms and hold their hands while they slept. But what if they woke? What if they caught her in the act? A desperate old woman sneaking into people's rooms to hold their hands. "Weirdo. Saddo." Joni wiped her running nose with the back of her sleeve and followed Olga from the medical bay. They crossed the dark hallway into the toilet block on the other side.

The same red glow in here as everywhere else. Water dripped somewhere in the room.

Plip!

Plip!

Plip!

Olga stepped from the toilet seat to the cistern. She pulled the maintenance shaft hatch open and climbed in like she'd done it a thousand times before.

Joni followed, dragged the hatch shut behind her, squeezed past Olga, and led the way. Her voice echoed in the quiet shaft. "Someone looked after me in the medical bay. Joni doesn't remember who. A man. He called me his …" She stopped. "Shit! He called me his little chick. He was kind. He gave me better food than before. It got rid of the woozy feeling in Joni's head and stomach. Joni got her strength back. They'd been drugging her all along. Louis would have killed him had he known he was helping me. Would have killed him dead. He left the straps too loose on Joni's bed one time. When she got her strength back. That's when Joni got away. Joni's been showing him who's boss ever since."

"And you are, Joni. You're one of the toughest people I've met."

"Joni is. We're better up in these tunnels. This is where Joni feels safe and in control." She pressed one side of her nose and blew. It drove another lump of flour from her nostril. "Let's stay up here."

"I think that's a good idea. Now let's get to the control room and close the gates."

CHAPTER 25

"How much longer, Olga?" Gracie had chewed the inside of her mouth red raw. She'd have an ulcer in the morning. Her hand ached from gripping her button. Her arm ached from holding it up for the wall of prisoners to see. And she'd best keep a hold of it because nothing else would keep them back. Her and Hawk versus a thousand or more prisoners. But at least they'd beaten them to the gates. They'd been holding them there for about fifteen minutes. It felt like fifteen days.

"We're getting there. Just keep them occupied."

Hawk snorted a laugh. He scanned the vast mob as if he could understand the thoughts buried deep in every pair of narrowed eyes. "Easier said than done."

But they were in control. For now. The mob William and the others had sent their way had grown. Maybe doubled. Two thousand or more? Hard to tell from the ground. But more and more stepped from the streets and alleys. Emboldened by their peers on the main road, they tested the fallacy of the flashing red lights and came out on top. Thankfully, they still believed in the button. Better that than finding out the hard way. For everyone.

A prisoner stepped from the mob. A woman, she had matted locks and wild eyes. Her black clothes hung from her like rags, and she had scars on her neck and face. Gracie's hand twitched with her urge to reach for Hawk, who now rubbed his own healed wounds. The scruffy prisoner's pale skin turned crimson, and she shook with the force of her cry. A flurry of words. Whether or not Gracie and Hawk understood them, they'd best listen.

The response from the two thousand prisoners slammed into them as a wall of sound. It rocked Gracie back on her heels. Her hand holding the button twitched. She pressed down a little harder, clamping her teeth as she fought to not press it fully. They'd not charged yet. Nobody needed to die because she'd lost her bottle.

Olga's tinny voice in Gracie's ear. "What was that?"

"They're getting restless. The threat of these buttons can only hold them back so long."

The raggedy woman stamped with every step. She paced up and down in front of her fellow prisoners. She thrust her skinny arm into the air and shouted again. The crowd met her call. Their cry a force of nature that lifted the hairs on Gracie's body. The will of thousands of people who'd had enough. And who could blame them? But no matter how she empathised with them, she still stood before them as the enemy. As their oppressor. She moved closer to the stairs leading back to the top of the wall. If they were to be chased anywhere, better they ran somewhere that took away the mob's advantage of outnumbering them.

The woman with the matted locks punched the air to accentuate her words. She let out a tongue-rolling war cry.

Those behind echoed her call.

The diseased in the meadow shouted back.

"Shit!"

Hawk spun towards the open gates. Diseased descended on them. He fired his gun. The stuttered clatter echoed off the high walls on either side. There might not be a siren, but they were certainly filling the space left by its absence.

Hawk's bullets slammed into the diseased. Some of them spun and fell. Some of their limbs flung out behind them. Two took bullets straight to the face. The impact tested the integrity of their rotting bones and shattered their skulls like overripe pumpkins. He'd taken down the first wave.

Silence fell over the crowd.

The colour had drained from Hawk's face. He held his gun as if his hands didn't belong to him. "What else could I do?"

The prisoners screamed and charged.

Gracie grabbed Hawk and dragged him from their path. Their backs to the wall, they held their buttons in front of them as the stampede passed. The prisoners gave them enough clearance to present no immediate threat. But if either Gracie or Hawk pressed the button, they were close enough to fall. And they must have known it. Maybe they accepted this truce. They both had their own agendas. They didn't need to battle today.

"We have to stop them." Hawk held his button higher.

"No!"

"No?"

"What good will it do? We've already lost control, so why kill them? We won't get them all, and they're leaving this place whether we like it or not." The prisoners flashed past. A fleeing herd. "They'll either die at our or the diseased's hands. And they've made that choice."

Gracie backed into the spiral staircase and ran up the stairs. The hard steel cold and unforgiving. She took them two at a time. Her gun swung on its strap. Her backpack heavy with unused magazines. Fatigue ran through her veins from being awake all night. Her panting effort got thrown back at her in the cramped space. The stairs made her dizzy. Round and round. Her thighs burned from her ascent.

The strong wind at the top of the staircase cooled Gracie's sweating face. She stumbled as she ran on tired legs to the side of the wall overlooking the meadow and the steep hill. The spot she'd watched the gates open from countless times before.

Thousands of prisoners spilled out. They met the diseased head-on. Many got past. Many climbed the steep hill. The uncoordinated creatures tried and failed to catch them. Many fought and scrapped, rolling around in the meadow with the foetid monsters. Screams and cries from the infected and uninfected alike. How long before they all sang the same tune?

"Gracie, we're here."

Her finger to her ear, Gracie winced as a child got hit by a fully grown diseased at a flat-out sprint. Both of them went down, the child's neck snapping against the ground before the diseased sank its teeth in. The kid lay limp. At least they wouldn't become one of them. "Hang on."

Olga said, "Hang on? *Again?*"

"You're too late to close the gates. The prisoners are running out in their hundreds. That ship's sailed."

The disease spread through the crowd. Prisoners turned on prisoners. The hill out of there packed with people. The front runners had climbed to safety, but there were so many prisoners on the hill, they were now getting held up. Easy pickings. The diseased dragged them off and attacked.

"Shit. So we're screwed? How long before we lose the prison?"

"We might not."

"What?"

The battle continued at the bottom of the hill. It attracted the diseased like a siren's call. It pulled them away from the prison's gates. "The diseased are following the escaping prisoners away from the prison. Many are falling, but many more are getting away. There are too many for the diseased to cope with."

"For now," Hawk said.

Gracie rested on the steel wall and caught her breath.

"So what do you want us to do?"

"Turn all the lights white."

Hawk and Olga said it in unison, "What?"

While replying to Olga, Gracie turned to Hawk. "We need to close the gates at some point, but not now. The prisoners were sneaking out before, and it was working, but that tactic's now lost to us. We can't go back to that. This is the last roll of the dice. I say we send as many as we can out of here while the gates are open. Because after this, there's going to be an army of diseased waiting in the meadow, and who knows how long it will take for them to clear."

"So turn the lights white?"

"Yep."

"You're sure."

"Yeah, and you need to do it before we lose the moment. The second there's a lull in the number of prisoners rushing out of here, the diseased will get curious and come in. And please stay close by. We will need to close the gates at some point. Hopefully, by then, the prison will be empty."

CHAPTER 26

"Close them, open them, close them, open them." Joni bashed the heels of her palms together and paced back and forth on the flat steel roof. The wind in her hair, flour in her nose.

"I'm just glad to be out of that place for a minute." Olga stretched her arms to the moon and inhaled. "And they're not doing it on purpose."

The white lights atop the walls stretched away from them in every direction. They stood on the roof of the guards' block, the dark heart of this dark prison. They could see everything. Wall to wall. On top of the world, where Joni liked to be. But they were close enough to the control room should they need to return. And if their past few hours had been anything to go by, they would have to return. They'd be calling on Joni again. "Close the gates, open the gates."

"But it's working." Olga pointed down the main road leading to the gates. Packed with prisoners on the run and more joining them from the side streets. "And at least it's sped things up. Get it all done under the cover of night and then get out of here. Head south."

"Careful what you wish for."

"Huh?"

Joni shook her head and filled her lungs. "Doesn't need to know. Now's not the time." She continued batting her palms together and strolled to the edge of the roof. So many prisoners on the main road. Pocket Rocket had a point. At least they'd achieved this. If nothing else, they've given plenty of prisoners a good chance at freedom.

Clack-clack.

A dog ran into the plaza.

"Huh?"

Clack-clack.

Another one. Accompanied by a drone. They both ran towards the guards' block. "With so many prisoners on the run, why are they coming back this way? Are they all coming back to charge?"

"Huh?" Olga moved close to Joni.

"Dogs. Drones. They've come back here."

"You think it's to charge their batteries?"

"I dunno. Joni doesn't know nothing about nothing about nothing." She leaned on the roof's perimeter wall and peered over. She gasped.

Olga peered over beside her. "Jeez. How many are there?"

"About three hundred in total. Minus the twenty or so William and the others have taken out."

"Are they *all* down there? They can't all be waiting to get in."

A jolt snapped through the machines as if they were all locking into the same central nervous system. "And they are."

"They are what?" Olga said.

"The same central nervous system. Dogs and drones unite. Come together and take back control. An army. All fighting for the same cause."

"The dogs and drones are all going to fight together?"

"Yes! Why don't you listen to Joni? She hates having to repeat herself. Dogs and drones unite."

"What does that mean?"

"Proper screwed. When they reach the prisoners, they're proper screwed. Only one winner, winner, prisoners for dinner."

"What can we do about it?"

"You want Joni to wipe your arse for you as well?"

Olga shook her head. "I don't understand. What are you saying?"

"You have friends who have buttons. Joni got them for them. You got trapped outside. A pack of dogs and drones is a deadly force. But with micro EMPs, they're also a massive target."

"William, Matilda, Artan." Olga pressed her finger to her ear. "We've found the dogs and drones. They're all here, out the front of the guards' block. They're pulling them together to send them out through the prison as one. There's about three hundred of them. My guess is they will take off down the main road after the prisoners. You need to get between them and the prisoners with your micro EMPs."

CHAPTER 27

William ran ahead of Matilda towards the main road between the guards' block and the open gates. They'd left Artan with the bikes, weapons, and earpieces. They couldn't be without transport in this place. "This feels insane." William held up his hands. "We're armed with two buttons each, and we're about to run into hundreds of dogs and drones and thousands of prisoners."

Matilda's usually tanned skin had turned pale. But she'd insisted on coming with William rather than being left to mind the bikes.

Close to entering the main road, they slowed their pace. William reached across and squeezed one of Matilda's hands. Her chest swelled with a deep inhalation, and she nodded. They had this.

Filling his lungs too, William raised his micro EMP and stepped out into the main road, facing the guards' block.

Matilda said, "What the ..."

Prisoners filled the main road between them and the block, and more joined them all the time. They burst from side roads. They shouted to one another. But none of them headed towards the gates.

"Where are the machines?" William rocked from side to side, but he couldn't pick out the dogs or the drones in the madness. "Olga said there were about three hundred of them, right? Right?"

Matilda had turned around and faced the other way. "Uh! I think we came out at the wrong point."

William turned too. "Damn!"

About two thousand prisoners ran for the open gates. They were being driven forward by a pack of machines. The three hundred Olga had warned them about. The glow of flames shimmered off their surroundings. Some people burned, and some were dropped by stuttered bursts of bullets. A ruthless slaughter.

"Well, what are we waiting for?" Matilda led the charge.

Had he not had someone to follow, William might have obeyed his body's commands and remained rooted to the spot. But he couldn't leave Matilda. He took off after her on wobbly legs. His throat dried, and his heart beat with such force it upset his running rhythm. But they had to do this. They owed it to the prisoners. And what better time than when the machines were preoccupied?

The amplified prisoners' screams drove needles into William's eardrums. The *whomp* of igniting balls of fire. Blood burst from bullet wounds. The air reeked of singed hair and the sweet tang of seared flesh. The machines executed the prisoners with cold efficiency. An organised wall of death, they mowed down their victims.

Matilda halted, and William stopped next to her. More prisoners burst from a side road ahead. About five hundred men, women, and children, they blocked their access to the machines. Many of the prisoners checked behind before returning their attention to William and Matilda. Confused scowls crushed sweating faces. They were trapped between the enemy and the enemy. They had to make a choice.

Every prisoner carried a weapon. Clubs, bats, and blades, they stepped towards William and Matilda. And who could blame them? The machines were chewing through bodies, dropping the prisoners in their droves. And what if the diseased got in too? William shook his head. Little point in thinking about that now.

The five hundred prisoners quickened their pace from a fast walk to a jog.

Matilda pointed down the road. Pointed straight at the charging prisoners. "Let us pass. We can deal with those machines."

Scowls deepened, and they quickened their pace.

She waved her micro EMP at them. "This button will kill the machines."

The prisoners slowed a little.

"Maybe they understand?" Matilda said.

William shrugged. "Or maybe they're conditioned to fear buttons that cause mass destruction?"

Many prisoners checked behind again as if they needed reassurance they were heading towards the lesser threat of the two.

The prisoners halted when Matilda raised her other button.

William gasped. "What are you doing?"

"They won't let us through, and they're more scared of the machines than they are of us. We have to change that."

The prisoners about fifty feet away, the massacre over two hundred. Matilda stepped forwards with her buttons in her hands. The prisoners stepped back. Tight jaws, hard scowls, white-knuckled grips on makeshift weapons.

His hands sweating on his buttons, William's legs weakened again. "They're not getting out of our way. And I'm not sure they will."

Just ten feet separated William, Matilda, and the prisoners. The *whomp* of fire and the burst of bullets behind them. Screams of the fallen. Wails of despair. Those towards the back of the crowd checked behind again. At what point would the machines turn on them? When would they be forced to decide? And what death would they choose? At least the buttons would be quick.

A croak in his voice, William pointed over the heads of the prisoners. "We need to get past."

The already deep scowls deepened. Weapons twitched in grips.

Matilda, now just a few feet from the crowd, dropped her button. The one that set off the prisoners' implants. Half the angry faces tracked it. The entire crowd jumped back when she stamped on it, shattering it between her heel and the rough concrete.

William copied Matilda. He stamped on his button too, crushing it into the ground.

Her hands pressed together in prayer. Matilda then pointed down the road. "We need to get through." She raised her micro EMP. "This button will take down the machines. You need to let us pass."

The front row of prisoners remained resolute, but those at the back parted. That parting moved forwards until just those at the front blocked their way.

One of the older women in the group came forwards and elbowed herself into the front line. She shouted at the prisoners and shoved one half of the line towards one wall and the other half the other way.

Enough room to get through them in single file, William led this time. He passed so close to the prisoners, their hot breath pushed against his face. The gap got so tight on the other side, he rubbed shoulders with several of them on his way through.

Matilda joined William on the other side of the mob. She raised her eyebrows, and her cheeks bulged with her exhale. Just a few hundred feet between them and the machines, William led them towards the massacre and shook his head. "I can't believe we begged to be let through to this."

Screams. Cries. The floor shone with spilled blood. The strong reek of charred flesh caught in the back of William's throat, and he gagged.

The machines focused on the prisoners. They didn't notice William and Matilda just fifteen feet away. William pressed his micro EMP.

A line of drones fell from the sky with a *crash!* They landed on the now limp bodies of the dogs.

Matilda pressed her button, and the next line fell. Their choice to clump together made them an easy target.

The ground a lake of blood that splashed up with William's steps. Some patches were dried to a tar, blackened from the flames. Corpses everywhere. Cremated and not, many of them fixed on the sky with glazed stares.

Crash!

The last of the drones dropped to the ground. The last of the dogs fell on their sides.

The prisoners screamed and cried. As William and Matilda backed away, many of them ran to the fallen. They dropped to their knees. They lifted limp heads and ran fingers along necks, feeling for pulses.

About three hundred dead machines mixed with three times that number of prisoners. William flicked his head back the way they'd come, his voice hoarse. "We might have ended this slaughter, but it by no means feels like a victory. Let's get back to Artan and see if the others need our help with anything."

The moonlight reflected off Matilda's glazed eyes. She turned several slow circles in the centre of the massacre and shook her head before following William.

The prisoners who'd let them through to get the machines now ran towards them. William winced as they drew close. Five hundred of them. All of them armed. William and Matilda had nothing. They'd smashed their only defence.

But the prisoners ran through them as if they weren't there. Through them and over their fallen comrades and the machines responsible for their deaths. The gates were open. If they wanted to get out of here, they had no time to grieve.

CHAPTER 28

A sea of white lights stretched away across the prison. Left and right, coast to coast, and all the way to the south wall. Despite Gracie's elevation, the boundaries for each were well beyond her sight. The moon added to the white highlight running along the tops of the walls. The tall and thick steel barriers were like small roads fifty feet from the ground. Small roads studded with sentry guns.

Many of the streets were too narrow to see into from Gracie's vantage point. How would she know when the charging prisoners were thinning out? When would she tell Joni to close the gates for good? For now, plenty still burst out onto the main road in groups, albeit fewer now than an hour ago when Joni and Olga had turned all the lights white. They still ran for the gates, crossing over the bodies of the fallen, the corpses of machines and prisoners alike. And Joni had been correct about the guards. Too lazy at the best of times for the night shift, and because they'd felt vulnerable enough to lock down their block, none of them had come out to patrol the prison's streets.

The latest group of prisoners to burst out onto the main

road comprised just four people. A man, woman, and two children. The woman held the boy's hand. He must have been about ten. The man carried the small girl on his back. Four or five, or maybe small for her age. Definitely younger than the boy. Gracie clung to the cold metal of her mum and dad's wedding rings and expelled a cloud of condensation with a hard sigh.

Hawk leaned on the wall beside her. "There are fewer prisoners coming out now."

"No, there's not." Like telling him the moon didn't hang over them in the sky, or the steel wall wasn't cold.

Hawk rubbed Gracie's back. "Let's see what's happening in the meadow."

Gracie remained rooted to the spot as the dad of the family shouted up at his little girl. She covered her eyes when they ran through the fallen bodies. The boy slowed down and took it all in, his face slack, his shoulders slumped. Protect the little one, but the older sibling had to face the harsh reality of this life. Everyone looked after the little one. She tightened her grip on her mum and dad's wedding rings.

"Come on." Hawk tugged Gracie's arm.

The family vanished from sight beneath them. Gracie joined Hawk in running across to the other side of the wall.

William's tinny voice speared Gracie's ear. "How's it looking up there? It looks like the flow of prisoners is slowing."

Gracie spoke before Hawk could. "We're fine for now." She reached the other wall and gulped, her voice weak. "We're doing okay."

Despite Hawk's attention burning into the side of her face, Gracie squinted into the darkness at the sea of diseased in the meadow below. The escaping prisoners on the hill had drawn most of them away from the gates. Many prisoners climbed to freedom. But with a wall of creatures between the open gates and the hill out of there, that route had been closed off to any more who wanted that same chance at a new life. And the most recent escapees didn't have the numbers on their side like before to drive the beasts back.

Gracie pressed her lips tight and refused to look at Hawk. Let him stare.

The family of four burst out into the meadow. They ran several steps and slowed their charge. They were free, but what now? Where would they go? A wall of snarling chaos between them and the hill out of there. Those who were going to escape that way had already done so, or were making their bid for freedom. The family had the shadows cast by the tall wall, but there were more diseased milling about in the meadow than before.

A pack of about ten prisoners burst out behind the family and ran past them. Armed with bats, clubs, and blades, they raised their weapons and charged at the hill and the horde between them and freedom.

Her right palm tingling from where she rested on the cold steel wall, Gracie clung to her mum and dad's rings with her left and twisted away from the massacre. Every prisoner fell. "They need to find another way around the diseased."

Gracie jumped at another shrill cry in the meadow. Her breaths quickened, and her heart pounded. Just one diseased, but it only takes one. It broke from the mob at the bottom of the hill, many of them still focused on the climbing prisoners. Slashing at the air with wild arms, it ran on the edge of its balance and made a beeline for the family of four. Since leaving the gates, they'd remained rooted to the spot. And who could blame them? The shadows along the wall might work, but with so many diseased in the meadow, their chances of survival were slim at best.

The little girl screamed louder than the creature. More diseased turned their way. The dad took off first. The girl on his back, he ran away from the diseased and away from the open gates.

Hawk sighed. "They don't stand a chance. A child on his back and her dragging a ten-year-old with her. There's only one winner here."

The diseased leaped towards the dad, arms outstretched. It caught the girl and her father, and all three of them fell. Hard. The girl flew from her dad's back. The diseased and the dad rolled on the ground, wrestling with one another.

The mum grabbed the little girl with her free hand and dragged her away. The children cried and pulled towards their dad, who lay on his back. Pinned by the diseased, he held the frenzied creature away from him at full stretch. The creature's greasy hair hung down at the sides of its face. It snapped and bit at the air between it and the man. It twisted and lunged, snarled and yowled.

The dad's arms failed him. Gracie's stomach clamped as tight as the diseased's jaw when it bit into him. The dad fell limp. But the mum had found the shadows. A way out of there.

The family of four now a family of three. They kept tight to the wall and ran away from the now diseased dad. Another group of prisoners broke from the gates and ran for the hill. They fell like those before them. But at least the family—

"Shit!" Gracie's grip on her mum and dad's rings hurt her palm. Two diseased hit the family of three. They connected skull to skull, the creatures taking down the mum and the boy at the same time. The girl ran.

Both diseased bit their victims. The girl remained in the shadows of the wall, her small arms pumping, her little legs moving fast despite her slow pace.

"What's she doing?" Hawk said.

The girl stopped and turned around.

"Run, girl. You can get away from here if you run."

"But wh—" Gracie's voice failed her. She sniffed against her running nose, and her view of the girl blurred through her tears.

The mum and the little boy twitched. Limbs spasmed and jaws snapped. The boy got up first and charged at his little sister.

The small girl sobbed and stared at the ground.

Crack! Her brother slammed into her, head to head. She turned limp from the collision. On top of her, the boy bit into her face.

Gracie's tears turned cold on her cheeks. She flinched at Hawk's touch.

"Do you need me to do it?" he said.

While biting on her bottom lip, Gracie nodded.

With one hand on Gracie's back, Hawk pressed a finger to his ear. "Olga, it's time to close the gates."

Gracie flinched at Olga's voice. "And you mean it this time?"

"Yes. This one's for real. If we leave it much longer, the diseased will be inside the gates."

A few minutes later, the gates' mechanism snapped through the steel wall with a *thunk!* The tone of the vibration played a single base note along the vast steel barrier.

"William," Hawk said.

"Yep?"

"Can you come and meet us at the gates? Gracie and I need to get out of here before things turn nasty."

"Sure thing. See you soon."

"Come on." Hawk tugged Gracie's arm. "We've done all we can. Let's get out of here."

CHAPTER 29

"Everything's done, so Joni can now focus on doing what she came here to do. The gates are closed and locked. The drones and dogs are down. She's blinded him by killing his screens, and now she needs to blind him by cutting his eyeballs from his skull." The knife handle against the base of her back. She reached behind and wrapped her hand around its familiar grip. "Yes, cut his eyes out. Sneak in like carbon monoxide. End him before he knows what's hit him."

His call snaked through the maintenance shafts. The small voice of a man alone in the observation room. "Let me out!"

Joni's tittering laugh called ahead of her. She sang to him. "Still trapped in there, little one? And you're never going to get out alive. You're Joni's now. The tables have turned. Time to put an end to you."

They were close to the observation room when Olga tapped Joni's feet. She halted mid-crawl and turned to her pocket rocket friend.

Olga pointed at the hatch. "I'll kick it open so you don't have to. You'll be able to get in much quicker that way."

"Yes! That's a good idea, Pocket Rocket. You smash open the grate, and Joni can slip in like a black widow. Drop from the hatch, stinger in hands, and poke his eyes out."

"Whatever you need to do, Joni. Just know I'm here for you."

Her small screwdriver in her back pocket, Joni fished it out and undid the lock on his door. "I might need a quick getaway."

"I'll keep track of you from up here," Olga said.

"Thank you."

"That's okay."

"For everything. For standing by crazy old Joni. For being her fr ..."

"Friend, Joni. I am your friend. And you don't need to thank me. You've done so much for us. Besides, we all need someone around. You've spent a lot of time on your own. That must have been hard."

"So hard."

"And I can see that you need to do this in order to heal. It's not a course of action I'd usually back, but this man seems like he's pure evil."

"The purest."

"Also, I had a ... someone close to me who needed my support. They just needed me around to give them the time and space to work their shit out."

"What happened to them?"

"They're dead now. They deserved much more than I gave them." Pocket Rocket dropped her focus to the steel she lay on. "They needed patience and kindness. I didn't give them enough. If I can help you ... I mean, it will never make up for what happened with him, but it might take even the slightest step towards it. You're a good person, Joni. Don't let anyone tell you otherwise. You're kind. Considerate. Selfless."

The lump in Joni's throat cut off her reply. She nodded at Olga and crawled to the hatch overlooking the control room. All the screens were out. He sat bathed in the crimson glow of the emergency lights. She slipped her gun from over her head and pushed it behind her in the shaft. Why take a gun to a knife fight? A knife slaughter.

Olga rolled onto her back, lifted her foot over the grate, and counted down with her fingers. Three. Two ...

Crash.

He looked up as Joni came down and landed in front of him. Her long and rusty knife, an extension of her arm, she pointed the tip at him, her teeth bared.

But he sat in his chair with his hands resting on his paunch. He raised an eyebrow at her. The slightest hint of a smile lifted one side of his mouth. "I wondered when you'd turn up. You've finally decided you want to meet her?"

Joni stepped back a pace. The hand holding her knife shook. "Who? Meet who?"

"Who?" He laughed, but his mirth quickly fell from his face. "You really don't know who I'm talking about, do you? Wow. I wondered how effective the drugs were. Very. Clearly. I'm talking about your daughter, Joni. *Our* daughter."

A wobble snapped through Joni's legs, and she fought to hold her balance. She rested a hand on her stomach. "Wha ... what?"

He scoffed, sending out a spray of spittle. "We had a baby, Joni. A daughter. She's not a baby anymore. She's twenty-four. You were ill at the time of her birth."

The small room amplified Joni's rasping shout. "Joni wasn't ill." She shook her head. "No, Joni wasn't ill. She was *sedated*. By you. You nasty little man. You controlled Joni. Locked her up. Kept her drugged. Bullied her."

Louis' smile spread wider, his face a gargoyle's leer in the deep crimson glow. He looked down at her hand on her stomach and raised his eyebrows. "So you remember? You had a C-section. What, you think you could have given birth? You couldn't deliver a coherent sentence most of the time."

"Then where's the scar?"

"We covered it with cosmetic surgery. We thought it might be too much if the evidence of your failed parenthood permanently marked your body. Seeing as you wouldn't see our daughter after that."

"You're lying." Joni's hand shook, and she struggled to hold her knife. The rusty blade wobbled, the point moving like the end of a divining rod over an underground river. "Joni doesn't believe you." Her voice warbled. "She would remember it. She'd feel it in her body still."

Again, Louis looked at her hand on her stomach. "We held you for another two years after the birth for you to recover. Recover and, I hoped, forget. You were a liability and in no fit state to raise a child. The farther we dragged you away from her, the better."

Joni jabbed the blade at him and sprayed spittle. "Lies!"

"No, it's true." The glow from his device's screen lit up his pudgy face. His pasty skin. His yellow teeth. He turned it so Joni could see the screen. A face she'd seen before in her dreams. Her own face, in a way. Her own face tainted by his.

"Tell me I'm lying now."

"No. No." Joni grabbed her stomach again. "What have you done to Joni?"

"Coming back now, is it? And you did it to yourself. You weren't fit to be a mother."

"Because of you."

"I hate it when people blame others for their weaknesses. Own your fragility, Joni. We did our daughter a favour by taking her away from you. You were just a host in this transaction. A vessel."

"Transaction suggests I had some agency."

"Come on, Joni. Look at yourself. You're not capable of agency. You never were, and you never will be."

"But Joni's survived in this place—"

"You've been living like a bug in this place. Scuttling around in the maintenance shafts like a strange little creature."

"You knew?"

"Of course I knew."

"You're getting inside Joni's head again. Manipulating her. Making her think things about herself she doesn't think. Lying to her. Again. All over again. You're poison. You're carbon monoxide."

"There you go again, blaming others for your shortcomings. Put that knife down. If you give up now, I might let you meet her."

Joni turned the blade in her hand. It had been in the bucket for years. Getting rusty enough to poison him when she plunged it into his soft flesh.

"Put the knife down, Joni."

The weapon heavier now than before. Joni laid it on the side.

"There we go. I acted with Antonia's best interests in mind."

"Antonia?"

"I named her after my mother. She's turned into a fine young woman. We did the right thing in keeping you away."

"Fuck you!"

"Now give me your hands."

"What? Why?"

Louis lifted a pair of handcuffs, hanging them on one

finger. "You want to meet her? I can't trust you, Joni. I need your wrists in cuffs before I take you anywhere."

"When has he ever done right by Joni? When has he ever been honest? Don't trust him. Don't trust him as far as she can kick him."

Click! Click! Louis clipped the cuffs to Joni's wrists. "You've opened the door now?"

"Yes." Tears stroked Joni's cheeks. Snot ran from her nose. She focused on the steel floor.

"Guards!"

Two women and a bear of a man came in. The women avoided Joni's glare, but the man frowned at her, his eyes pinched at the sides.

Louis flicked the air with his chubby hand as if wafting away a fly. "Take her to a holding cell. We'll decide what to do with her later."

"What? You said you'd take Joni to see her daughter."

"I lied."

"About her daughter?"

"*My* daughter, not her daughter. And no, that was the truth. I lied about her ever meeting her." He flicked his hand again. "Get rid of this trash now. Her presence is making me nauseated."

CHAPTER 30

The steel of the maintenance shaft cold against her cheek, Olga lay flat as the guards left with the now handcuffed Joni. Two women and one man. Louis sat in his chair and watched her out, his eyes dead. A chill snaked through her at his utter lack of empathy.

Olga backed away and crawled along the maintenance shaft after Joni and the guards.

Joni twisted against her restraints. "What are you doing to Joni? What has she ever done to you?"

"Uh ... you tried to burn us alive?" one woman said. "You stole our food. You took control of our prison ..."

"Not burn you alive. Joni didn't want to burn you alive. She just wanted to distract you so she could—"

"Set the prisoners free? You're not helping yourself here, love."

Olga crawled ahead of Joni and the guards and waited at each grate along the shaft for them to pass beneath her. With every glimpse, Joni fought them more than before until the guards overpowered her and dragged her with her feet trailing along the ground.

The maintenance shaft bent left at the end of the corridor. Olga waited over the final hatch for the guards to follow the bend. But instead of turning with the hatch, they stopped directly beneath her. The two women wore hard scowls. The man, twice the size of the others, had softer, kinder features. A massive black beard. He looked like he'd stumbled from out of the forest. Looked like he could pull up trees with his hands.

Only one woman had spoken to Joni so far. The next one shoved her and said, "You're not very popular in here, you know?"

"Joni doesn't care."

"You will wh—"

"Alma!" The man had a voice befitting his stature. Booming and authoritative. "Will you shut up? She's been through enough already. She doesn't need your poison on top of it all."

Ping!

"Shit!" Olga muttered. The guards were waiting for an elevator. How could she follow them? And where were they going to take her from here?

Rolling onto her back, Olga raised her foot over the hatch. If they got in that elevator without her, they'd kill Joni before she found her again. She had to take her now. After everything Joni had done for them, the odds might be against her, but hopefully she could surprise the guards and catch them cold.

One woman, the woman not Alma, stepped into the elevator first. Alma followed her in. Just Joni and the bear in the hallway. If Joni got in that elevator, they'd kill her. Olga's heart beat in her neck. She could do this. She lifted her right foot. She'd be fine. She'd—

"You're going to be okay, Little Chick."

Olga froze.

The man put his thick arm around Joni's shoulders and led her into the lift. His voice booming but kind. "You're going to be okay."

Ping!

The elevator's doors closed.

Olga had no chance of tracking Joni now, and even if she found her, how would she get her out? No way would they lock her somewhere with a maintenance shaft running through it. Not with Joni's track record. But if she could find that guard … He was the guard who had helped Joni in the past. Surely he'd help her again.

CHAPTER 31

Despite William's quad handling differently now he had Hawk as a passenger, he led them back to Joni's place with little trouble. They'd passed packs of prisoners on the way, but each time the quads were too quick and the distance between them too great to inspire either side into action. The prisoners watched them pass through hollow eyes. They wandered the place like docile diseased. They were aimless now the gates were closed. But they couldn't have kept them open any longer. Easing off his throttle, he slowed on their approach to Nick, who stood waiting for them by the hatch to Joni's lair. Both him and the entrance were bathed in the shadow of the guards' block.

Hawk rode on the back of Matilda's bike, and Artan rode alone. He jumped from his bike before it had stopped moving and ran to Nick. The two of them embraced. William winked at the smiling Matilda. Artan deserved happiness in his life.

After their hug, Artan turned his palms to the night sky. "Where are Olga and Joni?"

Nick shook his head. "They've not come out of the block yet."

"And we won't be."

William pressed his finger to his ear. "Olga?"

"I'm not coming with you. Neither's Joni."

The others let William speak. "What do you mean? What's going on?"

"You need to go south without me. I'm going to be here for a while. This is where I want to be."

"How can we leave without you?"

"You did it without Max."

Heat spread through William's cheeks. "And we realised our mistake. It's not one we'll make again."

"Look, after everything that's happened, I've decided I can't be around you all. It reminds me too much of Max. Besides, I can't leave Joni on her own."

"Bring her with us."

"She doesn't want to come. And I don't know how long I'll be. Right now is your best chance to leave, so take it. The guards are preoccupied. It's dark. There are no drones and dogs. The prisoners are more focused on getting out of here than attacking you. And you still have your quad bikes. Do you still have your quad bikes?"

The others all watched William. "Yes. We do."

"Then take this opportunity and go."

"But—"

"Go, William. Leave me be. Let me do what I need to do here. I've realised I can't grieve for Max while I'm around you all. I have too much anger. Make his death worthwhile. Make the lives of everyone who's died because they crossed our paths worthwhile. Do the right thing and leave."

"But ..."

"Fuck off, William. All of you. Get away from me. Go. I'm taking my headset out now. I don't want to see any of you ever again."

William jumped at the crackling sound of Olga's earpiece

from where she'd clearly stamped on it. The others remained focused on him. "So what do we do?"

"What can we do?" Gracie said. "She just made it pretty clear."

"What's happening?" Artan said.

Nick reached out to him and held his hand. "She's saying she doesn't want to come with us."

"I gathered that much."

"That she can't grieve for Max while she's in our company. And that now's the best time to leave the prison with the guards distracted and the machines down."

Matilda's voice was barely more than a whisper. "We can't leave her."

"But she doesn't want us around," Hawk said.

"I say we vote on it." Artan, still off his bike, turned full circle to elicit a nod from everyone. "Those who want to move on now, raise your hand." He raised his. Nick did the same.

"She seemed pretty clear." Hawk raised his.

Gracie shrugged and raised her hand.

Artan returned to his quad bike, and Nick got on behind him. "That makes four to two. Let's get out of here."

William straightened in his seat while Matilda shook her head. If she wanted to stay, he'd stay. "You ready to move on?"

The sides of her eyes pinched. A slight glaze covered her stare. Her throat bobbed with her gulp. She uttered one weak syllable that tore the air from William's lungs. The decision they needed to make. "Yep."

"Ok—" William lost his words and coughed to clear his throat. "Okay. You know, I think this is the last time I'm going to head south. We keep going, hoping we'll find a better life, but we're yet to come across anything better than what we've left behind in Edin. I'm not prepared to keep searching forever. Sometimes I think you have to accept your lot and make do."

"That's easy to say now …" Hawk looked around. "But if the south's worse than this shithole, I'm going to keep going."

William shrugged. "Fair enough. I suppose we need to get out of here to find out. Come on." He turned his bike's throttle and led them away, the ugly guard block at their back as they headed farther south than they'd ever been before. "Let's get out of here."

CHAPTER 32

The maintenance shafts were less creepy when Olga followed Joni through them. Even with her nonsensical wittering in her often haunting voice. Maybe because she now stared ahead into darkness punctuated by the red glow from below. Also, the responsibility rested firmly on her shoulders, and the only voice she had for company now rattled around inside her own skull. What if she didn't find Joni in time? After all she'd done for them. Hers and her friends' lives, plus the lives of thousands of prisoners had depended on Joni, and no matter how eccentric she'd been while getting the job done, she hadn't let them down. Did Olga have it in her to return the favour and get Joni out of there?

Cold steel against her stomach. Her gun slung across her back. At least she'd finally mastered Joni's technique of keeping it balanced there. She didn't need it knocking against the steel shaft and announcing her presence to anyone below.

Olga crossed another grate overlooking another crimson-lit hallway.

Thunk!

The red glow gave way to the dazzling white of fluorescent lights. So bright it lit the block like the sun and burst through the grates with an enquiring glare. An inquisitor's spotlight. It turned the entire block into an insomniac's worst nightmare.

A crackling came from speakers in the corridor. A man's voice. His voice. "Everyone to the sports hall now. Everyone to the sports hall now. Over."

"Shit." Where the hell was the sports hall from her current spot?

Whoosh! A door opened below.

Whoosh! Another door somewhere else nearby.

Whoosh!

Whoosh!

Whoosh!

Grey-uniformed guards flooded into the hallway. They chatted amongst themselves. The general hum of conversation masked Olga's swishing progress above.

Olga followed the crowd until she passed over the sports hall's door. The maintenance shaft changed direction, pointing straight up towards the high ceiling. The room stood twice the height of the corridors and other rooms. She braced against either side of the tunnel and climbed. At the top, she slid along until she peered down through the grate on the crowd below. Her stomach churned, and she drew deep breaths. If she fell from here, her skeleton would shatter on impact. But regardless of the height, every other shaft had supported their weight, so why not this one? She'd either fall or she wouldn't. Little point in wasting the energy worrying about it. Not that it stopped her stomach from turning.

There might not have been a stage like Joni had described when she'd last been there, and he had no guards held hostage and drugged beside him, but that didn't make the thickset man's demeanour any more palatable. Olga squirmed where she lay. She knew too much about him. If Joni didn't cut the vile man's eyes out, she would. He stood before the crowd with his shoulders hunched and his chin jutting forwards. The bright lights shone off his bald head. His wild red hair poked out at the sides like a crown of ginger thorns. His fists balled, he stared out at the gathered guards like he'd fight every one of them. He waited for total silence.

Olga gasped and clapped a hand to her mouth. The guard who'd called Joni *Little Chick* stood amongst his peers. Huge, hairy, and built like he could take on half the room by himself.

Louis clicked his tongue several times. Each snap whipped around the cavernous space. His puce face matched his red hair. He drew a deep breath, reminding Olga to do the same, her lungs tight, her pulse accelerating.

Stressing his point by punching his open palm, Louis said, "Today's been a bad day for this place. A bad fucking day. And I won't stand for it. *We* won't stand for it."

Many of the guards in the crowd shook their heads. Some folded their arms across their chests.

"Now, we've fucked up."

Glances passed between guards. Had they fucked up? Were they going to take the blame for what happened?

Louis continued. "We've let the south's worst fears come to pass, and we need to fix it. We've lost control of the prison. But we *can* fix this. *And*"—he wagged a finger at the guards— "the south never need to find out about it. I have a plan."

His hands clasped behind his back, his paunch thrust out before him, Louis paced up and down, his heels clicking against the steel floor. "The plan is to keep this place in lockdown while it's still dark. Get the block in order first. Once we've done that, we'll move out to regain control of the prison. This has been a glitch, nothing else. And from what I can tell, the diseased are still in the north, and the gates are closed. We've lost prisoners, but who really gives a shit about the prisoners' lives?"

A few guards snorted and scoffed. Many nodded.

"At first light, we'll open up the block again. We'll retrieve the dogs and drones and get them back online. They're our eyes and ears in this place. They'll help us regain order. Then we'll get the prisoners back to their relevant sections. The sensors on the white lines are still down and might take a while to get online again, but we still have the handheld triggers." He paused and grinned, displaying a mouth filled with yellow teeth. Olga twisted where she lay. "So, on our way back to reminding the prisoners who's boss, if we need to make an example of a few of them, then have at it. Fill your boots." He laughed. "I know I will.

"Our output from the industrial sections won't be what it was, but I'll deal with those awkward questions from our partners in the south as and when I have to. Part of our recovery will involve repopulating this place with prisoners to get it back to full capacity. We have plenty of diseased in the north, and while the show must go on, and the chance to run south must still be offered to the prisoners and broadcast to everyone else, we can thin the numbers a little so we don't lose as many prisoners as before. We believe the people who broke into the prison are still inside these walls. We need to find them. Their punishment will be severe." He punched his open palm again. "I want to torture the fuckers."

Silence descended on the room. A space where many people holding a meeting would ask if there were questions. But Louis clearly had no interest in discourse.

Olga jumped when he clapped his chubby hands, the snap of their connection whipping around the room. "So, I'm sure you can all see there's no need for the south to find out what's happened here. We'll tell them we've had technical difficulties, and normal service will resume shortly. We control what they see, so as long as we're vigilant, we won't need to show them how we've screwed up and failed to look after this place. For the next few hours, we'll get things in order in here, and when we have the light of a new day to aid us, we'll take our prison back."

He hadn't mentioned Joni once. They had the woman responsible for most of the chaos, and he'd kept it to himself. What did he have planned for her? Whatever it was, Olga wouldn't let it happen. No chance.

The bear of a guard joined the crowd queuing to leave the sports hall. Olga moved down the vertical shaft much like she'd climbed it. Hands and feet pressed against the walls on either side, she shuffled a few inches lower at a time.

An easy man to spot in the crowd, Joni followed the guard when he left the sports hall. Dressed in the same grey uniform as the others, he stood a head taller than most. But, while easy to spot, how could she get his attention when he had so many people around him?

Whoosh!

Whoosh!

Whoosh!

Doors opened on either side of the hallway, and the guards vanished into rooms and down corridors. But the bear of a man still walked with a crowd of at least twenty of his colleagues.

Olga ruffled her nose at the burned reek in the air. They were clearly close to the kitchen.

Whoosh!

She pressed her cheek against the cold steel shaft and peered through the next grate. The monster of a guard joined a group going into a room on their left.

Olga followed the guard towards the kitchen. The charred reek of what they'd done grew stronger. She gulped several times, dragging the taste deep into her throat.

Six guards stood in front of the ovens. One had her hands on her hips and shook her head. "Look at the state of this place."

"It's going to take an age to clean." The guard's booming voice damn near shook the maintenance shaft. He pointed back towards the door. "I need to use the toilet, and then I'll be back."

The guard with her hands on her hips cocked her head and raised an eyebrow. "Make sure you come back!"

"Of course."

The man walked with a swaying roll like he had a skeleton made from boulders.

Olga spun around in the shaft and overtook him. Across the grates overlooking the kitchen and back to the junction in the shafts. Back at the hatch she'd used to watch them into the room in the first place, she lay flat and focused on the door again.

Whoosh!

The monster of a man rolled out into the hallway and headed her way.

At every grate, Olga halted and let him pass beneath before she moved along to the next one. When they got far enough away from the kitchen, she'd drop in front of him. He wanted Joni to be okay too, so surely he'd listen to her. He had to.

"Ralph!" A man's voice farther along the corridor.

Olga snapped rigid in the shaft.

"How's it going in the kitchen?"

"It's a mess."

"They've not broken the ovens, have they?"

"No, I don't think so. But they'll take a lot of effort to get them clean enough to use again."

"Do you think we'll find the people responsible?"

"Who knows?" Ralph turned his huge palms to the ceiling, each one the size of a dinner plate. "Maybe they had good cause to do what they did?"

"What, you on their side or something?"

"No. Of course not."

He sounded like he was on their side. He sounded like the man Joni had described. The guard with a conscience. If Olga could get him alone, surely he'd help her find Joni and bust her out of there.

The other guard reached up and patted Ralph's right shoulder. "Just be careful what you say. That level of empathy might get you in trouble in a place like this."

"Don't worry about me. I know what I'm saying. This level of empathy makes me human. I won't give that up for anything or anyone."

The guard shrugged and left, their heels clicking against the steel floor. The place alive with guards, Olga couldn't drop from the ceiling in the hallway. She'd get rumbled in seconds.

Ralph turned left and hit the button to open a door.

Crack!

Whoosh!

Another junction in the maintenance shaft, Olga followed him. Just one grate between her and a dead end. The room below had a toilet and a sink inside. Olga rolled on her back and lifted her foot over the grate. But before she could kick down, the *clack* of a belt buckle hit the steel floor.

"Shit!" Turning around again, Olga peered down on the bear of a man sat on the toilet, his trousers around his ankles. "Shit!"

Olga shuffled back towards the junction. She needed this

man's help. How likely would he be to give it to her if she dropped on him while he sat on the can?

"How long does he want us up here?"

Olga froze.

"He said we need to check out the entire block."

Two voices in the maintenance tunnels. Two men. They were close and getting closer.

"*All* of it? Why?"

Olga poked her head from the end of her small section leading back towards the toilet. The shaft stretched left and right along the corridor. They were coming from the left. Right led her back towards the kitchen. No matter which way she went, they'd see her before she turned off again.

"He didn't say why. Other than we're vulnerable to intruders up here."

"So we have to crawl around on our bellies searching empty tunnels because he's paranoid?"

"Pretty much. He said bring back anything we find."

"Maybe we should sack it off now, get some rest, and tell him we found nothing."

The swish of the two men crawling along the shaft called ahead of them. Joni and Olga could teach them a thing or two about keeping the noise down in these shafts. The weight of her gun on her back. Maybe she could use it to scare them away? To give her a chance to get out of there. She shook her head. No. Do that and she'd justify them being in the shafts. She'd justify his paranoia.

Back over the hatch above the toilet. Above the shitting Ralph. Olga scrunched her nose at the stench from below. But she couldn't be appalled. After all, she was the one intruding on his privacy.

Olga slid her gun from her back and laid it down in the shaft. If she came down armed, she wouldn't stand a chance of getting him onside.

Crash!

Olga kicked the hatch, and it swung down into the toilet. She slipped backwards into the room, stood on the edge of the sink, closed the hatch behind her and dropped to her feet.

Ralph watched her, his mouth hanging open.

Olga pressed her finger to her lips. "I'm really sorry to interrupt."

His jaw hung slack, and his brow locked in a frown.

Her words were driven by her rapid pulse, her breaths stolen by her tight chest. Olga launched into her explanation. "I'm sorry. I didn't want to come down here, but what else could I do? There are guards up in the shafts, and they would have caught me. I needed to speak to you. You're the only guard in this place I trust." She gasped.

"And you had to do it while I was taking a shit?"

"I'm sorry. I—"

"What do you want?"

"Joni."

"What?"

"Joni. Little Chick. You helped her before. You cared about her in the past, and I think you still care about her now. I saw you take her into that elevator. You were kind to her when the others weren't."

"How do you know I was kind to Joni before?"

"She told me. She'd forgotten about her daughter because of the drugs they'd fed her, but she remembered your kindness. How you looked after her when they were treating her so awfully. You're not like them."

"And who are you?"

"I'm a friend of Joni's. Like you."

He shifted where he sat. "So you're responsible for the chaos too?"

"I helped her. And can you blame her? After what he's done."

"But the prisoners?"

"We only let them go north. We set them free. Do you think that's such a bad thing? We even closed the gates after them so the diseased didn't get into the prison. Tell me honestly, how do you feel about how they run this place?"

"I'm not sure what I think matters. What else am I supposed to do? It's not like there are many employment options for someone like me. This is food and board. That's more than most have in this world."

"Please, Ralph."

"How do you know my name?"

"I was in the shaft when you were talking to the other guard about cleaning the kitchen. I nearly came down to talk to you then, but he appeared. It sounded to me like you understand where Joni's at. Please, Ralph, help me. Help me get Joni out of here. Help Joni reunite with her daughter."

Ralph nodded. "Okay."

"Okay?"

"Yeah. Okay. But"—he raised his right index finger and turned it in the air—"can you please turn around for a moment."

"Yes. Of course. Sorry."

After a few seconds, Ralph flushed the toilet. Olga cowered in his presence when he walked over to her by the sink. He washed his hands and wiped them dry on his uniform. "Right, follow me."

CHAPTER 33

William still had Hawk on the back of his bike. He rode with Matilda and Gracie on his left, and Artan with Nick on his right. He squinted against the strong headwind and rolled his shoulders to deal with the weight of his rucksack. A bag filled with more magazines than he could ever use. But better to have them than not, even if his back paid the price. "Doesn't she know how much we all regret what happened with Max?"

"I'm sure she does." Matilda remained fixed ahead. "But she clearly has to get her mind straight. And she's right, this is the best time to leave. While the guards are in disarray. While the drones and dogs are down. It sounds like getting through the last section of this place will be hard enough as it is. We have to take this opportunity."

William jumped when Hawk leaned forwards and shouted in his ear. "I also wish Joni could have given us a bit more information about what we're running into."

The only one of them who seemed impervious to the effects of the headwind, Artan sat with his back straight and his face at ease. "But she had no more information. Did you see anything on the screens, Nick?"

"Honestly? I didn't know what I was looking at half the time. If I watched the screens for too long, it gave me motion sickness."

Their three sets of tyres against the rough concrete gave off a bass note hum. The wind flapped in William's ears. Side by side on the main road, they all focused on their destination. Still too dark to make out exactly what lay ahead. The wide main road ended. That much he could tell. The north led straight to gates, but the south appeared to be a dead end. They needed to get closer to be sure. What would they do if they had to turn around? Where would they go? William drew a deep breath to settle his churning stomach. One step at a time.

"We didn't save enough of them," Gracie said. "We should have kept the gates open for longer."

Hawk leaned closer to Gracie, and the entire quad leaned with him. "I was with you up there. If we'd left them open for much longer, we would have lost the prison. That wouldn't have been any good for anyone, including those prisoners still yet to escape. We did what we could. We closed the gates when we had to. We saved their lives."

"What life is this in here? Is it even worth saving? There's still, what, fifty thousand prisoners in this place? That's a lot of people being left to suffer."

"If your figures are right, that means one hundred and fifty thousand prisoners had a chance at freedom. We did what we—" Hawk's grip tightened on William's waist, and he pressed against his back, shoving the metal magazines into him.

A group of prisoners burst from a side road on their right. They spilled from it like a diseased horde, several hundred of them filling the road. William twisted his throttle and guided his quad over to the left wall. He shot through the ever-decreasing gap.

Matilda followed William.

"Til—"

William turned as several prisoners tore Artan and Nick from their quad. The riderless bike flipped several times as it barrel rolled down the main street.

Hawk tapped William's shoulder and held the button for the prisoners in front of him. "Take us back."

At least three hundred prisoners in the road, they swarmed Artan and Nick, laying into them with kicks and punches.

No time for debate. William turned the bike hard, the two right wheels lifting from the ground and slamming down again as he straightened out and headed back for the prisoners.

Hawk waved his button, and most of the crowd backed off. Five prisoners remained, zealous in their attack. Three still laid into Artan, and two beat Nick.

William pulled up close, and Hawk jumped from the back of the bike. He slashed at the air between him and the main crowd with his button, driving them back. He kicked one of the prisoners attacking Artan, sending the man stumbling. "Get back. Now."

But the prisoner ran for Artan again.

Gracie's shrill scream snapped William's shoulders into his neck. It reverberated in the wide road. "What are you doing? Don't you dare use that thing!"

Both Artan and Nick stayed down, covering their heads with their hands. The four remaining prisoners wouldn't quit, and the ones who'd run looked ready to come back.

"Hawk," William said, "if we don't take these few down, we'll be overrun."

Hawk pressed the button.

The five prisoners coughed blood as one. They crumpled to the ground. Artan and Nick scrambled to their feet and scurried to their upturned quad. Both of them dishevelled and flushed, but still mobile enough to get away from there.

All five prisoners curled into foetal positions and held their stomachs. William twisted where he sat as they haemorrhaged from every visible orifice.

William turned his bike around and faced away from the suffering prisoners. "Come on, Hawk. Let's get out of here."

The bike rocked with Hawk's heavy and graceless mount.

William pulled up alongside Artan and Nick. Artan sat in the driver's seat, and Nick climbed on behind him. "Everything all right?"

"No." Artan peered back over his shoulder at the prisoners gathered in the small side road. He gripped his gun.

"They've left you alone now, Artan. Drive away. At least you can. They're stuck here."

Artan let go of his weapon. His hard scowl softened when he turned to Hawk. "Thank you. And I'm sorry you had to do that."

Hawk sighed. "Me too. Me too."

CHAPTER 34

Her heart pounding, her eyes itching from both the headwind and what she'd just witnessed, Gracie faced Hawk on the back of William's bike and threw a wild arm in the air. "What the hell was that?" The quad wobbled with her sudden movement.

"Will you piss off?"

Gracie pulled her head back. "What?"

"We've already put our lives on the line to save *thousands* of prisoners."

She snorted a laugh. "So you've got a few executions in the bank now? Is that what you're saying?"

"Will you listen to yourself?"

Heat spread through Gracie's face, and she ground her teeth. "Will I listen to myself? You just murdered innocent prisoners."

"Look." Hawk's cheeks puffed, and he softened his tone, his voice coming through their headsets. "What you've done for these prisoners is admirable. You've helped many people in need."

"You were with me."

"But we did it at your behest. If it were down to the rest of us, we'd be south of this wall already."

"So you're blaming me for that now?"

"Will you just listen? I'm trying to praise you, Gracie. You have a kind heart, b—"

"But?"

"It's getting in the way of the group's needs and safety. No matter what happens, we have to put our own survival first. Trust me, I got no pleasure from that back there, but I'd do it again to save *anyone* in this group. And you need to see these prisoners for what they are."

"Vulnerable people in a shit situation?"

"The *enemy*, Gracie. They're the fucking enemy. And we no longer have the safety of being two hundred feet above them. We're on the ground with them now, and they're a genuine threat to all our lives."

"I think this is it," William said.

The hum of their tyres changed when they passed over a thick white line in the road. The lights on top of the walls on either side remained white from where Joni had changed them. What had looked like a dead end from a distance was, in fact, a street running across their path. They might not be able to continue straight ahead, but they could turn left or right.

A thick red painted line ran along every wall past the white line. A band about a foot thick and five feet from the ground. The paint had dripped and dried like spilled blood. Like a gash had been torn in the steel to reveal flesh beneath.

Matilda eased off in time with William, which left Gracie level with the scowling Hawk. Although, how he felt justified to look at her in that way ... With what he'd just done.

All three quad bikes rolled to a halt. Artan sighed. "So this is it?"

"Do you think it's as bad as Joni says?" Hawk said.

William killed the conversation dead with one syllable. "Yep!"

"Uh …" Nick peered behind them.

"Shit!" Hawk said.

Gracie's heart kicked when she turned back. More prisoners on the main road. Only about twenty this time. A group of men and women, they carried crude weapons and wore dark scowls. They were about twenty to thirty feet away, and they approached the white line, most of them dividing their attention between the lights on the walls that gave them permission to cross, and Gracie and the others on their quads. These were the enemy. Maybe Hawk had a point. No matter how she empathised with them, they clearly didn't return Gracie's compassion.

The quad rocked when Matilda looked back. "Why are there so many of them down this end?"

"It makes sense," Gracie said. "Maybe they didn't know the gates were open. How would they this far away? They might have come a certain distance because of Joni changing the lights to amber, but they clearly didn't get driven far enough north. I wouldn't mind betting the bulk of the remaining prisoners are in the far south, east, and west."

The mob paused on the other side of the white line. About ten feet away from Gracie and the others, they spoke amongst themselves, nods passing from one to the next. As one, the group stepped forward.

Gracie slapped Matilda on the back. "Go. Now! We don't need to kill this lot."

All three quads took off, shooting towards the street running across their path and deeper into the section marked with the blood red stripe.

Into the first road, Matilda and the other drivers paused. They could go right or left. Both options stretched away from them and offered no hint of which choice would be best.

The prisoners closed in.

Hawk raised his button, and Gracie pointed at him. "Don't you dare!"

"Tell us which way we need to go, then!"

The prisoners sped up, emboldened by their ability to cross boundaries that had previously kept them contained.

Although she worked her mouth, opening and closing it like the action would somehow inspire her to find an answer, Gracie had nothing. How could she tell them which way to go?

All the while, Hawk looked from her to the prisoners, his thumb hovering over the button that would turn their innards to liquid.

"We should go right!" William pointed with his right hand and led them away.

Gracie hooked an arm around Matilda's waist so she didn't roll backwards off the bike.

The prisoners ran into the red-lined section behind them.

It started as a distant ticking. Like rain against a faraway windowpane. If they'd have turned left, they would have headed straight for it. Glints of light shifted in the air. Small shards of steel caught the moon's glow. They closed in on the prisoners and Gracie's group. Thousands of tiny reflective flashes punched through the darkness.

Gracie's tight plait kept most of her hair in, but when she looked back, the loose strands at the front tickled her face and ran into her eyes. She blinked repeatedly and kept her attention behind. They were pulling away from the prisoners, but the micro bugs were gaining on both of them. Small metallic insects. A plague of tiny machines. They filled the road from wall to wall. They raced along it like a flood.

It took less than thirty seconds for the slowest prisoner to scream. Swallowed by the bug cloud, they were there one moment and red mist the next.

Matilda took a sharp left and then another right. Gracie gripped the handle on the back of the bike, her hands aching from where she fought to stay on against the sudden changes in direction.

William and Artan rode with them. Hawk and Nick clung on like Gracie. They had to trust the drivers to make the correct choices. What else could they do?

Another T-junction in the road. A split second to decide. William and Hawk turned left. Matilda turned right with Artan and Nick. Gracie watched Hawk and William away before the cloud of bugs shot out behind them. They filled the road, blocking her line of sight. A wall of shifting razor-sharp chaos, made up of thousands, but driven by a sole intention. That sole intention the destruction of Gracie, Matilda, Artan, and Nick.

"Hawk?" Gracie pressed her earpiece. "Hawk, don't follow us. You'll have to meet us somewhere else. Keep heading south."

Nothing.

Gracie pressed her earpiece again. "Hawk?" She tapped Matilda on the shoulder. "Can you hear them?"

"No." Matilda shook her head. "I think the earpieces have stopped working."

"Nick?" Gracie leaned across to him. "Can you hear the others?"

Most of his attention behind, his face slack, Nick looked at Gracie and shook his head before returning his focus to their impending death.

The two quad bikes whined with their acceleration. The bass note hum of tyres against concrete. They might have been at full speed, but the flood of bugs were faster.

CHAPTER 35

Olga followed Ralph from the toilet. The bear of a man slapped the button to open the door with a thunder-strike blow.

Boom!

Whoosh.

Ralph poked his head out into the hallway and waved Olga on with his massive hand. "Clear. Follow me." He paused, turned back to her, and raised a bushy eyebrow. "Although I'm not sure I need to tell you that. Anyone who'll intrude on a man taking a shit ..."

Olga winced. "I'm sorry. Again."

His brown eyes glazed as if he went somewhere else for a moment. He refocused. "Me too."

Ralph a step ahead of her, Olga followed, ready to take cover behind the wall of a man should anyone appear.

They reached the lift, and Ralph attacked the call button like he had the one to leave the toilet. This man didn't do subtle or gentle. He turned his back on the elevator's doors and folded his arms across his chest.

Olga slipped in behind him, away from sight.

Ping!

The elevator arrived.

Whoosh!

The doors opened.

Olga backed in first, and Ralph followed. He pressed the button to close the doors and let go of a hard sigh.

The elevator had the same aesthetic as the rest of the place. Made from cold steel and lit with a bulb that belonged in an interrogation chamber. It forced Olga to lower her gaze, and she still had to squint to block out the glare. It demanded subservience. How did anyone live in a place like this?

The doors closed.

"Wait up!"

"Damn!" The elevator's acoustics turned Ralph's rumble an octave lower.

A hand reached through the closing gap and pulled the doors open again. Ralph moved across in front of Olga and stepped back, forcing her against the steel wall.

Crushed between the wall and Ralph's broad back, her hands pinned to her sides, Olga took shallow breaths to slow her rampaging pulse.

The person who'd entered said, "Thank you." They pressed a button, the click preceding the *whoosh* of the closing doors.

The guard must have seen her. Maybe Olga should shove Ralph forwards and knock him out before he could report back to anyone important. She only needed him unconscious for long enough to find Joni and get out of there. Surely they'd have the time to do that. But what if he hadn't seen her? Ralph's broad frame could hide a lot. Joni had trusted him, so Olga should too. He'd know the best thing to do. And if it came to a fight, she'd be ready.

The elevator's rapid rise made Olga's stomach tingle.

Her heart kicked when it stopped. Were her hands not pinned to her sides, she would have thrust them out for balance.

Ping!

Whoosh!

Trapped between Ralph and the wall, Olga held her breath and waited.

The man in the elevator with them said, "This isn't your floor?"

"Nope!" Ralph's entire back vibrated with his reply. "Changed my mind."

"You changed your mind?"

"You worry about you, yeah?"

Ping!

Whoosh!

The doors closed, and Olga squirmed behind Ralph. The atmosphere had been bad enough before the doors had opened. No wonder Joni preferred to move around in the maintenance shafts.

Ping!

Whoosh!

Olga tracked the man's steps from the elevator.

Ping!

Whoosh!

The doors closed again, and Ralph stepped forwards. Olga filled her lungs, and this time thrust her hands out for balance when the elevator dropped again.

"Not used to riding an elevator?"

Her head spinning, Olga kept her arms out to the sides as if it would aid her balance. "How did you guess?"

Ralph smiled for the first time. It changed his entire face. His eyes turned to slits, laughter lines stretching across his temples. "And sorry I crushed you."

"Better to be crushed than discovered sneaking around

this place. I can't imagine Louis has much charity in his heart for me right now."

The elevator halted with another jolt. Olga slipped behind Ralph again. Someone could be waiting to get in.

The doors opened, and Ralph stepped forwards, poking his head out into the corridor. "We're good to go."

Olga let go of her tension with a sigh. She understood being crushed by Ralph, but she didn't welcome it. She followed him out.

While their surroundings were familiar, and this corridor could have been any corridor in the place, it stood out as different because of the lack of ambient sound. No whispers of guards' movement, no whoosh of opening and closing doors, no clips of conversations around bends and inside the rooms they passed. Olga shivered. Had she imagined it, or had they lowered the temperature too?

After he'd led Olga down a corridor and around a few bends, Ralph stopped in front of a door unlike any other in this place. At least any she'd seen. It had no button beside it. Instead, a large key hung from the wall on a hook. Like everything else, they'd made the key from gunmetal grey steel. A hatch in the centre of the door, Ralph pinched the small handle with his large fingers and slid it open with a *crack!* He pressed his face to the door and peered through before closing it again. *Crack!* Each action snapped through their quiet surroundings like a gunshot.

Ralph's massive hands dwarfed even the large key. He slid it into the slot and freed the lock. *Clunk!*

The door's hinges cackled when he pulled it wide, the door opening out into the hallway. He stepped aside for Olga.

The lithe and lean Joni sat on the steel bench in the room. Her long blonde hair hung down, framing her face.

"Joni! It's great to see you!"

Joni looked up. Regardless of her many ramblings, her azure gaze had always remained sharp and focused. Like she had some kind of agency over her state of mind. Like her babbling commentary had been a choice. An agreement made between her and insanity. She'd give the madness what it needed, but she'd keep a shred of herself in reserve. She raised a hand towards Olga. "No. Don't. Look o—"

Crash!

Ralph slammed the door shut behind her.

Thunk!

He locked it.

Olga's entire being sank, and Joni said, "Out!"

CHAPTER 36

The quad wobbled when William turned to look back. "Shit!" He let go of the throttle, and his bike slowed.

Hawk leaned close to him and shouted in his ear, "What are you doing?"

"We've been separated from the others."

"I know!"

"We need to get after them."

"You saw those things, right?"

"Yeah. And it's not the first time I've seen them either. Olga and I ran into them in the rat run."

"And you think we can ride through them to get to Matilda and the others?"

"Well…"

"Did you see what they did to those prisoners?"

"I was focused on where we were heading."

"Well, I can tell you, it wasn't pretty."

The cloud of bugs had vanished from sight. The road behind them empty, the blood red line running down either wall just about visible in the shadows. Matilda and Artan had been ahead of the small, deadly insects. Hopefully they still were. William pressed his finger to his earpiece. "Tilly, are you okay?"

Silence.

"Hawk, is your headset working?"

Hawk looked back to where the bugs had gone and then returned his focus to William and shrugged. "No. Dead as a diseased with an axe in their head."

"A simple no would do."

"No."

"Shit!"

"We have no other choice but to keep moving, William. They'll head south. We'll have to just focus on getting there ourselves."

William fought his own reluctance, turned the bike's throttle, and accelerated away.

With no bugs on their tail, William drove slower. The narrow roads twisted and turned, leading them who knew where, and giving them too many options to follow. William followed his gut. Left. Right. Left. Right. Left. Left. Hopefully, they were still heading south.

"Shit!" Hawk jumped, and the bike wobbled. He twisted and turned on the back, shaking the bike again. "What was that?"

William turned around. "Wha—"

Something behind them shot from the left wall, hit the right, and fell to the ground.

"Bullets!" Hawk slapped William's back, the sharp magazines in his backpack digging in. "We need to go faster."

Another bullet shot from a small hole in the left wall and hit the right. And then another. Each one a foot or two behind them.

William sped up, setting off more bullets than before, but they were faster than the traps. For now.

Too many options, William might as well have ridden with his eyes closed. He turned right, left, right, right, right.

The bullets stopped, but Hawk still clung onto William's waist like a constrictor. He squeezed the air from him and pressed his loaded backpack into his spine.

"You can let go—"

Thunk!

The bike bucked from the back. Hawk and the two rear wheels lifted into the air before it slammed down again.

"Spikes!" Hawk's voice rose in pitch. "They've got spikes in the ground."

They'd passed over a steel hatch in the concrete. The hatch had flipped up, lifting the quad with it. It sent them away from the thick steel spikes that punched up from the ground. Had they come this way on foot, they'd be filled with holes by now. If they'd come this way on foot, they'd have been shredded by the tiny insects the second they entered the place.

William's eyes burned because of the headwind and his refusal to blink. He kept the bike at full throttle and scanned the road ahead. The shadows made it hard to see if there were any more hatches in their path.

The slightest glint on William's right. "Duck!"

He threw himself over the bike's tank as a scythe swung from the wall with a horizontal slash. He remained over the vehicle, Hawk pressing on him as a dead weight against his backpack. "Hawk, are you okay back there?"

Hawk tapped William's shoulder. "Yep."

Thunk!

Another scythe swung out from the left wall. A large curved blade designed to remove heads.

William turned right. The next road ran straighter than the others. A decent run out of there. Where he'd eased off to manage the twists and turns, he opened up his throttle again.

Thunk! It came from behind them.

"What now?" William sat up and twisted in his seat. They'd turned onto this road and could only go one way. The other way a dead end. That dead end now opened. A door had dropped into a sleeve in the ground.

"What is that thing?"

A mechanical beast the size of a horse. It grunted, snorted, and stepped from its prison with slamming steps. Covered in black steel-wire fur made from short bristles like a hard brush, the tips covered in red rust. Like blood. Like the thick red stripe on the walls on either side. Its brushed steel teeth glistened, catching what little light came down from the moon. Its red eyes glowed. It had the power in its thick jaws to turn them to paste. It charged after them, breaking into an awkward lolloping gait and gathering speed with every step.

Hawk slapped William's shoulder. "Do you know what that thing is?"

His throat dry and his stomach in knots, William twisted his throttle. "That's Old Tom the tomcat."

"Tomcat? It looks like a fucking lion. Shit. I would have rather taken my chances with the bugs."

CHAPTER 37

A sharp sting ran from the end of Olga's toe all the way up her shin, but she kicked the door again anyway. "What the hell, Ralph? I trusted you, you piece of shit."

The hatch in the door remained closed. The lock remained locked.

"Don't ignore me, Ralph!"

Snap! The hatch shot open to reveal a small section of Ralph's face. Thick eyebrows and a hard scowl. "Shut. Up!"

"You shut up." Olga jabbed a finger at him. Were it not for the sharp steel panel that could have taken it clean off, she would have thrust it through and poked him in the eye. Her stamp echoed around the metal cell. "Why have you done this to us?"

"Just keep your mouth shut, you idiot."

"Wha—"

Ralph lowered his voice. The Ralph she thought she knew returned. His hard edges softened. "Trust me, okay?"

Joni grabbed Olga's arm in a tight grip and dragged her away. "You need to listen to him."

"Weren't you the one who just told me to look out when I came in here?"

Joni shrugged and swiped her wild blonde hair away from her face. "I saw him closing the door behind you. I didn't know he planned on locking you in here. When I saw him doing it, I reacted. But we're trapped now—"

"So we just give up?"

"So we might as well let this play out. He said we could trust him."

"But he's just locked us in here."

"What other choice do we have?"

Ralph had left the hatch open. It let in the voices of the two approaching women. The same ones who'd brought Joni down here?

Their heels clicked as they walked in step with one another. One of them said, "Who were you talking to, Ralph?"

"The prisoner."

"I know she's on her own, but she's not earned the right to have your company. Not after what she's done."

"Are you kidding?" Ralph scoffed. "She deserves everything she's got coming to her. I was just about to tell her as much."

Olga raised her eyebrows and tilted her head to one side.

"But I think she's hurt."

Joni's lips tightened. She shrugged.

"Hurt? How?"

"I don't know. She doesn't look right."

Joni shoved Olga away, dropped to the floor, and held an arm across her stomach.

One guard unlocked the cell door, the *thunk* snapping through the room, the vibration of it against Olga's back from where she leaned into the wall beside it.

The door opened.

Olga swallowed a dry gulp.

One of the female guards from earlier stepped into the room, and Joni groaned. "Ow!"

Her fists balled, Olga rocked forwards on her toes, but paused until the second female guard entered.

"Argh!" Olga punched the second guard in the back of the head. She caught her clean, and the woman folded like wet card.

Joni sprang up and drove an uppercut into the other guard's chin. The *clop* sent a wince through Olga, and the guard dropped to the floor, both women unconscious.

"Now come on." Ralph stepped into the room and beckoned Olga and Joni forwards.

Joni first, Olga followed her out.

Crash!

Ralph slammed the door shut, locked it, and closed the hatch. His red face glistened with sweat. "We need to get out of here before someone finds out what we've done. Come on."

They arrived at the elevator Olga and Ralph had ridden. But when he reached for the button, Joni grabbed his arm. "Stop. I know a better way out of here." She pointed up at the maintenance shaft running over their heads.

His mouth hanging open, Ralph looked from the hatch to Joni and back to the hatch. He passed Joni a walkie-talkie. "Take this with you. It has a tracker on it. I'll be able to find you again."

With a single sharp nod, Joni took the walkie-talkie and clipped it to her belt.

Ralph dropped onto one knee and linked his fingers together. He held his hands towards Joni, offering her a boost. She stood on, and he lifted her towards the grate, holding her steady while she tugged it open. He then lifted her higher so she could crawl in.

After Joni had vanished from sight, he did the same for Olga. Before she stepped onto his hands, she patted his shoulder. "Thanks, Ralph. Sorry I didn't trust you."

"It's okay. It's hard to know who to trust in this world. I'll see you soon."

Olga nodded, stepped onto Ralph's hands, and crawled into the open maintenance shaft when he lifted her higher. Joni was already a few feet ahead of her. She reached back, closed the grate, and followed her friend out of there.

CHAPTER 38

Gracie clung to Matilda's waist, holding on against the sudden changes in direction. The chatter of thousands of metallic wings behind grew louder as the creatures gained on them. Nick was on the back of Artan's bike beside her. He too held on. If either of them slipped, the cloud of razor-sharp insanity on their tail would consume them. It'd chop them into tiny pieces in seconds.

The wind in her face, Gracie peered over Matilda's shoulder. They were on a straighter section of road. The bleeding red line on the walls on either side stretched away from them. But they had a chance here. She patted Matilda's shoulder. "Stay on this road."

"What?"

Gracie shouted over the wind, "Stay on this straight. Don't take any turns."

"Okay."

But Gracie froze.

Matilda shouted back to her, "Why am I staying on this road?"

Gracie spun around on the bike. The road might have been rough, the hum and the vibration through the bike bordering on maddening, but at least it was level. No surprise bumps to throw her off. Now facing the other way, she gripped the back of the bike between her legs. Hopefully the road's flat surface would remain that way, her one-handed grip on the bar on the bike's back tenuous.

With her free hand, Gracie aimed her gun back at the cloud of bugs and opened fire. The kickback sent aching streaks through her forearm, and she clamped her jaw against her effort. But she kept the end pointed at the creatures and unloaded.

Nick did the same next to her. Spinning around, he gripped the bike between his legs, bared his teeth, and fired like Gracie.

Gracie ran out of bullets first.

Nick, a few seconds later.

The bugs moved like a flood and were still getting closer. She would have probably had more success shooting water. What a moron.

A grenade on her hip, Gracie removed it, bit down on the pin and pulled it out with her teeth. She threw it at the bugs.

They parted and passed over it.

Several seconds later, the *whomp* of the exploding grenade mocked her. Did she really think she could beat these things with bullets and explosions? The wall of bugs now closer than ever. The shifting and glinting chaos sent her mind reeling. Just a matter of time before they caught up to them. She shared a glance with Nick, who shrugged back at her. They were screwed.

Matilda took a sharp right.

Gracie held on with one hand.

It wasn't enough.

She tilted, her left leg lifting with her tumble. Her momentum dragged her over. She took the bike with her. It lifted onto two wheels, but this time, instead of slamming back down to the ground, it kept going.

CHAPTER 39

Olga paced back and forth. The click of her heels echoed in Joni's home. The last time she'd been in here, there had been more of them to deaden the sound. Joni sat at her laptop computer, the clickety-click of her keystrokes a match for Olga's pacing steps. How had she spent so much time in here on her own? Maybe the screens had provided a welcome distraction, but for over twenty years? Cold. Damp. And quiet. In the space between the noises they made, the silence became so complete Olga could hear the function of her own organs. Hardly surprising it had turned Joni somewhat eccentric. Olga would have been barking at the moon within a year.

But at least the blank screens meant the drones and dogs were still out of action. Louis might have a plan, but it would take time. Time for the others to get away from this cursed place. A pang twisted through Olga's chest. She should have asked them to wait. But what about Joni? She couldn't leave her on her own again. Not now she knew she had a daughter. Joni needed her more than the others did. Like Max had needed her.

And what if Ralph turned out to be a bad egg? He'd led them true so far, but that didn't mean he'd continue flying straight.

Bathed in the glow of her screen, Joni sat hunched over her laptop, her fingers alive on the keyboard. She stared at her recorded footage, but Olga had already seen enough the last time they were down here. She didn't need to see any more horrors. She got it. This place was awful.

"What if Ralph sells us out? What if he doesn't mean to, but he accidentally gives us away? Or if he has a situation where he has to choose between saving himself and saving us? We can't expect him to protect us then."

Joni shrugged and continued typing.

"You're right," Olga said. "That's a lot of *what-ifs*. Too many to consider. I suppose I don't enjoy sitting around waiting for someone to turn up. I don't know when he might arrive, or if I even want him to arrive."

Again, Joni shrugged.

Click!

Click!

Click!

Olga's heels tapped against the damp concrete ground. "He was immune, you know?"

"Who?"

"Max."

Joni stopped typing. She turned towards Olga. "The person who's the reason you're staying with me?"

"Part of the reason, yeah. He was immune to the disease. So he did all the killing for us. When we needed somewhere clearing of those damn creatures, he went in and took down tens, even hundreds of them at a time."

"Wow." Joni's face fell slack. "That must have been hard on him."

Her words slammed into Olga's stomach, and she laid her

hand against her abdomen. "I wish I'd had your foresight. We were just trying to survive. We all did our bit. Did what he could to help. None of us stopped to think about what it was doing to him. He kind of lost the plot."

"Kind of?"

"He lost the plot."

"I know how that feels."

Tears itched Olga's tired eyes. "We should have done more. Both to prevent him from getting into a state and then to help him heal afterwards."

Joni reached out and held Olga's hand. She had a firm and reassuring grip. The sharp intelligence remained in her azure stare. "I really appreciate what you've done for me, but please don't feel you have to. And while I get you're doing this for Max as well as me, know that you did the best you could for him. If you had your chance to relive it all again, you'd make the same decisions. You can't undo the past. You can only learn from it. Thank you for everything you've done. Max would be proud."

Olga filled her lungs with the damp air. "You sound different."

"Huh?"

"You're saying *I* not *Joni*."

She shrugged. "The battle's moved to the inside. But that's a step in the right direction, eh? The time we just spent in the block has done something to me. Things are making a lot more sense now than ever before. For years, the pieces of my puzzle have been in the air. Now they've all fallen to the ground. At least I can start putting them back together."

The walkie-talkie crackled, and Olga jumped back from it.

"Joni, it's me, Ralph. The tracker's telling me we're close, but I don't know where you are ..."

"This is it," Joni said. "Do we reveal ourselves? Give up this last hiding place? I trust him, but are you on board?"

"I'd say by this point we're already all in."

One sharp affirmative dip of her head, Joni stood up and climbed the ladder. She reached the top and shoved the hatch aside with the scrape of steel over concrete. Moonlight flooded into the dark hole, and Joni gasped.

Olga balled her hands into fists. She scanned her surroundings. She had nothing to use as a weapon.

But Joni climbed back down of her own free will.

Had Olga been asked to bet on it, she'd have put all she owned against Ralph being able to get through the hole, but the large man slipped in and descended after Joni.

Joni jumped off the final rung with swollen and bloodshot eyes. Olga reached across to her. "You okay?"

Joni bit her bottom lip and nodded.

Olga gasped and stepped back when Ralph alighted the ladder. He'd blocked her line of sight until that moment.

A woman followed him down. A female guard. She had beautiful long hair. Dead straight and even redder than Gracie's. It ran to her bottom and shone like it had its own light source. She descended the ladder with the grace of someone who'd been sent from the heavens to this damp dungeon.

Tears ran freely down Joni's cheeks, and she fought to get her words out. "I'm sorry about the state of this place. It's a real mess."

With eyes as swollen as Joni's, Ralph breathed in, his broad chest rising with his intake. "I would have done something much sooner had I known. But I had no idea where you'd gone."

The back of her hand pressed to her nose, Joni nodded several times.

Olga swallowed against the lump in her throat.

Ralph spoke with a warble in his voice. "Joni…"

Joni continued nodding.

"From the day you left, I've kept an eye on her to make sure she's been okay. Louis has always been kind to her. When she got older, I didn't want to turn her against her dad, but I slowly told her about her mum. How her mum loves her and never wanted to leave."

Joni nodded like she couldn't stop.

"How it was a difficult situation and how she had no choice. When I knew I could tell her without it getting back to Louis, I set the record straight. Not to turn her against her dad, but to be the antidote for the poison he'd spread about you."

Racked with heavy sobs, Joni dropped her focus to the ground and wailed.

"Joni," Ralph said.

Joni looked up. What little colour she had in her face had gone, turning her chalk white. Her nose ran. The light from the laptop screen glistened off her sodden cheeks.

"Please allow me to officially introduce you. Joni, meet Antonia. Your daughter."

CHAPTER 40

Another weaving getaway, William flung his quad left and right.

Old Tom made it around the corners after them, but at least one in every three sudden turns ended with the monster slamming into a steel wall with a loud *thud!*

The ground a blur, the turnings they could have taken flashed past them on either side. The red line remained a constant. A dirty scar on the dirty walls.

Hawk tightened his grip around William's waist again.

William twisted and shoved down on Hawk's arms. "Not so tight!"

"It's not working." Hawk had become William's rear-view mirror. Other than gripping on, he checked Old Tom behind.

Not that William needed Hawk's feedback. Old Tom's thunderous charge grew louder until the vibration of every step shook all the way from the ground to his choking grip on the handlebars. Even with the beast slamming into walls, each collision making the prison sing like a gigantic bell, he moved faster than they ever could.

William thrust his left hand into his pocket and removed

his micro EMP. He passed it to Hawk. "This is our last hope. When Old Tom gets to within a few feet, press it."

"That's all I have to do?"

"Yep."

"Really?"

"Yep."

"What if I get it wrong?"

"Just press it!"

The quad lost its power. William twisted the throttle, but no matter how hard he turned, he couldn't wring life back into the dead vehicle. He twisted it again, gripping so hard his right hand ached. The throttle unresponsive. The engine's whine faded. The hum of the tyres lowered in pitch, and Old Tom, still about thirty feet away, gained on them quicker than before. "I said to wait until he got to within a few feet."

"And then you said *just press it*. So that's what I did."

William snatched the button from Hawk. He clung to the handlebars with his left hand and guided them through the maze. He gripped the button in his shaking right and held it back towards Old Tom.

The massive machine galloped after them like a landslide.

Fifteen feet away.

Ten feet away.

Five feet.

So close William ruffled his nose against the beast's coppery reek. Blood or metal? Hard to tell.

William pressed the button.

The beast's red-eyed glare died. His gallop abandoned him mid-stride. His front legs turned limp, and Old Tom's face slammed into the concrete. The monster slid after William and Hawk. Sparks kicked up from his chin. He slammed into the rapidly decelerating quad bike and launched the pair from the seat.

William hit the concrete and rolled. His gun and backpack flew away from him, and he lost his grip on the micro EMP. Turning over and over, he came to a halt against a steel wall, Old Tom sliding and stopping just a few feet away.

His ears ringing, his body battered from the fall, William sat up and rubbed his head. Hawk had landed a few feet farther down the road. "You okay?"

A bleeding nose and a fresh graze on his cheek, Hawk patted himself down and nodded. "Yeah. I think so." He stood on wobbly legs, retrieved William's gun, backpack, and the micro EMP, and handed them to him. "Now let's get back on that bike and get away from here."

"We can't do that."

"What?"

William waved the micro EMP. "Weren't you listening when we were taking down the dogs and drones?"

"We kind of had our own shit to deal with."

"This thing kills anything electrical within a small radius."

"Shit." Hawk raised his gun. "At least we have these!"

William pulled his lips tight.

"We don't have these?"

"Look at the red number on the top."

Hawk turned the gun to see the red number. Or lack of red number. "These are dead too?"

William removed his earpiece and threw it to the ground. "And even if we do get the radio back online, we've just fried our headsets."

Discarding his earpiece and then his gun, Hawk threw his shoulders up in a shrug. "So, what now?"

"We walk." William set off and re-shouldered his backpack. "And we hope if we come up against anything else, we can beat it with our fists or we'll be able to outrun it. But, hey, look on the bright side, at least Old Tom's deactivated. Given a choice between walking away from here and not, I choose walking away every time."

CHAPTER 41

It made everything worthwhile. Just to see Joni reunited with her daughter and reunited with Ralph, the one guard who had her back. Olga smiled as she settled into Joni's seat in front of the twenty blank screens. They'd blinded the prison, so she had no clue what was going on outside. Hopefully her friends had found a way out.

"What I have on here"—Joni lifted her laptop to show Antonia—"is awfully condemning of your father. He's done some heinous things, and I believe he deserves to be punished. I take no pleasure in exposing him, not because I care about him, but because I care about you and your relationship with him. Someone like him shouldn't be in charge of a place like this. I want to help others see that, but I won't do it without your permission."

A younger version of Joni stared back at her. Her father's colouring, but she had Joni's features. Antonia fixed her mum with her sharp and intelligent azure gaze. "I understand. And a few years ago, I might have objected. But I'm an adult now. I'm under no illusion about what Dad is. What he's like. I've seen his cruelty to others first hand. And how he justified it by saying some people deserved to be treated like crap. That's something I won't stand for."

"Okay." Joni gulped. "I've had access to their broadcasting channels for the longest time. I could have done this a lot sooner, and maybe I should have, but it would have been too quick. I held on for years because I felt like I owed him the torture and torment he put upon me. It's petty."

"No." Antonia shook her head. "It's not. Not after what he's put you through. You needed to take back control. I understand that."

"And I think I knew about you." Joni tapped her heart, her cheeks flushing red. "Deep down. I mean, even if a mind gets lost, how can a body forget about being pregnant?" She looked at the floor. Her long blonde hair fell across her face. "I knew I had unfinished business with Louis. I knew I couldn't put an end to him because there was something missing. Now I know what that was."

Joni's hand shook when she held it over the keyboard. She took a calming breath before tapping a single button.

One screen in front of Olga burst to life.

Joni, Antonia, and Ralph came over and stood around her chair.

Olga pressed against the armrests to stand, but Joni put a hand on her shoulder and gently pressed her back into her seat. "Stay there; it's fine."

Since they'd been down in Joni's dungeon, Ralph had spoken little. He pointed at the screen. "This footage is playing somewhere else?"

"Yeah." Joni nodded. "On every screen in the prison. On every broadcast channel outside the prison. Anyone who would see an eviction or the rat run or the arena will have a chance to see this."

Despite having already seen it once, Olga squirmed in her chair as Louis rode through the communities, pressing the button that turned the prisoners' insides to mush. Her stomach churned with every kick he drove into the head of the leader of the unregistered army. Again and again until he decapitated it.

Both Ralph and Antonia watched on, their faces slack. Antonia bit her fist, and her blue eyes filled with tears. Joni touched her forearm. "I'm sorry you're seeing this."

But the footage didn't stop there. The next few minutes showed Louis and three of his guards on the roof of their block, taking potshots at prisoners. They had guns that shot targets much farther away than any weapon Olga had seen before. They cheered the loudest when they hit a child.

Olga filled her lungs to settle her roiling stomach as Louis and several guards threw prisoners from moving tanks. Their limbs snapped, and many had fallen limp by the time they came to a halt. Every one of them had grenades strapped to them. Every one of them got blown to pieces as the grand finale to their abduction and torture.

Antonia said nothing beyond a few gasps and groans. But when Louis and several guards led two other guards from the block at gunpoint, she said, "No. Come on, now. Really?"

They marched their hostages over to the warehouse. They stopped before the large building and pressed metal devices to the backs of their necks. Each cylindrical device fitted in a guard's grip. They were about a foot long.

"What are they doing to them?" Olga said.

Ralph's sombre tone echoed in Joni's underground den. "Implanting them with the same chips they've forced into the prisoners. Once inside that place, if they try to leave via any of the exits, they'll bleed out. He's putting them in there to be lost amongst the next batch of those due for execution in the warehouse. No one will be any the wiser with so many of them in the crowd."

Olga jolted when the footage changed. A warehouse filled

with diseased. Chaos. Fury. Some of them spilling from the open doors. The footage focused on the two guards, still in their uniforms. They both cried crimson tears.

The next piece of footage moved to a room with a large table in the middle. Louis sat at the head and led a meeting with a group of men in suits. Olga said, "Huh?"

"Listen," Joni said.

"Yes." Louis stroked his scruffy goatee. "I can get hidden cameras all over the block. You can have unrestricted access to the guards' lives."

One of the suited men bit his fingernails. His voice trembled when he said, "Nothing's off limits?"

Louis turned his palms to the ceiling. "Voyeurism sells, right? Especially when those being observed don't realise they're being observed. What viewer doesn't want to see their favourite guards whenever they want. We'll make a killing."

The footage changed to two guards having sex. A woman sitting on a toilet. Several people taking showers.

"My god." Antonia clapped a hand to her mouth. "Please don't tell me that people saw ..."

"I'm sorry, but he gave unrestricted access to the entire block. The only privacy he protected was his own." Joni returned to her laptop as more footage of Louis' violence played out on the screen. She picked up a microphone, her words ringing out through the prison. "So, Louis, you recently told me I wasn't capable of agency. That I'd been scuttling around the prison like a bug. A nuisance, but no real threat to you and the life you choose to live. Well, what do you think of my agency now? It's not just the prison who have seen what you're like, this is going out live to everyone who watches the games you play with these prisoners. They might share your hatred for our enemies, but I doubt they can forgive your sadism when faced with the naked truth of just how nasty you are. How you'll sell out your colleagues in a heartbeat. Even your own daughter. They know you shared footage of your daughter showering too, right?"

Olga winced, along with Antonia. No one needed to hear that of their parent.

"And now they know you've lost control of the prison. Maybe they could put up with the rest, but how can they abide your utter incompetence?"

Joni placed the microphone down next to the laptop. She sighed, deflating with her exhalation. "I expected that to feel a lot better. I've focused on what it would do to him. I didn't stop to think about what it might mean to the other guards. I didn't care about any of them enough until now."

Antonia cleared her throat. "You did what was necessary. They'll understand."

"I hope so."

Olga rocked forwards in her seat and stood up. The other three turned towards her. She pointed at the ladders. "I need to go. I reckon if I'm quick, I might catch up with my friends. It's time for me to move on."

"You're going to do the run through the south section of the prison?" Joni said.

"I have to." She looked from Ralph to Antonia. "And you're both staying with her, right?"

"I will if Joni wants me around," Ralph said.

Antonia simply nodded.

Joni came forwards and held Olga's hands. The crazy Joni she'd first met had taken a back seat. Hopefully, she'd gone for good. Calm. Composed. Focused. Her piercing blue eyes fixed on Olga. "Thank you. For everything."

Olga pulled Joni in for a hug. She forced her words past the lump in her throat. "I would wish you all the best, but I don't think you need it. You're awesome, Joni Muldoon. Don't ever let anyone tell you otherwise."

CHAPTER 42

Milliseconds passed between the quad bike tilting at the edge of its balance, rolling, and throwing Gracie and Matilda from the turning vehicle. The crash threw them both into the wall, and they dropped to the hard concrete. Gracie's ears rang. Her head pounded. Her body ached from the skeleton-jarring collision. Her world spun, and what little light they had from the moon dulled. The silver bugs closed in.

But Nick and Artan streaked past them. Both of them on their feet. Artan had a button in his right hand. He pressed it.

The bugs at the front of the pack fell and crashed to the ground in a splashing wave.

Gracie covered her face as several slid into her, cutting the backs of her hands.

Artan pressed his button again.

Another wave of the creatures crashed down.

Yet another press of his button dropped the rest of the cloud. Now utterly useless, they formed a pile of pieces. Scrap metal.

Gracie got to her feet on unsteady legs. She rolled her

shoulders to resettle her backpack. The coppery taste of her own blood ran down the back of her throat. She nodded at Artan. "The micro EMP?"

"Yep."

"Wow. I heard you using it on the radio, but I didn't expect it to be quite so …"

"Effective?"

"Yeah. And why are you only using it now?"

Artan slipped his gun over his head, gripped it by the barrel, and swung it through the air. A tiny bug hit the wall on his left and dropped with the others. He turned his gun towards Gracie. The red number showing how much ammo he had left had gone. "Because it's just killed all our equipment. Our bikes. Our guns. Our grenades. Our earpieces."

"Damn!"

"Yeah. But it's what we needed to do, right?"

Gracie rolled her shoulders again. The aches would be with her for a while. "Right." She followed Artan away from there, turning her back on the tiny metallic insects. Now they were without their weapons and vehicles, how would they deal with whatever they ran into next?

CHAPTER 43

A twitch ran through William's body with every step. It urged him to run as if that would somehow make him safer in this highly volatile section of the prison. Chances were he'd set off more traps, and they'd probably die sooner. They were screwed. He knew it, and Hawk beside him knew it. A point they'd both clearly realised was best not discussed. Why shatter the small hope they had, even if they both knew it to be an illusion?

They walked along one of the wider roads they'd been on since entering this section of the prison. The blood red line ran down the walls on either side. Maybe this path led to the gate out of there? Wider because they were on the home straight? But how did they even know if they were heading the right way? The mazy paths could lead anywhere.

Fatigue buzzed through William's legs. His feet ached, and his mouth had dried hours ago. Every time he gulped, his throat locked with the phlegmy paste that had lodged there.

"Stop!" Hawk slammed his arm across William's chest, knocking him back. He stood before a hatch in the ground like the one they'd passed over on their bike. The one that had nearly flipped them.

Hawk tapped it with his toe.

Thunk!

The hatch flew open, shooting up from the road like a trapdoor, driven wide by thick spikes beneath.

William scrunched his feet in his boots. Any of those spikes would have ripped straight through them. Would have turned their feet to paste.

Hawk led the way, skirting around the outside of the trap. William followed, his back to the rough steel wall. The thick spikes were decorated with chunks of old flesh, and they glistened in the moonlight with blood. The stench of rotting meat hung in the air. It turned William's stomach, and he screwed up his face. "Even a scratch from one of these would probably give you an infection you'd never recover from."

"This place is awful." Hawk shook his head. "I hate it here."

"I suppose if you want to reassure the people in the south that if there's any kind of prison break, those in this prison will remain in the prison, then this is the way to do it." William stepped clear of the pit and the spikes protruding from it. "Most of the time, the prisoners won't even get past the white lines leading into the place."

"Get down!" Hawk tackled William to the ground.

A spray of bullets ran over their heads. They peppered the steel wall, each one falling to the rough concrete just inches from William's face. "Thank you."

Hawk got off William and shrugged. "I had to do something while I was on the back of the bike. I saw some triggers for the traps when we avoided them the first time. Fool me once and all that." He pointed at the holes in the wall. "This is where they shoot from."

"Wait." William grabbed Hawk before he stepped off again. "See those marks?"

Were it not for the thick red line, William might not have seen them himself, their surroundings still swamped by the night's deep shadows. Charred marks from where a flame had burned one side of the wall, the crimson paint several shades darker because of fire damage. Barely more than a pinhole on the other side of the wall, he pointed at it. "The flames must come from there."

"Damn." Hawk looked back, the hatch still open behind them, the spikes poking from the ground. "We've got no chance of getting past here. We have to find another way around."

"Yeah." William nodded. "Hopefully we don'—"

The hum of an engine called to them. William's heart raced. A tank appeared a second later. "They must have seen what we did to Old Tom."

"So what do we do no—"

William raised his hands in the air.

"What are you doing?"

"If you have a better option than surrender, I'd love to hear it. But I don't fancy our chances against a tank, so what else are we going to do? We either die here—"

"Or die in their custody. No doubt at the hands of a sadist."

"The longer we live, the more chance we have to exploit their mistakes. We've walked away from everything else so far."

"Doesn't mean we'll walk away from this."

"We're trapped between a tank and flamethrower. Do you have a better solution to our predicament?"

"Damn!" Hawk tutted, shook his head, and also raised his hands.

The tank's hum quietened from where it slowed and

rolled close to William and Hawk. It hit the spikes with a *thunk* and rolled right over them, bending them so they were now useless.

His mouth drier than ever and his heart in his throat. His collar itched with sweat. Spasms fired the length of William's legs. They dared him to make a break for it. But where? Into a fiery death?

The tank stopped just a few feet away, and the door opened.

"Tilly?" William dropped his hands.

Matilda hunched down to avoid the tank's low roof as she stepped out. She ran to William and threw her arms around him. She kissed his face. "I'm so glad we found you."

William stepped back and held her hands. "I was worried yo—" He shuffled where he stood.

"We're all okay." Matilda stepped aside.

William followed Hawk into the tank. Gracie, Artan, and Nick were already in the back. They sat on the two steel benches running along the side walls, a gangway between them. He gulped. "You made it!" Gracie handed him a bottle of water. He took a sip, the cool liquid a balm for his sore throat. "You all made it!"

Olga sat in the cockpit. Dwarfed by the massive padded chair, she spun around and beamed a grin at him.

"Where did you get this tank from?"

"Joni and her daughter—"

"Daughter?"

"It's a long story. They helped me. They showed me how to access the map with the route to the south gates. They showed me how to use the heat sensor to find you all, and how to emit a signal that disables all the booby traps in our way."

"How long are the traps disabled for?"

"I had a choice."

"And what did you choose?" William said.

"Permanently. There are still a lot of prisoners in this place. I know the south hate them, but what if a life in the south is better for them than staying here? I didn't want to be someone who leaves and then pulls the ladder up behind me."

Gracie leaned back in her seat and grinned.

"And I'm ..." Olga cleared her throat.

"I'm ..."

William leaned close to hear her better. "You're what, Olga?"

"I'm fucking sorry, okay? Jeez, what do you want, blood?"

William fought to suppress his smirk.

"I didn't mean what I said to you when you were waiting for me. I just needed you to go. I'd made a promise to myself to stand by Joni for as long as she needed me. I owed it to her. I owed it to Max. And I couldn't have asked you all to wait. It only took a few hours, but it could have taken days or even weeks."

"You *could* have asked us."

The others nodded along with William.

"I chose not to."

William reached forwards and squeezed Olga's shoulder. "It's good to have you back."

Spinning around so she faced the windscreen again, Olga nodded. "It's good to be back. Now let's get out of this shithole." She pressed a button, closing the door on William's right.

William sat down on a bench next to Artan. A weapon rack dominated the tank's back wall. They had guns, grenades, and ammo. At least they were leaving this place armed.

The gates in the south had nothing on their northern counterparts. They were much smaller and no doubt easier to operate. They were less ceremonious, dwarfed by the two-hundred-foot-tall wall that housed them.

Olga pressed a button in her cockpit.

Clack!

Nothing happened.

She did it again.

Clack! Clack!

William leaned forwards. "Everything okay, Olga?"

"Joni said this might happen."

"What?"

"The tanks can't open the gates. The place has gone into lockdown, so the gates are closed too. But"—she held up a small device—"she gave me this."

Gracie said, "What's that?"

"Follow me." Olga hit the button to open the side door. She spun around in her chair and left the tank first, William close behind.

The gates, like many doors in this place, had a control panel beside them. Olga's small device had a cable protruding from it like a tail. A small metal end, she plugged it into the hole in the panel. Three red lights came to life on the device. Each one turned green, one after the other.

Thunk!

The gates wobbled and shifted. They parted down the centre. When they'd opened to just a few feet, they froze.

Olga pressed the door button, but the gates remained stuck. The lights on her small device turned back from green to red. She unplugged it and plugged it back in again. The lights remained red. "Well, I'm guessing this is it." She looked from the tank to the gap in the gates. "This is as far as they open."

"So we're on foot again?" Hawk said.

"Yeah." Olga shrugged. "Unless you have a better suggestion?"

"I don't care as long as we get away from this place."

"Okay." William clapped his hands together. "If we're going to leave the tank here, we need to take as many weapons as we can carry."

"Oh." Olga raised her right index finger. "And leave the micro EMPs. Joni and Ralph said they don't work in the south. They're designed as an extra measure of control in the prison, but they're useless everywhere else."

William removed the button from his pocket and discarded it. Artan and Matilda also tossed theirs to the ground.

~

THE LAST ONE of the group to leave the prison, William turned sideways to get through the gap in the gates. His gun hung across him, and he still wore the backpack filled with ammo from Joni. Hopefully, this would be the one time they didn't have to fight, but they'd be foolish to go unprepared.

Signs of a new day diluted the black sky. Now dark blue and well on the way to dawn. Dew clung to the steel surfaces like the place perspired.

His body leaden with fatigue, William stumbled away from the open gates with heavy steps. A small camera sat above them, mounted on the wall, recording anything that approached the prison from the south. Gracie had kicked the one when they came into this place, and she'd shot this one before any of them emerged. It now hung shattered and limp.

William flipped the dead camera the bird before turning around to join his friends. Exhausted both physically and mentally, but still he smiled. His words came out as a croak. "We did it."

CHAPTER 44

The one screen that had shown the others Joni's footage of Louis had turned black after she'd finished her broadcast. But she'd since brought several back to life with her own cameras. Cameras she'd stolen from him over the years. She'd snuck out and placed them in various spots so they focused on the guards' block. So far, very little had happened.

"We've got something!" Ralph leaned closer to one of the central screens. Several guards dragged Louis from the block and shoved him away. He stumbled and fell to his knees. He pleaded with the guards, his hands pressed together in prayer. One guard took a run up and kicked him in the face, sending him sprawling.

Joni's heart sank. It should have felt better. And it would, had she not been watching it with his daughter. No matter how cruel, the man was her father. And who wanted to see the ugly truth of a father like this?

Joni leaned across to turn the screens off, but Antonia reached out to her. "It's fine. Leave it."

"You're sure?"

Her focus on the screens, her face tight, Antonia nodded. "Yeah. Leave it."

CHAPTER 45

William rolled his shoulders to adjust how his backpack sat. His gun hung across his front, and he held Matilda's hand. They'd left the south gates well behind them, but the road out of there had clearly been designed to be travelled by vehicles. They'd been walking for an hour or two along the monotonous corridor. Tall steel walls on either side, the rough grey concrete beneath them. Had they not passed through the gates, William might have questioned if they were even heading out of the prison. The sky had turned from dark to light blue, and dew hung in the air, the cool pricks of moisture a welcome relief against his sweating skin.

The group didn't speak much, each lost in their own thoughts. If the others were anything like William, they were processing what it had taken to get them to this point, and what it might take to get them further.

A gap opened up in the prison wall on their left. They'd seen it from about a mile away, and it had been the focus of their attention since. But before they reached the exit, every other person in the group halted. They all watched William.

William paused too, but they smiled at him. Olga laid her arm out in front of her. "Go on. You first."

Like he'd done so many times before, William filled his lungs. What would they discover next? He stepped forwards. For a few seconds, his words abandoned him. It took for Matilda to come to his side and rest her hand on his back before he finally let go of a breathy, "Wow!"

The others joined William and Matilda. Each of them struck with awe by the view. Artan and Nick hugged. Olga and Gracie smiled at one another. Hawk's eyes shone with his tears.

"I've never seen anything like it," William said. The exit to the south of the prison sat on a hill and looked out over what they'd fought so hard to reach. A collection of eight towers unlike any William had ever seen. They stood as tall as the prison's north and south walls. They shone in the morning sun from where the light reflected off their mirrored windows and glossy metal frames.

Roads stretched between the buildings like webbing. From the ground, right to the very top. And there were no guards watching the south exit. They clearly had a lot of faith in Louis and his management of the prison.

William reached down and grabbed Matilda's hand. He grinned at her. "Let's hope this is as promising as it looks."

She returned his smile. "Anything has to be better than what we've left behind."

CHAPTER 46

"What's he doing now?" Antonia had sat on the chair in front of the screens for the past half an hour.

Joni had walked away after the guards had thrown Louis from the block and he'd vanished from her cameras' line of sight. Chances were he'd run into prisoners who hated him and had been killed.

Ralph ran over, and Joni joined a second later. The bright glare from the screens made Joni's eyes itch. She'd sleep for days when she finally got her chance.

About twenty prisoners appeared on one screen, Louis behind them with a button in his hand. No audio to go with the footage, but his flapping mouth and red face showed Joni all she needed to know.

He drove the prisoners on, forcing them forwards. When he came into the next screen, Joni's entire being sank. "Oh, shit!"

"What?" Antonia looked from the screen to Joni.

"He's taking them to the warehouse. That can only mean one thing."

"It only takes one?" Antonia said.

Ralph sighed. "And he has about twenty with him."

On her way to the ladders out of there, Joni grabbed her gun. She scaled the rough and rusty rungs, shoved the hatch open. She crawled out, Ralph and Antonia close behind.

The warehouse hidden from sight, but a diseased scream rang out, turning Joni's blood cold. "We're too late."

The creature grew gradually quieter.

Ralph said, "It's running the other way."

The butt of her gun in her shoulder, Joni looked down the barrel with one eye closed. "They've not locked the guards' block. We need to keep them from getting in there. At least if the guards are still active, they might regain control of this place. They have the weapons and the means."

A diseased appeared from around the side of the block. Like every other one of its kind, it ran, leaning forwards, permanently on the edge of its balance like it could face-plant at any moment.

Joni steadied her pulse with several deep breaths. The creature still a few hundred feet away. She pulled the trigger and nailed it with one shot. A red splash burst from the back of its head. Its legs buckled, and it went down.

Two replaced it.

Joni took them down with three shots.

"Jeez," Ralph said, "we could have done with you—"

Six more came around in a pack. They descended on the block. Antonia said, "Do the guards even know what's happening?"

Joni pulled the trigger. Once. Twice. Three times. Four. Five. Six.

She took down four of the six. Her final few bullets slammed against the steel wall next to where the creatures entered the block.

The diseased screams vanished inside the building and

faded to silence. Joni slumped and lowered her gun. "We're screwed."

Another scream. Joni raised her gun again.

Antonia gasped when Louis appeared. His jaw slack. Crimson tears streaked his cheeks. His arms flicked away from his body, spasms firing through him. His head snapped one way and then the other.

One eye closed, Joni looked down the barrel of her gun and pulled the trigger.

The gun kicked. The back of Louis' head burst away from him. A cloud of red mist. A bullet hole in the centre of his face. His legs failed him, and he flopped. Joni released a long sigh.

Screams erupted from the guards' block, and Ralph's eyes widened. "What do we do?"

Fixed on her fallen father, Antonia's glare steeled. "If that bastard's taught me anything, it's that it only takes one. And how many went in there?"

"Two," Joni said. "And who knows how many went the other way, deeper into the prison."

"So the guards' block is lost, as is the prison." Antonia shook her head. "We'd be mad to go rushing into that block now. We won't last five minutes. And if the disease spreads through this prison, how many prisoners are left who could turn?"

Joni sighed. "Still tens of thousands."

Ralph returned to the entrance to Joni's home. "I reckon the safest place right now is down here. We should hide and let this play out. The south are probably already on their way."

Joni dragged air in through her clenched teeth.

"What?"

"I didn't send the broadcast out of the prison. There was a

delay between transmitting it inside the prison and outside. I pulled it before it made it beyond these walls."

"Why?" Antonia said.

"I felt sad for him. He's lost so much already. And I have no loyalties to the south."

"So the south don't know what's happened?" Antonia said.

"No. They're none the wiser, and who knows how long it will take for them to realise what's gone on here."

"Damn." Ralph scratched his head. "Even more of a reason for us to lie low. When we come back above ground again, we need to do it armed with a solid plan." He backed down the ladder into Joni's home, and Antonia stood close by, waiting to follow him in.

More screams from the guards' block, Joni waited for Antonia to jump from the ladder at the bottom before she too backed into her home. Halfway down, she pulled the steel cover across, shutting them in. What would the prison look like the next time they came to the surface? She shook her head to herself. One step at a time. She now had a friend and a daughter. Regardless of what happened above ground, she had more than she'd had in a long, long time.

EPILOGUE

The midday sun shone on the discarded tank, but the diseased still ran straight into it. It connected with the steel body, *tonk!* It stumbled back and fell on its arse.

Standing on wobbly legs, always on the edge of its balance, it shambled past the tank to the slightly open gates. A tight gap, but not so tight the beast couldn't get through after a couple of tries.

The creature tripped again on the other side of the gates. It fell to the rough concrete under the now blind security camera. Nothing to see here.

Back on its feet, the wide road stretching ahead of it, the creature leaned forwards and quickened to a teetering run. Free at last. It had spent too long inside those walls. Whether it knew it or not, it needed to see what the south had to offer.

Flanked by tall steel walls, the creature travelled alone along the wide road. A solitary escapee for now, but if the gates remained open, more would follow it out. But even if they didn't …

. . .

MICHAEL ROBERTSON

... IT ONLY TAKES ONE.

END OF BOOK TWELVE.

Thank you for reading *Escape:* Book twelve of Beyond These Walls.

It Only Takes One: **Book thirteen of Beyond These Walls is now available at: www.michaelrobertson.co.uk**

Have you checked out *Fury:* Book one in Tales from beyond These Walls? It's a standalone story set in the city of Fury. While it can be read independently of the main

ESCAPE: BOOK TWELVE OF BEYOND THESE WALLS

Beyond These Walls series, and features new characters, the story occurs at the same time as Between Fury and Fear: Book eight of Beyond These Walls.

If you're yet to read it, go to www.michaelrobertson.co.uk to check out *Fury:* Book one in Tales from Beyond These Walls.

∽

Support The Author

Dear reader, as an independent author I don't have the resources of a huge publisher. If you like my work and would like to see more from me in the future, there are two things you can do to help: leaving a review, and a word-of-mouth referral.

Releasing a book takes many hours and hundreds of dollars. I love to write, and would love to continue to do so. All I ask is that you leave an Amazon review. It shows other readers that you've enjoyed the book and will encourage them to give it a try too. The review can be just one sentence, or as long as you like.

ABOUT THE AUTHOR

Like most children born in the seventies, Michael grew up with Star Wars in his life, along with other great stories like Labyrinth, The Neverending Story, and as he grew older, the Alien franchise. An obsessive watcher of movies and consumer of stories, he found his mind wandering to stories of his own.

Those stories had to come out.

He hopes you enjoy reading his work as much as he does creating it.

Contact
www.michaelrobertson.co.uk
subscribers@michaelrobertson.co.uk

READER GROUP

Join my reader group for all my latest releases and special offers. You'll also receive these four FREE books. You can unsubscribe at any time.

Go to www.michaelrobertson.co.uk

ESCAPE: BOOK TWELVE OF BEYOND THESE WALLS

ALSO BY MICHAEL ROBERTSON

THE SHADOW ORDER:

The Shadow Order

The First Mission - Book Two of The Shadow Order

The Crimson War - Book Three of The Shadow Order

Eradication - Book Four of The Shadow Order

Fugitive - Book Five of The Shadow Order

Enigma - Book Six of The Shadow Order

Prophecy - Book Seven of The Shadow Order

The Faradis - Book Eight of The Shadow Order

The Complete Shadow Order Box Set - Books 1 - 8

∼

NEON HORIZON:

The Blind Spot - A Cyberpunk Thriller - Neon Horizon Book One.

Prime City - A Cyberpunk Thriller - Neon Horizon Book Two.

Bounty Hunter - A Cyberpunk Thriller - Neon Horizon Book Three.

Connection - A Cyberpunk Thriller - Neon Horizon Book Four.

Reunion - A Cyberpunk Thriller - Neon Horizon Book Five.

Eight Ways to Kill a Rat - A Cyberpunk Thriller - Neon Horizon Book Six.

Neon Horizon - Books 1 - 3 Box Set - A Cyberpunk Thriller.

∼

THE ALPHA PLAGUE:

The Alpha Plague: A Post-Apocalyptic Action Thriller

The Alpha Plague 2

The Alpha Plague 3

The Alpha Plague 4

The Alpha Plague 5

The Alpha Plague 6

The Alpha Plague 7

The Alpha Plague 8

The Complete Alpha Plague Box Set - Books 1 - 8

∼

BEYOND THESE WALLS:

Protectors - Book one of Beyond These Walls

National Service - Book two of Beyond These Walls

Retribution - Book three of Beyond These Walls

Collapse - Book four of Beyond These Walls

After Edin - Book five of Beyond These Walls

Three Days - Book six of Beyond These Walls

The Asylum - Book seven of Beyond These Walls

Between Fury and Fear - Book eight of Beyond These Walls

Before the Dawn - Book nine of Beyond These Walls

The Wall - Book ten of Beyond These Walls

Divided - Book eleven of Beyond These Walls

Escape - Book twelve of Beyond These Walls

It Only Takes One - Book thirteen of Beyond These Walls

Beyond These Walls - Books 1 - 6 Box Set

Beyond These Walls - Books 7 - 9 Box Set

~

TALES FROM BEYOND THESE WALLS:

Fury - Book one of Tales From Beyond These Walls

~

OFF-KILTER TALES:

The Girl in the Woods - A Ghost's Story - Off-Kilter Tales Book One

Rat Run - A Post-Apocalyptic Tale - Off-Kilter Tales Book Two

~

Masked - A Psychological Horror

~

CRASH:

Crash - A Dark Post-Apocalyptic Tale

Crash II: Highrise Hell

Crash III: There's No Place Like Home

Crash IV: Run Free

Crash V: The Final Showdown

~

NEW REALITY:

New Reality: Truth

New Reality 2: Justice

New Reality 3: Fear

Audiobooks:

CLICK HERE TO VIEW MY FULL AUDIOBOOK LIBRARY.